# A Masquerade for the Baron

## Barrington's Brigade
## Book 6

# Ruth A. Casie

## ARE YOU SIGNED UP FOR DRAGONBLADE'S BLOG?

You'll get the latest news and information on exclusive giveaways, exclusive excerpts, coming releases, sales, free books, cover reveals and more.

Check out our complete list of authors, too!

No spam, no junk. That's a promise!

### Sign Up Here

www.dragonbladepublishing.com

*Dearest Reader;*

*Thank you for your support of a small press. At Dragonblade Publishing, we strive to bring you the highest quality Historical Romance from some of the best authors in the business. Without your support, there is no 'us', so we sincerely hope you adore these stories and find some new favorite authors along the way.*

*Happy Reading!*

*CEO, Dragonblade Publishing*

# Additional Dragonblade books by Author Ruth A. Casie

**Barrington's Brigade Series**
A Marriage for the Marquess (Book 1)
A Dilemma for the Duke (Book 2)
A Redemption for the Baron (Book 3)
A Vow for the Viscount (Book 4)
A Reckoning for the Earl (Book 5)
A Masquerade for the Baron (Book 6)

**The Ladies of Sommer-by-the-Sea Series**
The Lady and Her Quill (Book 1)
The Lady and the Spy (Book 2)
The Lady and Her Duke (Book 3)
The Duke's Lost Love (Novella)

**Pirates of Britannia Series**
Donald
Hugh
Graham
The Pirate's Jewel
The Pirate's Redemption

**The Lyon's Den Series**
The Lyon's Gambit
The Lyon's Alliance

# Chapter One

THE SCENT OF roses, beeswax, and far too much perfume lingered in the parlor at Lady Wilmot's country home in Sommer-by-the-Sea. Heat pressed at the back of Leticia's neck. Her fan was a poor defense against the prickle of rising impatience. The weather had begun its slow shift into autumn, and with it came the first of the indoor entertainments, a musicale. Lady Leticia Salisbury stood near the refreshment table, fanning her cousin Felicity's dance card with thinning patience. Across the room, the girl had vanished into a cluster of young ladies fluttering around the footmen who'd just brought in a fresh tray of ratafia cakes.

The musicale had been her aunt's idea, respectable enough, with just over sixty guests, a competent quartet, and more conversation than music. Leticia had agreed to attend. A favor, nothing more. Her only duty was to chaperone, guide, and ensure her cousin didn't flirt too freely, overindulge in sugared almonds, or commit the unforgivable sin of dancing with the same young man twice. It had taken less than an hour for Leticia to regret every syllable of her promise.

She looked down at the card. "Three blank spaces," she muttered, and turned toward the edge of the room just as the orchestra launched into a country reel. Laughter erupted from the far corner.

"Lady Leticia?" someone called, far too brightly.

She turned. Mr. Denby, freckled, flushed, and already waving, headed straight toward her, something white clutched in his hand. A misplaced glove, perhaps, or a crumpled handkerchief. Or, heaven help her, another poorly composed poem about her cousin's smile. Her stomach sank. Poor Felicity would never survive another verse about her dimples.

Leticia took a decisive step forward, intent on intercepting him before he reached the punch bowl and said goodbye to his dignity.

Unfortunately, someone else moved at the exact moment, and they collided at the corner of the table. Her slipper grazed the heel of a well-polished boot, and she let out a soft *oof* as a firm hand caught her elbow.

"Terribly sorry," she murmured, regaining her balance.

"I believe that's yours," said the gentleman.

Leticia looked down. Her cousin's dance card had fallen to the floor. She bent to retrieve it just as he did. Their fingers brushed.

"A dance card," he said, glancing at the names. "And I see I'm on it. Twice."

She arched a brow. "Are you?"

He studied the card for a moment and gave a quiet huff of amusement. "That explains it. This isn't yours."

She reached for it. "No. It's my cousin's."

"I owe her an apology," he said, handing it over, "and my friend a warning. Too much time and far too little supervision."

Before she could respond, two gentlemen approached, untitled, judging by the look of them, their gait, and their complete disregard for the sanctity of conversation gave them away.

"There he is," said the taller of the two, clapping the stranger's shoulder. "Ash, romancing young ladies already?"

"He's fulfilling the obligations," said the other with a grin. "It's in the patent, you know, romance, charm, and a fondness for dreadful poetry, just beneath property rights and moral deportment."

Leticia's gaze sharpened. *Ash.* Short for Ashcombe. Baron

Ashcombe. The name suited him. Crisp. Precise. Quietly inconvenient.

Ash sighed, as though he'd been suffering fools all evening. His shoulders stayed square, feet planted with a soldier's steadiness. This was no idle society man.

"Gentlemen, your timing is as impeccable as your taste in fiction."

"We aim to please," said the taller one with mock solemnity. "Carry on," he said with a careless wave of his hand.

The pair drifted off, and Leticia tucked the card into her reticule, amusement flickering at the corners of her mouth.

Once again, the music began.

Ash turned back to her. "May I have the honor of this dance?"

She hesitated. "I'm afraid you're not on my card."

"Perhaps I can remedy that, at least unofficially," he said. "One dance. No mischief. No poetry."

She studied him for a moment. He stood with unhurried confidence, no smile, no posturing. Just waiting.

The orchestra struck up another country reel. Across the room, Mr. Denby had reached her aunt and was bowing toward her cousin, clearly congratulating himself on delivering whatever he'd been holding. Her cousin looked horrified.

Leticia turned back to him. "Very well. But only one. A second dance, and someone will draw the wrong conclusion."

"And we mustn't have that," he replied evenly, offering his arm.

They stepped onto the floor together, matched only by height and timing.

Leticia had danced with a dozen partners in a dozen ballrooms, but this felt different. It was as if she'd stepped into a perfectly rehearsed play she'd never auditioned for. His touch was assured, his silence deliberate, and her pulse had the audacity to skip, just once. The warmth of his palm steadied hers, and against her will, her chest tightened, a treacherous thrill chasing through her ribs.

Ash didn't fill the silence with compliments or charm. He simply danced, precisely, and well.

"Are you always so serious?" she asked during a turn.

"Only when I'm expected to be entertaining," he said.

She nearly laughed.

When the reel ended, Ash bowed. "Thank you, my lady. I shall endeavor to limit my appearances to a single line on future dance cards."

"That would be safest," she said lightly.

They parted with a nod. Ash disappeared into the crowd, and Leticia turned to find her cousin threading her way toward her, cheeks flushed and eyes wide.

"Who was that?" Felicity whispered, tugging her aside in a swirl of silk and whispered scandal.

"A baron, apparently," Leticia murmured. "New to town. Dances well. Understands sarcasm."

Felicity's eyes sparkled. "He looked at you like he knew something the rest of us didn't."

Leticia handed over the slightly crumpled dance card. "He looked at me like I'd rewritten it. Honestly, three blank spaces? You mustn't be so choosy."

"I was saving one for Mr. Denby," Felicity said shyly. "Though he tried to hand me Aunt Margaret's lace cap, thinking it was mine. I didn't have the heart to correct him."

Leticia smiled despite herself. "Perhaps you'll marry for mercy, and I'll marry for silence. That would suit us both."

They turned toward their aunt, who was waving her fan with quiet authority at the card table.

And somewhere across the room, Ash's gaze found Leticia again, just once, with something unreadable behind it, cool and intent, as if testing her mettle rather than admiring her gown.

THAT EVENING, WHEN Leticia returned to Eastbury Manor, her aunt's home, she sat at her dressing table, pins in her lap and her hair half undone, while her cousin perched cross-legged on the edge of the bed, still in her evening gown and clearly unwilling to surrender the night.

"I'm only saying," Felicity insisted, "he looked at you like he meant something by it."

Leticia met her gaze in the mirror. "He looked at me like he was trying to decide whether I was the problem or the solution."

"That's worse," Felicity said, appalled. "He's a baron. He's supposed to be charming."

"He was polite," Leticia replied, tugging another pin loose. "And he danced with precision, which is more than can be said for Mr. Denby, who nearly turned a country reel into an act of war."

"That's unfair," Felicity protested. "He means well."

"Most missteps in life begin with good intentions and poor rhythm."

Felicity laughed, flopping backward across the coverlet, skirts and ribbons spilling around her like an overturned bouquet. "Do you think he'll call on you?"

Leticia lifted a brow. "We haven't even been introduced."

"Doesn't seem to have stopped him."

"That," Leticia said dryly, "is what makes it remarkable. And slightly improper."

"Improperly intriguing," Felicity countered.

Leticia stood and turned from the mirror, her gaze lingering on her reflection a heartbeat longer than necessary. A baron, a dance, and a smile she hadn't meant to give, unsettling. She drew a breath, steadying herself before facing her cousin. "You're still in your gown."

"I was waiting to see if you'd admit you liked him."

"Get up," Leticia said, gesturing toward the screen. "If you crush that hem, I shall never hear the end of it from your maid or mine."

Felicity giggled and scrambled upright, half-skipping toward the screen with her slippers in hand. "You're terribly serious for someone who smiled at a baron."

Leticia paused, letting the smirk form before turning away. "I smile at all manner of men. It keeps them from asking questions."

Behind the screen came the rustle of fabric and a low, satisfied sigh. "Do you think he'll call anyway?"

Leticia, now in her nightdress, returned to the dressing table and resumed the slow work of braiding her hair.

"He struck me as the sort of man who doesn't call unless there's a purpose. And one dance at a middling assembly may not qualify."

"You remember it."

"I remember the conversation."

A pause.

"You liked him."

"I said no such thing."

"You didn't dislike him."

Leticia secured the end of her braid with a ribbon and met Felicity's eyes in the mirror.

"He was… not uninteresting."

Felicity grinned. "Which, coming from you, is the same as declaring undying affection."

"If I ever declare undying affection," Leticia said calmly, "you have my permission to faint with style and summon the physician."

Felicity laughed again and slipped under the coverlet just as Leticia dimmed the lamp. The room fell quiet, still enough for her own thoughts to sound louder than the night.

Leticia slid into bed and lay still, staring at the ceiling.

Her cousin would return to London in the morning. She, on the other hand, had no desire to go back. Her aunt had taken her in after her parents' passing, and Eastbury Manor had been her home ever since.

The baron's expression came back to her, cool, assessing,

almost distant. And yet he'd offered his arm, asked her to dance, and thanked her as though it mattered.

Not uninteresting, she thought again, and closed her eyes.

THE NEXT MORNING brought fog, a lingering haze of perfume, and secrets. Before breakfast, Captain Gabriel Ashcombe had received a gold token, his summons.

Now he stood in front of Lord Barrington's townhouse. It was square, respectable, and entirely unimpressed with itself. He resisted the urge to adjust his cravat. He hadn't worn his uniform in months, but something about Barrington always called the soldier in him to the surface, even in a civilian's coat and polished town boots. The ballroom's laughter clung faintly to him still, a reminder that he belonged more to campaigns than assemblies.

He rapped once, brisk and efficient, and was immediately admitted by Barrington's butler. "Good morning, Mr. Sanderson."

"Good morning, my lord. Upstairs, sir. First door on the left."

Barrington's study looked more like a campaign room than a gentleman's retreat. Papers lay in meticulous stacks across the desk. Maps flanked the wall beside a half-filled brandy decanter. At the far end of the mantel, a lone vase of wilting roses spoke of a recent feminine touch. Likely his longtime friend Mrs. Bainbridge's attempt at softness.

Barrington stood at the hearth, sleeves rolled, spectacles perched low. He glanced up briefly.

"You're late."

"I'm titled now," Ash replied. "Baronial grace takes time."

"You move like a man trying to avoid an assignment," Barrington said as he poured two glasses. He handed one over. "Don't bother. You'll take it."

"Will I?"

Barrington didn't answer. He crossed to the desk and laid a page flat.

"Three thefts," he said. "All local. One during the Wycliffe Assembly, another at the Fairchilds' garden supper, and the third after a card party at the Harringtons'. Each theft was quiet and precise. No alarm was raised."

Ash took the paper and scanned it. "Jewels?"

"Mostly. Valuables, but none were unique. What matters is the aftermath. Each victim received a letter, unsigned and explicit. Pay, or private affairs will be exposed."

Ash frowned, examining the paper in more detail. "Blackmail?"

Barrington nodded once. "All couched in language meant to suggest ties to the Order."

Ash looked up. "The Order's finished, isn't it?"

"Their known leadership has been captured or scattered. Edward's final report is still forthcoming, but from what we've discovered, the structure is gone. The Order, as it operated, no longer exists."

Ash narrowed his eyes. "But..."

Barrington met his gaze. "We never identified the true leader. Not conclusively. Every name we traced led to another shadow. And now, someone is picking through the wreckage, rebuilding, or repurposing. They're using stolen funds and the threat of scandal to piece together something new."

Ash's jaw tightened, half reflex, half memory. "So this thief."

"We've taken to calling them the Raven," Barrington said.

Ash's chin lifted. "The Raven. That was the Order's mark."

"Yes. Clever. Silent. This is no common criminal. This is a threat to study, not chase. Like a raven, this is someone who is at home in the dark and drawn to glittering things."

"Poetic."

"Unavoidable."

Ash took a slow sip of brandy. "And you believe they'll strike again?"

"I do. These thefts weren't random. They were deliberate. Targeted. Someone is testing our reach while they build influence, one gem, one secret, one whispered threat at a time."

Ash set the glass down. "You want me to stop them."

"I want you to observe," Barrington corrected. "The Marchmont Masquerade is in two nights. Nearly every person of consequence will be there. I expect the Raven will be among them."

"And you're sending me?"

"You're newly titled, unmarried. More importantly, you're on the guest list. You'll draw no attention. You're the perfect man for it."

"Splendid," Ash said. "I've always dreamed of serving His Majesty in lace and a mask."

Barrington reached for a sealed envelope. "This one actually opens doors. Try not to misplace it."

Ash accepted the invitation, slipping it into his coat. "And if I don't dazzle with my wit and charm?"

"Observe, report, and try not to insult anyone titled."

Ash smirked. "A challenge."

"A worthy one," Barrington replied, lifting his glass. "For a man who's mastered cannon fire but not conversation."

They shared a glance, wry, familiar, edged in mutual trust.

Ash finished his brandy and put the glass down as he stood.

Barrington gave a nod. "Godspeed, Ashcombe."

Ash lifted two fingers in a half-salute and stepped out into the sharp morning air. A masquerade. God help him. He would rather face gunfire than a ballroom full of marriage-minded mothers. But orders were orders, and a baron, it seemed, was still a soldier.

# Chapter Two

T HE AUTUMN LIGHT filtered through thinning trees, casting long golden streaks across the gravel path. The Sommer Castle Gardens were dotted with promenaders and carriages, all pretending not to notice one another, as if visibility alone fulfilled the obligation of society. The masquerade was only a day away, its anticipation rustling through the gardens like the first breath of autumn wind.

Ash kept pace beside Lady Erica Notley, careful and unhurried, as mannered as the conversation they were expected to share, though his chest tightened, reminding him he'd rather be anywhere else. The air smelled faintly of damp leaves and salt from the sea, and each breath felt more like endurance than leisure.

The stroll had been her suggestion, a harmless opportunity for fresh air, mild conversation, and no expectation of fireworks. She wore a soft blue walking gown that matched her eyes almost too precisely, and her bonnet was trimmed with ivory lace. Altogether, she looked as though she'd been painted for the express purpose of putting others at ease.

Ash shifted his weight slightly, the tightness in his shoulders refusing to relax. Something about her perfection made him feel out of place, as if he were an ink stain on parchment too pristine to bear it.

"I do find the coast lovely in autumn," she said, watching the leaves swirl near the base of a tree. "There's something orderly about the change. Summer fades, and the world turns quietly inward."

Ash glanced sideways. "I suppose that's one way to see it."

"You don't agree?"

"I've never thought of the seasons as orderly," he replied. "Weather is a battlefield, always shifting, and often insufferable."

She laughed, a soft, elegant sound, perfectly timed. "You sound like a man still expecting cannon fire in the hedgerows."

"Force of habit."

They continued for another dozen paces.

"I'm glad we did this," she said. "You're easy to speak with."

Ash was not certain that was true, but he inclined his head. "Likewise."

Their conversation had wandered from books, a recent musicale, to the current state of the newspapers. She asked nothing of consequence, and he offered little in return. She was pleasant, gracious, and unquestionably suitable.

And yet, despite her kindness and quiet humor, something in him fell flat. The silence between their words pressed heavier than the words themselves.

He wasn't in love with Erica, but her family was respected, her manner composed. She was everything a baron's wife was expected to be, and everything he wasn't ready to fight. It should have been enough. It was not.

Still, suitability was what mattered. He was titled now and expected to settle, to marry, to build a life that would outlast his years of service. Erica struck him as the sort of woman who would not flinch from duty. Who would not question the long absences, the silences between letters, the public decorum that came with the role.

She would make a proper baroness.

She excused herself at the corner of Park Lane, thanking him with a smile that left nothing resolved and nothing promised.

Ash watched Erica disappear down the walk with her maid, her posture unchanging even as the breeze tugged lightly at her bonnet. She never looked back. He stood still for a moment, as if trying to feel something definitive, a decision made, a chapter closed. But all he found was the same hollow pause that had followed them through each step of the garden. It had been a lovely day, by any measure.

ASH TURNED, INTENDING to return home, when a familiar voice called from the other path.

"There he is! Our resident baron and battlefield poet, Baron of Romantics!"

Ash groaned softly.

Two figures approached, his untitled, unabashedly impertinent friends, still in riding coats and clearly enjoying the chase. Trenton, the taller, grinned as he tipped his hat in mock solemnity.

"We heard you've taken to the parks. Next thing, you'll be writing sonnets in the shrubbery."

"Did she look at you with admiration?" asked Henry, the shorter and more dangerous of the two. "Or mild confusion? We're betting on confusion."

"She laughed," Ash said.

"She laughed?" Trenton clapped a hand to his chest. "You'll be engaged by Wednesday."

"Don't be ridiculous."

Henry leaned in. "We're merely encouraging. The baron must uphold his sacred duties."

"Romance, charm," Trenton recited, "and a fondness for reading aloud by candlelight."

"It's in the patent," Henry added. "Just under land stewardship and foxhunting."

Ash stopped walking. "If either of you says the word courtship again, I shall enlist you both as footmen at the masquerade."

Trenton raised a brow. "So, you're attending."

Ash nodded once. "On orders."

Henry gave a theatrical sigh. "Ah, nothing says romance like government-sanctioned espionage."

Ash huffed. "Only when the gentleman is newly titled, unexpectedly bold, and apparently unfamiliar with reading the fine print."

Trenton paused, brow arched. "That sounds personal."

Ash didn't answer.

They resumed walking, their laughter trailing behind them as the wind picked up slightly, carrying with it the scent of turning leaves and early frost.

Ash said nothing else, but as they reached the gates, his thoughts lingered not on Erica's perfect posture or her careful turn of phrase, but on another voice entirely.

Sharp. Amused. Discerning.

*Only when the gentleman is newly titled, unexpectedly bold, and apparently unfamiliar with reading the fine print.*

A wry smile tugged at his mouth.

"Not uninteresting," he murmured to himself.

Ash arrived home just before dusk, the long walk from the park doing little to ease the tension that had settled between his shoulders. The house, no longer his father's and not yet fully his, still bore the stiffness of old ownership. Portraits he hadn't chosen lined the walls. Books he would never read sat in neat, dustless rows, as if ordered to impress rather than enjoy.

He set his hat on the nearest table and glanced around, frowning faintly. The fire had been laid but not lit. The decanter on the sideboard was full, though he didn't recall asking for it to be refilled. A letter rested unopened on the mantel. And the blasted boots, the ones he preferred for evening wear, had been moved. Again.

He stooped to peer beneath the escritoire, found nothing, and straightened with a sigh.

The staff meant well. They were efficient. Loyal. They simply didn't know his habits, and he hadn't the patience to train them. Not yet.

It was a small thing, misplaced boots, unfamiliar chairs, but the accumulation wore at him. A title might settle on a man's shoulders overnight, but belonging… that took time. The barony sat on him like a uniform that didn't yet fit.

He moved toward the hearth, stooped, and struck a match with slow precision. Flame flickered and caught as shadows danced across the paneled walls.

The room warmed as the light grew, but the unease didn't fade. The tension in his shoulders held firm, as though his body refused to be fooled by heat or hearth.

He sat in the armchair nearest the grate, legs stretched out, posture relaxed in the way of a man who had spent years teaching his body to be still. The stillness had once been a useful and reliable skill. Tonight, it felt like armor that no longer fit.

Erica's voice drifted through his memory, all soft inflection and social poise. She had said all the right things, had dressed with impeccable care, had walked at exactly his pace, and smiled at exactly the right intervals. Everything about her had been… correct.

She met every standard the title required. On paper, she was perfect. And yet, he could not make the pieces fit.

So why did it leave him hollow? Because the decision had already been made.

He leaned forward and reached for the newspaper on the side table. The Times, folded twice over, had been abandoned unread. He unfolded it, stared blankly at a column about dock tariffs, then dropped it again.

It wasn't the memory of Erica that lingered.

It was the other woman. The one who had looked him dead in the eye and accused him of not reading the fine print.

Ash let out a slow breath and rubbed the back of his neck.

The woman near the punch bowl filled his mind.

There was nothing showy in her demeanor, no calculated

elegance or well-placed compliments. She'd met him as though he were a challenge she intended to solve, not charm. And when he'd offered the expected banter, she'd parried without blinking.

*Not uninteresting.*

It had been a deflection, and a cowardly one at that.

She had caught him off guard, and worse, she had done so without title, without introduction, without apparent effort. And still, he remembered her. Not the fall of her hem or the color of her ribbon, but the tilt of her chin. The curve of her smile was not entirely amused or forgiving. Her presence unsettled him in a way no cannon fire ever had.

Ash rose, crossed to the sideboard, and poured himself another half-measure. He didn't usually have more than one drink, but tonight felt like an exception, though he couldn't say why.

He returned to the chair, drink in hand, and glanced at the small notebook resting beside the lamp. It was a military habit he'd never entirely abandoned, recording notes, reminders, and impressions from the day. Never anything personal. Just enough to remember where things stood.

He opened to a blank page and dipped his pen.

*October 3 – Walked with Lady Erica Notley in Sommer Castle Gardens. Discussed music, publications, and seasonal observations. Appropriate in all respects. Suitability confirmed. Entirely unremarkable.*

He paused. Considered the word *unremarkable*, and underlined it once with steady precision, a quiet finality in the motion that was heavier than he intended.

He hesitated before dipping the pen again. The pen hovered, then dropped to the page.

*The lady with the dance card. The one I forgot to forget.*

Another breath. He had to find out more about that woman.

He closed his notebook. No flourish. No underlining this

time, just a line on a page and a flicker of something he couldn't quite name, warming in his chest like the fire across the room.

# Chapter Three

L ETICIA HAD NOT slept well.

Not for lack of comfort. The bed was warm, the linens fresh, the house respectfully quiet. But her thoughts had looped themselves into knots, tugging at the edges of her rest each time she began to drift off. The moment she closed her eyes, the memory of a bow, a hand, a look returned with unwelcome precision.

It had been one dance. One conversation. Nothing that should have lingered.

And yet, a chill ran up her neck at the memory of his gaze. Not with admiration, but with interest. As though trying to decipher something that wasn't entirely legible at first glance. Most men looked at her and saw only what they expected: polite charm, practiced ease, and inherited grace.

She had read three pages of *Camilla*, stared at the same corner of the ceiling for what seemed like hours, and once considered going downstairs for tea, except that would mean explaining herself to Alice, her lady's maid, or Aunt Margaret. Heaven forbid.

But he had tilted his head, just slightly, as though cataloguing something unexpected. Evaluating, not admiring.

And he had danced like a man trained to follow orders, not instincts.

Leticia rolled onto her side and muttered to the ceiling, "Not uninteresting."

She didn't know whether to be flattered or insulted.

The morning light was soft, unhurried, and far too gentle for the restlessness curling beneath her skin.

She lay in bed longer than usual, her eyes tracing the shadowed curve of the ceiling above her. The house was quiet. Someone, probably the maid, had opened the curtains just enough to let in a spill of golden light across the foot of her bed. Dust motes danced in the beam like so many idle thoughts.

It had been only a dance. A single conversation. Nothing to stir the heart. Nothing to keep her awake.

Leticia exhaled and swung her legs over the edge of the mattress, letting the chill of the floor remind her where she was and, more importantly, where she wasn't. Not in the ballroom. Not in the soft, suspended moment when the stranger who turned out to be a baron, newly titled, had thanked her with such deliberate formality. *My lady.* Spoken like a question he meant to answer later. The echo of his voice still chased through her like an unfinished melody, persistent and unwelcome.

Her maid, Alice, entered quietly, arms full of linens.

"Morning, my lady. The kettle's just on. Your aunt says Lady Alfreda means to call this afternoon. Shall I lay out something pale or bold?"

Leticia blinked, startled from her reverie. "Pale," she murmured. Then, realizing what she'd said, amended, "No. Bold. Something with shape."

The word surprised her. Brazen, almost. She stiffened, as if daring herself not to retract it again.

The maid curtsied, lips twitching as if to smile, and slipped from the room.

Leticia stood, wrapped her robe tight, and crossed to the window. Beyond the window, the world was waking calm, unhurried, and indifferent to her unrest. The day had begun, ordinary and indifferent.

The world had resumed without pause, which only made her more vexed with herself for lingering.

She turned away from the window, trying to shake the heaviness that clung to her thoughts like fog. There was nothing to be done about it now. One dance. One remark. It shouldn't have meant anything.

And yet.

She stepped into her day dress slowly, letting Alice fasten the back while her mind wandered elsewhere. The sash was still in her hands when the maid re-entered with a salver in her hand.

"A note, miss. Delivered not ten minutes ago."

Leticia took it, noting the familiar crest embossed in the wax, Notley House. Her smile came involuntarily. Erica's notes were always carefully penned, full of flowing script and casual charm, as though written in a sun-dappled garden with nothing more serious than a poem in mind.

She broke the seal and unfolded the paper.

*Darling L,*

*Last night was a triumph, but our season's mischief is far from over. The masquerade draws near, and I do hope you'll attend. I shall be there, plumed, painted, and pretending nothing at all.*

*They say masks reveal more than they hide. I wonder what I might learn if I spot you behind one.*

*Promise you'll come. I've half a mind to make it a game, but perhaps we're past such things.*

*Ever yours,*
*Erica*

Leticia read the message twice. Her fingers tightened around the edges, just enough to crease the paper before she caught herself.

It was exactly the sort of note Erica always sent, light, lovely, and designed to leave one feeling special. And yet, there was something in it… the suggestion of a challenge, the hint of secrecy beneath the silk. Her friend's hand always sparkled with gaiety, but this time it pressed more deliberately, like a bell she could not unhear.

She folded it again, slower this time, and looked toward the window.

She told herself she hadn't yet decided whether to attend. The idea of a masquerade seemed indulgent and unnecessary. However, the idea had settled beneath her skin, persistent and irrational. She told herself it was an obligation, a social expectation, but some part of her craved the escape.

The gown was already ordered. The mask was chosen. The invitation was accepted weeks ago. It would be noticed if she didn't attend. And there would be resulting gossip. She let out a deep sigh. She had no intention of being the brunt of that.

Leticia tapped the folded letter against her palm.

A single dance wasn't a scandal. Unless one kept thinking about it the next day.

She set the letter on the dressing table and turned back to Alice, who stood waiting near the armoire.

"Something with shape," Leticia said again, more firmly this time. "And the green slippers."

Alice's brows lifted slightly, but she offered no comment. Only a nod, and the faintest suggestion of a smile.

Leticia turned her attention back to the letter, still folded on her dressing table.

She should have forgotten him by now.

The dance hadn't lasted more than five minutes. He had said nothing remarkably, that maddening phrase, *not uninteresting*, and her name as though it were a secret he meant to carry away with him. Yet there had been something about the way he stood. As if accustomed to command, but unused to amusement. As though he didn't quite know what to do with someone who answered him honestly.

He had danced like a man who followed patterns, not instincts. Each step was precise, measured, not mechanical, but as if he'd been trained to move with efficiency, rather than joy.

It had intrigued her. And more than that, it had stayed with her long after the music ended.

She stood, pacing lightly before her mirror, absently adjusting the fall of her sleeve. Memory slipped in where discipline should have been of a summer afternoon at Ridgemoor, Erica laughing in the garden, tossing bread to the ducks with unapologetic aimlessness.

"You can't always be composed, Leticia," words she'd deflected at the time with a practiced smile, though they'd pricked sharper than she let on. Only now did she begin to understand the warning behind them. Erica had said, tugging a blade of grass between her fingers. "Someday you'll want to be entirely unreasonable, and I do hope I'm there to see it."

Leticia hadn't known whether to be flattered or insulted. She smiled, of course. That was what one did. But even then, she had felt the divide between them. Erica was carefree and radiant, and herself… reliable.

She glanced at the clock on the mantel, at the small velvet drawer in her dressing table where the masquerade mask had been tucked away since it arrived from the modiste.

She hadn't so much as lifted the lid. Perhaps she was afraid of who she'd find behind it.

A knock came at the open door, followed by the unmistakable silhouette of Lady Eastbury. She wore her dark shawl wrapped elegantly over one shoulder, a small book in her hand, and the faint scent of lavender trailed after her.

"You're up early," her aunt said lightly. "Good. I've been awake for hours and had no one to share in my indignation at the latest from the Morning Post."

Leticia turned. "What has society done now?"

"An article named a viscount's pug one of the ten best-dressed attendees at Lady Withersby's garden party."

Leticia blinked. "Was it well dressed?"

"Impeccably," her aunt allowed. "But I object to its inclusion on principle."

Leticia smiled despite herself and gestured toward the chair near the window. "Shall I prepare a protest? Or merely have Alice remove the fashion section before your tea arrives?"

"No, no. Let the world be absurd. It makes our restraint appear virtuous." Her aunt settled gracefully, added, with the slightest arch to her brow, "I hear your friend Miss Notley is preparing something especially grand for the masquerade."

Leticia raised a brow. "Already?"

"She's had it planned since July, I suspect. She merely let the rest of us catch up."

There was a pause. Leticia folded her hands. "You're looking forward to it?"

"I am." Her aunt smiled softly. "There's a kind of delicious freedom in not being recognized. Anonymity, just for an evening, can make one surprisingly bold."

Leticia considered that. "Or dangerously foolish."

"Possibly both." Her aunt looked up. "But there is something to be said for stepping out of one's role, even briefly. One can try another way of being. A different voice. A secret self."

Leticia glanced again at the drawer. A mask was a hiding place. But also a mirror. It could conceal just enough to let something truer slip through.

She was not so composed as she had once believed. And if she let herself want something, someone, with that same honesty, she wasn't sure she'd know how to stop.

She watched the sunlight shift across the floorboards and, for a moment, imagined who she might be if no one expected her to be anyone at all.

# Chapter Four

ASH SAT IN the morning room, a half-read letter in one hand and a cup of coffee gone tepid beside his untouched breakfast.

The house, for once, was still. No mislaid boots, no absent-minded footmen rearranging things for reasons that defied logic. Only silence, and a steadily growing pile of correspondence. The faint tick of the mantel clock cut through the stillness, each second louder than it should have been. The stillness pressed on him more than the noise ever had, leaving him restless.

He turned back to the letter, though he had already read the first line three times.

*Ash,*

*There's been another quiet incident. Unconfirmed, but consistent with the pattern. All connected to elite events, high attendance, and minimal oversight. The masquerade may offer an opportunity to observe. Attend as planned. No action unless something feels off. Quiet presence only.*

*– B.*

No name. Just the initial. Barrington's hand, spare and unmistakable.

Ash folded the letter and set it down beside his cup. The masquerade had always been on his calendar. It was one of those events that straddled the line between social obligation and political presence. Harmless, in theory. A night of music, wine, and anonymity.

He wasn't fond of anonymity. This time, though, he wasn't dreading it. He reached for the coffee, found it cold, and set it down again. He would endure masks and frivolity for duty, but his pulse had not quickened because of Barrington's order.

He'd been informed that his presence would be "socially beneficial." Observation in evening clothes. No need for a uniform. Just a mask, and a partner.

And that was the problem. He didn't want a partner for duty. He wanted…her. His grip on the cold cup tightened involuntarily, the porcelain shifting with a quiet scrape against the saucer.

The woman from Lady Wilmot's musicale.

Not Lady Erica. Not one of the whispered-about heiresses or perfectly polished debutantes. Those were the women who made sense. The ones who would not undo him. The ones who wouldn't matter.

That was the point?

Her.

The one who had called him out with a smile. Who had made him feel like a man, not a title. The memory unsettled him in a way battle reports never had.

He scrubbed a hand across his mouth and stood, pacing toward the window. There was no reason to believe she would attend. No promise. No certainty.

But if she did…

He exhaled through his nose and turned back toward the desk. He still had reports to review, questions to frame, and details to memorize. None of it felt as real as the woman who had taken up residence in his mind, a woman with a discerning smile and eyes that had seen straight through him.

A sharp knock at the front door interrupted his thoughts.

A moment later, the butler appeared with the solemnity of a man well-acquainted with interruptions he had no authority to refuse.

"Mr. Trenton and Mr. Winthrop, my lord."

Ash didn't bother to rise. "Let them in."

Trenton entered first, hat in hand, his coat slightly askew and mischief clearly brewing. "Your man's excellent. Only flinched once when I mentioned we might be bearing scandal."

Winthrop followed behind, already eyeing the breakfast tray. "We thought you might be reading dispatches. Or issuing them."

Ash gave them a measured glance. "Those days are behind me."

"True," Trenton said, dropping into a chair as if he weighed half as much. "Now you defend against duchesses, not foreign powers."

"And you're doing a poor job of it," Winthrop added. "That coffee is a crime."

Ash said nothing, but he did remove the offending cup.

"We heard you are attending the masquerade," Trenton went on. "Your name's on the list, beneath someone titled and forgettable. Which does make you look rather impressive."

Ash raised a brow. "And you're here because?"

"To supervise," Winthrop said. "Masquerades are dangerous territory. Masks, mistaken identities, a dangerous concentration of satin."

"You've no idea what you're walking into," Trenton added. "One misstep, and you'll be engaged before the second waltz."

Ash returned to the papers on his desk. "Not likely."

"Because you're immune to charm?" Trenton asked.

"Because I'm not dancing."

Winthrop leaned on the hearth, clearly enjoying himself. "He'll dance if she's there."

Trenton's grin widened. "The one from Lady Wilmot's musicale."

Ash could still see the way the candlelight had caught the edge of her profile, the quick turn of her head before she'd spoken, precise, direct, unafraid. A moment that should've faded, but hadn't.

Ash didn't look up. "You presume too much."

"We were there," Trenton said. "We saw your face."

"You looked," Winthrop said, "like a man trying not to be caught thinking."

"She spoke to you like a person, not a prospect," Trenton added. "Must've been terrifying."

Ash closed the folio in front of him.

Trenton, more serious now, said, "Just don't forget where you are, Ash. At a masquerade, everyone sees what they want to. That doesn't mean it's true."

Ash studied him. "You think I'm in danger of being deceived?"

"I think," Trenton said, rising, "you've already been noticed. And you haven't stopped wondering what it meant."

Winthrop clapped a hand on Ash's shoulder as he passed. "Try not to fall in love with the wrong woman."

"And for heaven's sake," Trenton added, "make sure it's the correct woman when you ask her to dance."

They left in a burst of laughter and long coats, arguing about the worst dance partners they'd ever suffered.

Ash remained where he was, the fire at his back, the echo of their parting words heavier than he cared to admit.

He wasn't planning to propose to anyone. Not yet. Not exactly. But the words had been there, unspoken, waiting.

Still, the thought lingered, unwelcome and unshakable, like the echo of a dream one hadn't meant to remember.

Ash stood motionless long after the front door had closed.

The fire crackled behind him, low and steady. A log split with a sharp hiss, and the sound echoed too loudly in the stillness.

Their words had been meant as teasing. Mostly.

But he had seen the glance Trenton and Winthrop shared when they thought he wasn't looking, one part amusement, two parts concern. He'd known men who trusted him with their lives, and those two fools were among them. That made their warning harder to ignore.

He walked to the side table and opened the guest list. It had arrived two days ago, neatly folded and already annotated by his secretary.

He told himself he was checking for familiar names, potential allies, likely guests.

But his gaze skimmed the columns without focus, pausing now and then as if recognition might strike.

She would be there. He didn't know how he knew it—only that he hoped she would.

The woman from the musicale, as elusive as her name, as impossible to forget.

He read the list again, slower this time, searching for something he couldn't name. A trace. A hint. Something.

There was nothing, of course.

Still, he folded the page carefully and set it aside, unwilling to admit even to himself that he had been looking.

He glanced at the mantel clock. Late afternoon already. Not long now.

⟫⟪

HIS VALET ARRIVED precisely at five, as expected.

"I've laid everything out as requested, my lord," the man said, discreet and composed. "Do you wish to dress now, or closer to your departure?"

Ash glanced at the mirror and nodded. "Now."

In the dressing room, the garments waited in quiet obedience: the black evening coat with its fine silver embroidery, the waistcoat of deep midnight blue, the mask, leather and satin, a dark half-face that shadowed the eyes but left the jaw bare.

He ran his thumb along its edge. The leather was cool beneath his fingers, faintly scented with polish. The smell reminded him of the armory, of shields before parade. Not protection, appearance.

He dressed in silence while his valet adjusted the cuffs and brushed the coat. The boots gleamed. The cravat folded in an unfussy knot. Layer by layer, the uniform of civility replaced the man beneath it.

When the valet withdrew, Ash took up the mask again. It wasn't ostentatious. Just enough to grant anonymity or distance. He couldn't decide which he needed more.

He held it a moment longer, thumb resting over the curve where cheek met temple, as if the leather itself might answer. Then, deliberately, he raised it to his face. The ribbon drew tight behind his head with the soft sound of silk.

The man in the mirror was familiar and foreign all at once, composed, deliberate, and unreadable. The mask suited him too well.

It wasn't a disguise. It was a threshold. And standing on its edge, he realized how easily the world mistook silence for strength. The soldier in him welcomed the concealment; the man resented it.

He adjusted the mask, watched how the light caught its angles. It did not make him someone else. It only made him *invisible.*

He had walked into battle with less hesitation than this. But battle had never asked him to risk the one thing he had always guarded...hope.

# Chapter Five

THE BRONZE GOWN caught the light like dusk through cathedral glass—soft, warm, and easily overlooked until one truly looked.

It wasn't sumptuous, but it was beautiful, graceful in a quiet, deliberate way. The silk caught the light like breath, shifting from bronze to honey as she moved. For one unguarded instant, she had expected the mirror to offer someone else back to her. Someone braver. Someone less careful. But the image that met her gaze was unchanged. The same composed young woman, who always did what was right and never let the world glimpse what it cost her, stared back at her.

The gown had done its part. It was Leticia who had not changed.

Her throat tightened, the smallest tremor of longing threading through her composure. She would try the mask later, just to see if it might do what the gown could not. But the thought carried its own unease, as if daring to hide might reveal more than she was ready to face.

"A simple pin," she murmured, reaching for the tortoiseshell comb on the dressing table. Her hair was already twisted into a precise chignon, a quiet rebellion in its simplicity. "No sparkle."

Alice nodded, quick, capable, and wise enough not to argue.

Her aunt entered a moment later, her own gown a subtle dove-gray trimmed with silver thread. She looked Leticia over once, smiled with a warmth that didn't reach for words.

"Lovely," she said. "Exactly enough."

Leticia smiled faintly. "I wasn't aware elegance had a measurement."

"Oh, it does," her aunt replied, sinking into the armchair by the window. "Too little, and you disappear. Too much, and you invite judgment. Exactly enough, and they spend the whole night trying to remember you properly."

Leticia's soft laugh caught halfway to her throat. The words struck with a truth she didn't wish to name. Too little, and no one would see her. Too much, and they might never stop.

Her aunt's gaze drifted toward the window. "I never liked masks," she said after a pause. "They give people permission to be cruel—or to pretend kindness. But when I was your age, I wore one anyway. A red one with gold trim. I told myself it was for the thrill of it. Perhaps I only wanted to see who I might be if I weren't myself for a night."

Leticia turned toward her, surprised by the confession.

Her aunt's smile curved, soft and rueful. "I danced twice with a man who never learned my name. He made me laugh. Then he vanished into the crush, and I never saw him again."

Leticia absorbed that in silence, uncertain whether it was meant as a warning or nostalgia.

"Do you regret it?" she asked quietly.

"No." Her aunt's eyes warmed, though her tone stayed wistful. "But I never told your mother. She would have asked what I thought I was looking for, and I wouldn't have had an answer."

She stood, smoothing the folds of her skirt. "You don't have to wear that mask, Leticia. But if you do, make certain the person behind it is still you."

She pressed a quick kiss to Leticia's temple, unexpected, fleeting, and left the room.

When the door clicked shut, the stillness folded around her again. The mask lay waiting nearby, deep green velvet edged in bronze thread, peacock feathers catching the light. It was more daring than anything she owned. The sight of it embarrassed and thrilled her in equal measure, as though wanting it revealed something she hadn't meant to show.

She reached for it but stopped short. The mask seemed alive in the lamplight, its colors shifting, promising a courage she wasn't sure she possessed.

Leticia breathed out slowly. Perhaps she would only hide behind it. But even that, she thought, might be something.

She turned the mask over once in her hands and then set it down again.

A sharp rattle startled her. The tea tray trembled as Alice, reaching for an earring, brushed against the edge. The cup tipped. Porcelain struck wood. The liquid spilled in a bright arc, steaming and amber.

It splashed across Leticia's bodice, running down the bronze silk in blooming trails that darkened as they spread. The heat caught her breath. Then came the chill.

Alice gasped, horror written across her face. "Miss—I didn't— I'm so sorry!" She seized a cloth and began blotting helplessly. "I'll fix it, I swear—please—"

Leticia stood motionless, the scent of tea rising sharp and bitter around her, the fabric already ruined. Her mask lay forgotten on the table, its feathers quivering as if in sympathy.

The door opened again a moment later. Her aunt's calm voice preceded her. "I heard a commotion…"

Before Leticia could answer, the butler appeared behind her aunt, his tone uncertain. "Miss Notley has arrived, my lady."

"Show her in," Lady Eastbury said, stepping aside.

Erica entered with a wrapped bundle in her arms and an expression of gentle alarm. "What happened? I saw your butler's face and feared catastrophe."

Leticia's lips curved faintly. "There was tea."

Erica's gaze swept the room and saw the stained gown, the cloths, and Alice's stricken face. Something unreadable flickered in her eyes before she crossed to the chaise and laid the parcel down with care.

"I wasn't sure you'd have something ready," she said lightly. "I brought this earlier, but hadn't sent it up. The color didn't suit me, too deep, but I knew it would be perfect on you."

Leticia blinked. "On me? But what about your gown?"

Erica shrugged, easy and unconcerned. "I have another. I came only to be certain you had no excuse to stay home. It seems I arrived at the right time."

Lady Eastbury studied her, curiosity flickering but unspoken.

Leticia's gaze moved to the parcel. There was no reason to refuse, yet for a breath she only stared at it. A moment ago, the evening had seemed lost. Now, as the light caught the edge of the folded silk, it felt as though the night itself had changed its mind about her.

Minutes later, Leticia stood while Alice adjusted the bodice of the new gown, her earlier apology still pink on her cheeks. The maid's hands moved with reverent care now, each gesture an unspoken attempt to mend what had been spoiled.

The hunter-green silk shimmered as it settled into place, richer and deeper than anything Leticia would have chosen for herself. The fabric caught the lamplight like forest shadow after rain; it whispered when she moved, a sound both unfamiliar and intimate. The shawl lay nearby, crimson, gold, and russet, like something gathered from the edge of an autumn wood.

"It's beautiful," Alice said softly, not looking up.

Leticia didn't answer. Her hands rested at her sides, the hush of the silk a reminder of how quickly a moment could change. One instant she'd been ruined by a cup of tea, and the next she stood reborn in borrowed splendor.

Erica stepped behind her, smoothing a faint crease at the shoulder. "I told you it would suit you," she said, smiling at their reflection. "It's the contrast. You'll be the first thing anyone sees. And the last they forget."

Leticia's breath caught. The words brushed a hope she hadn't dared to name."

Alice passed her the mask.

Leticia hesitated only a moment before taking it. The velvet was soft beneath her fingers, the feathers light and cool against her temple. The ribbon slid into place with a whisper of silk as Alice tied it behind her hair.

She didn't feel like herself. Not entirely. But she wasn't someone else, either. The moment hung between the two, poised, uncertain, shimmering with possibility.

The door opened behind them.

Her aunt entered, one gloved hand still fastening her bracelet. "Leticia, are you ready?"

She stopped.

Leticia turned slowly.

For a moment, no one spoke.

Alice blinked, wide-eyed. Erica's lips curved just enough. And her aunt, ever composed, let out a soft breath as she took in the sight.

Even the butler, waiting discreetly in the corridor, took a moment too long to announce the carriage.

Leticia stood still beneath their silence, unsure whether she had stepped into a gown or vanished inside it.

In their eyes, she had become something new. But she wasn't yet certain who that was.

# Chapter Six

THE CARRIAGE LANTERNS cast long shadows as Ash stepped onto the front walk of Marchmont Hall, where the masquerade was already well underway.

Music drifted from open windows, lilting and indistinct beneath the low murmur of voices and laughter. Light spilled from the grand entry, warming the stone steps and the wide double doors thrown open to the autumn evening.

He paused, adjusting his mask. It sat snug against his face, leather and satin worked into smooth lines that shaded his eyes and revealed just enough to be recognized—if someone wished to recognize him.

He wondered if she would.

The footman offered his name to the steward inside, though Ash doubted it would be written down. Tonight was meant to be remembered for everything but names.

He stepped into the hall, the heat of the room brushing his skin, thick with perfume, wax, and rose petals scattered across the marble floor.

The ballroom was already crowded with feathers, jewels, and laughter tinted with wine.

Ash's gaze swept the room, not searching. Not exactly. But alert. He told himself he wasn't looking for anyone. His pulse betrayed him.

He made his way toward the refreshments table, drawn less by the wine than by the familiar figures holding court nearby. He saw Winthrop first, lounging with the casual posture of a man who had no intention of dancing. Trenton, of course, was speaking far too loudly.

"There he is," Trenton said, raising his glass. "Lord Unflappable himself."

Winthrop grinned and offered Ash a drink. "You're late. We were wagering whether you'd show up in uniform."

"Thankfully not," Trenton added. "Though you've missed the early entertainment. Word is Erica will be the gem of the evening."

Ash accepted the glass but didn't drink. "And how do you know that?"

"Saw her through the dressmaker's window yesterday," Trenton said. "Or at least a green gown she was being fitted for. Hunter-green. The sort that says: I intend to be admired."

"She waved to us," Winthrop added, "although her smile was clearly meant for you."

Ash's reply was dry. "Clearly."

But the word snagged inside him. Hunter-green. Feathers. Erica. She would definitely make an unforgettable entrance.

He lingered only a few moments more, listening to Trenton muse about the politics of flirtation and Winthrop's exaggerated opinions on the dangers of punch bowls. Then, without excuse or farewell, Ash stepped into the crowd drawn less by curiosity than by something already pulling him forward.

They let him go. Friends often did, when they recognized that words would only get in the way.

He moved further into the room. The music changed.

A trio of masked women swept past, and one of them turned, briefly, to glance at him. Her mask glittered with sapphires. It was not her.

He looked away. And stopped.

Across the room, at the top of the small staircase that descended into the main floor, a figure had just entered. The gown was deep green silk, shadowed and striking.

The shawl draped across her arms caught the light like autumn itself, gold, crimson, amber.

The mask, velvet, adorned with soft feathers, framed a pair of eyes that stopped him cold. He stood still as guests moved past him in a glittering swirl.

That was Erica. Hunter green, feathers, and a grand entrance designed to be admired. That was what he had come tonight to find, the suitable choice, the safe one, the woman who would steady a baron's life instead of upending it.

And yet... something in the stillness around her tugged at him. A hesitation in her breath, perhaps, or the hint of wonder in the way she looked at the room, as if she hadn't expected to be seen.

Madness. This was Erica. He would not let a single glance undo weeks of reasoning. He had come tonight to silence the echo of another voice, not feed it.

She stood just beyond reach, her face half-lit, her posture quiet but assured. Others glanced at her, but no one was brave enough to approach. They hovered, uncertain, as if waiting for her to choose whom she'd favor. That was how Erica always held court—cool, composed, untouchable.

She said nothing to correct them. Nothing to contradict the identity they all assumed. Of course, she didn't. There was nothing to correct.

And when she turned, the gesture, subtle, composed, was eerily familiar. Something Erica had done once before.

His shoulders eased. The tightness in his chest unknotted, reason reclaimed ground.

Every detail confirmed it: her gown, her poise. There was nothing to question. Nothing to correct.

Trenton's voice echoed somewhere in his memory: *"At a masquerade, one sees what they want to. That doesn't mean it's true."*

And Winthrop's final parting shot: *"Try not to fall in love with the wrong woman."*

He had laughed at the time. But now, standing at the edge of the crowd, he wasn't laughing.

*"No one knows who you are here,"* Trenton had said once. *"That's the only time a proposal might actually be romantic."*

He took a slow breath. It was the way she moved, like someone who hadn't expected to be watched. And the way his body eased when he looked at her, as though recognition itself restored the breath he hadn't realized he was holding.

He crossed the floor slowly, careful not to rush the moment, one step at a time, as though approaching a ledge.

She did not see him at first. Or if she did, she gave no sign. He waited until he was close enough to speak without raising his voice.

"You've stolen the night," he said quietly. "And possibly a few hearts."

She turned, just enough for the light to catch her eyes. Her mouth curved wryly, uncertain. A flicker of something unguarded beneath the mask.

"Should I apologize?"

"Only if you intend to give them back."

He couldn't see her smile, not fully. But he *felt* it.

She dipped her head. "And you, my lord? Have you come to claim one?"

His voice was steady, but not light. He had come to claim certainty, to end the torment of guessing. To choose Erica and be done with the ghost of another woman. "Perhaps just one."

"One might argue," she said lightly, "that the true danger of a masquerade isn't losing one's heart, it's revealing it."

Her breath caught. He felt it in the slight tension of her hand, the shift in her stillness. The mask gave her freedom, but not immunity, especially not from him.

"Would you care to dance?" he asked, though he already knew her answer.

She nodded.

He offered his arm. She took it. Her gloved hand brushed his sleeve, soft silk against fine wool, and something inside him settled. Recognition. Rightness.

They stepped onto the floor as the musicians shifted into a waltz, slow and romantic, timed not for precision but for intimacy. He guided her into the first turn with practiced ease. She followed, gracefully and assured.

He did not speak.

Neither did she.

Their silence was not awkward. It was full. Unspoken. Daring.

Each step deliberate, as though they danced on the edge of something unspeakably fragile.

He studied her. The way she moved, the slight tilt of her head when the violins swelled, how the flicker of candlelight caught in her hair. Erica. Every detail said so. The gown, the entrance, the voice. This was the woman he had come to find, poised, intelligent, exactly right. And at a masquerade, what one wanted and what one believed could blur until they became the same.

He had not called her by name. Not once. But the echo of it lingered in his mind. Erica.

She met his gaze once, steady and bright, and the quiet between them deepened. He'd been in battles where silence meant death. Here, it meant surrender.

The final notes of the waltz hung in the air like smoke. Ash held her gaze for a moment longer, released her hand, only to catch it again as she turned to step away.

"Forgive me," he said, voice low, "but I find I've no interest in letting you vanish into the crowd."

She stilled, her wrist warm beneath his fingers. He felt her breath hitch, a delicate tremor, confirmation that he was not alone in this sudden, reckless certainty.

"You deserve better than to be approached again by someone who might forget your name." He paused. "So allow me to be the one who never forgets it."

The words were simple. Courteous. But his voice gave them shape, and for the first time in years, he spoke without armor.

She smiled, a faint, luminous curve, and something inside him shifted. Clarity. At last.

"Marry me," he said.

Around them, the music stopped, but the crowd did not.

One gasp, then another, followed by a ripple of startled silence cloaked in silk and candlelight.

# Chapter Seven

THE WORLD DID not stop.

The music continued. The chandelier sparkled overhead. A footman crossed the far side of the ballroom with a tray of wine as if nothing had happened.

*Marry me.*

He had said it aloud. In front of everyone who mattered and everyone who didn't.

Someone had gasped. She didn't know who. It might have been her.

Ash stood motionless, his expression unreadable behind the mask. But she could see the truth in his posture. The steadiness. The sincerity. This was no jest. No mistake.

Except it was.

A chill ran up her spine. He believed she was someone else.

She had not meant to let the deception go that far. Hadn't meant to answer him at all. But here she was, caught in green silk, borrowed feathers, and a name that was never hers.

But her voice had gone missing along with her breath and her reason.

Leticia opened her mouth and heard herself say it before she understood why. He didn't know her name, but somehow, he had found her. And for one reckless heartbeat, she wanted the illusion to be true.

"Yes." Not loud. Not strong. But it was enough. Enough to move through the ballroom, the crowd, her bones.

A few guests clapped. And then a few more. The sound grew. It was not jubilant, but obliging, like a celebration offered more out of habit than certainty.

Ash reached for her hand, not with triumph, but with reverence. His eyes never left hers as he lifted it gently to his lips. The kiss was soft, formal, and entirely public. And like a vow.

"You've made me the happiest man here," he said softly. "He was wrong, you know."

Leticia blinked. "Who?"

"Trenton. He said you didn't believe in romance."

Her heart folded in on itself. Of course. He believed she was Erica.

Before she could speak, a call went out from near the musicians' gallery.

"Another waltz!" someone called. "Let them have the floor!"

The conductor nodded, and a new melody began lush and slow, as the dancers around them stepped aside.

She let him lead her again. One more moment she told herself. One more dance before the truth found her.

Just one more moment, she told herself. One more dance. In the morning, she'd explain everything.

Tonight, she could pretend that she danced in a sea of rose petals alone with him.

She had never danced like this before. Never been seen, wanted, cherished. For the span of a waltz, the rest of the world ceased to exist.

The music faltered beneath a sudden scream.

"My necklace! Someone has taken it!"

All eyes turned.

A woman near the edge of the floor clutched at her bodice with both hands, her fingers trembling. She looked down in disbelief, patted her neckline again, as if the necklace might reappear by magic.

"No, no. It was just here!" she cried, spinning halfway toward her companions, her face drained of color. "Someone's taken it!"

Gasps rang out around the ballroom. The conductor dropped his baton, and the violins stuttered to a halt mid-phrase. One or two guests instinctively placed hands over their own necklaces or gloves, checking what had not yet been taken.

He moved with a soldier's precision, placing himself between her and chaos. She should have been grateful. Instead, she could only feel the cold certainty that he did not even know whom he was protecting.

"Where were you standing?" he asked the woman who had cried out.

She pointed toward a cluster of chairs near the refreshments. "There. Just before the last dance."

A footman had already gone to summon the house steward. Ash nodded once, turning to Leticia.

"Come with me," he said. "Barrington will want to know."

Leticia nodded, her voice still caught behind her ribs. She followed him through the thinned crowd, aware of every eye, every whisper. The music had not resumed.

They rounded the edge of the ballroom toward a quieter corridor, only to pause as a familiar figure emerged from the alcove ahead.

Erica Notley.

Dressed in dove gray, elegant and composed, she looked every inch the darling of society.

Ash stopped. So did Leticia.

"Well," Erica said lightly, "I see you've found someone to dance with after all."

He looked at her, at Erica, and said quietly, "You nearly fooled me."

The words were gentle. Grateful. Final.

Her pulse stopped. The world tilted, the truth plain at last—he hadn't seen her at all. Before she could speak, Barrington showed from the opposite corridor.

"Ashcombe," he said urgently. "We've just had another report. This one from the retiring room. I need you. Now."

Ash's gaze darted back to Leticia, as if he might still explain. But she stepped back. It was too late.

Leticia looked at Erica, not a rival. Simply the woman he had meant to propose to.

She had danced in borrowed feathers and let herself believe he saw her. But he hadn't. Not ever. Her hand fell from his arm. The space between them grew wider than the ballroom.

"I should go," she said softly to no one in particular, or perhaps only to herself.

Neither of them stopped her.

Leticia slipped away down the corridor and stepped into an alcove. The silence pressed in around her, heavy and close, like a corset drawn too tight. The mask was no longer elegant or mysterious. It represented a part she was never meant to play.

She lifted trembling fingers to untie it, letting the ribbons slip through her hands. The velvet mask fell to the table beside her like something shed, not discarded. Her reflection in the mirror above the table startled her. She looked young. Flushed. Uncertain. Not at all the woman the ballroom believed her to be.

She would go back. She must. There was no room for retreat now. But she would go back armored in stillness, not hope.

With careful hands, she retied the mask.

She walked without direction, slipping into the warren of hallways that led away from the ballroom, through a service corridor, past a powder room, until she found herself in a side drawing room dimly lit and blissfully empty.

Leticia stood with her back to the door, chest rising too quickly. The gown was too tight. The mask, too heavy.

Footsteps approached behind her, paused. A soft knock. "Leticia?"

Her aunt stepped inside, closing the door behind her. She said nothing at first. Just looked at her niece for a long moment.

"You cannot undo it," she said gently.

Leticia turned, stricken. "He doesn't even know who I am."

"I know."

"I'll tell him the truth. In the morning. We'll straighten it out."

Her aunt's voice softened, but it did not bend. "And do you think society will forget what it heard tonight? What it saw? You said yes, Leticia, in front of half the ton. If you retract that now, it will follow you. It will follow your family. Your parents."

Leticia looked down. Her fingers trembled against the silk of her gown. "What am I to do?"

Her aunt crossed the room and held her close.

"You are to be brave, as you always have been. But you are no longer a girl who can choose and unchoose at will. You're a woman now, and your next step must be taken with your eyes open."

Together, they returned to the ballroom.

The music had resumed. Soft, unobtrusive. A few couples moved across the floor in quiet figures, trying too hard to appear unaffected.

Leticia held her head high. Her steps were sure, her mask secure. But the hush as she entered rippled like a breeze across still water. People turned. Murmured. One woman curtsied too deeply. Another leaned toward her companion, whispering behind a fan.

"Is that her?"

"So young."

"I thought it was Miss Notley."

Lady Eastbury's presence was a shield beside her, calm and composed. Leticia kept her gaze forward, her smile nonexistent. The ballroom blurred at the edges.

Ash stood at the far end. He didn't move toward her, but his gaze found hers. There was something unreadable in it, concern, perhaps. Or confusion.

She didn't look away. But she didn't approach him either.

A familiar voice rose nearby. "There you are! You've been the subject of every whisper."

Mrs. Bainbridge swept toward them in a flourish of tulle and pale blue silk. "Come now, my dear. The look on half these ladies' faces is enough to give me indigestion. Let me rescue you before one of them offers you a bridal crown made of peacock feathers."

Leticia allowed herself to be led, grateful for the distraction. She did not know whether to laugh or cry, only that she was still standing.

But as they passed beneath the arch of the ballroom's far alcove, there it was again, that flicker of warmth and ache and dread. The way he had looked at Erica. The words he had spoken. *You nearly fooled me.*

He had looked into her eyes and seen someone else. That was what she would remember long after the music, the gossip, and the glitter had faded.

Let the ton whisper.

Let them cheer.

Let them print their announcements in the morning papers.

Leticia would remember that look for the rest of her life.

# Chapter Eight

LETICIA STOOD STILL long after the ballroom erupted, not applauding, not invisible either. Guests glanced her way with curiosity, perhaps even approval.

A fairy tale unfolding, except the tale had a borrowed gown and the wrong ending.

The jewels had vanished. The music had stopped. And Ash, no, Lord Ashcombe, had proposed to her in the most public, irreversible way possible.

Not to Leticia Salisbury, exactly. But to the woman he believed her to be.

The shock of it hadn't landed until well after the dancers had scattered, the whispers had started, and Barrington's sharp command had drawn Ashcombe away. Then her aunt appeared at her side.

"I suspect that wasn't planned," her aunt said, her tone dry.

She hadn't answered for Erica. Or him. She had answered for herself. Leticia could only shake her head. Her hands trembled, but she kept them clasped tightly at her waist.

"I'm told the jewels were real. And now they are very much not here."

Leticia glanced at her. "Do you believe I had anything to do with it?"

Lady Eastbury arched one eyebrow. "I believe you wore a gown that didn't belong to you, attended a masquerade you weren't meant to enjoy, and accepted a proposal that wasn't yours to receive. That's an impressively full evening."

"I didn't plan any of it."

"I rather assumed that." She squeezed Leticia's arm gently. "You needn't explain yourself to me. But you'll need to decide how you mean to proceed."

"I don't know."

"Then be certain of your next step, Leticia, because you may not get another. Now go. Get some fresh air. A walk in the garden will do you good. Breathe. Decide."

So Leticia had stepped into the garden. Not to flee. To think. Her slippers crunched softly on the gravel. The air was cooler here, tinged with sea salt and something quieter. Moonlight, perhaps, or the hush that follows catastrophe.

She stood near the edge of the path, the sounds of the ballroom muffled by distance and clipped hedges. Lanterns glowed along the walkways, soft and low. The pulse in her chest had not yet settled. She stood between two lives, the one she had borrowed and the one she might lose.

She heard his footsteps before he spoke.

"You left quickly," Ash said.

"I needed air." Her voice was thinner than she intended.

He stopped a few paces behind her. "I didn't expect…" He paused. "None of it went how I planned."

Leticia turned. The moonlight caught the edge of his jaw, the line of his mouth drawn tight.

"You didn't plan to propose?"

"I didn't plan to propose to you."

The words were blunt. Not cruel, but close.

She nodded once, as if confirming something she had long suspected. "And yet, I said yes."

He looked away. "You didn't correct me," he said quietly.

"No."

A moment passed between them, too full of all the things neither knew how to say.

"I was aware the moment Erica showed," he admitted. "I

should have seen it earlier."

"Too many masks," she murmured. "And borrowed gowns."

He looked back at her then. Not with regret. Not with apology, only awareness.

"Why didn't you stop me?"

She inhaled slowly. "Because it was already done. Because the room had seen and heard and decided."

His brow furrowed. "But you knew. You knew I..."

"Yes, I knew."

He stepped closer. "Why?"

Leticia looked at him fully. "Because I wasn't ready to let go of that moment." Her voice cracked faintly at the edge of the confession.

The silence stretched.

He stood with his hands at his sides, not reaching for her, but not retreating either. She wrapped her arms more tightly around herself, as if bracing for something that hadn't yet struck.

"Everyone believes it now," he said.

"Yes."

"We'll be expected to make announcements. Host dinners. Be seen."

"That's true."

He looked down, his voice quiet. "We could end it."

"We could."

A shift in the air. He wasn't looking at her now, but she could feel him beside her.

"But it would create a scandal."

"Yes."

He looked up and met her gaze again. "Perhaps... we don't end it. Not yet."

Leticia unfolded her arms, then folded them again, holding them tightly across her ribs. "What are you proposing?"

"A temporary arrangement. Two weeks. That should be enough time for the story to settle. For me to..." He paused. "To finish what I came here to do."

Leticia's voice was steady. "And afterward?"

"We dissolve the engagement quietly. Blame a difference of temperament."

"And the public?"

"They will have tired of us by then."

Leticia hesitated. "Do you make a habit of false engagements, Lord Ashcombe?"

"No," he said. "But I appear to have made one tonight."

A breath of laughter escaped her. Dry. Unbelieving.

She nodded. "Two weeks."

He bowed his head. "Thank you."

She looked back toward the ballroom. "This is not what I imagined."

"Neither did I."

And yet neither moved.

The music resumed behind them, a waltz.

Leticia didn't turn to go.

"I knew it was you," he said. "Not by name. But in the way you moved."

She went still.

The wind stirred the lanterns and her hem, but she didn't turn toward him. Didn't speak. Not yet.

He stepped beside her, not close enough to touch. "I danced with you before. At the musicale."

"I remember."

A pause. "I should have known then."

She looked up at him slowly. The lines of his face were unreadable in the half-light.

"You do now."

"Yes."

The air between them held, not with tension, but with the fragile burden of possibility.

She looked toward the ballroom windows, where music bled out faintly into the night.

"Two weeks, my lord," she said. Her voice was softer now, as if testing the shape of it.

He nodded, hesitated. "If we are to maintain the illusion, perhaps you should call me by my given name, Gabriel or Ash, if you wish."

She looked at him, something flickering behind her eyes. "That would complicate things...Gabriel. You must call me Leticia."

A small smile tugged at the corner of his mouth, but he said nothing more.

Leticia breathed in the salt air. Her skin tingled beneath her borrowed gown.

She had stepped into the garden to clear her thoughts. Instead, she'd stepped deeper into uncertainty.

Neither of them moved. Neither of them spoke.

And neither knew how it would resolve.

# Chapter Nine

THE LIGHT WAS too bright. Leticia blinked against it, her temples pulsing with a dull ache. Even the softness of the pillow could not soothe the tension that had crept into her bones. She hadn't cried. Not last night. Not even when the mask came off and the gown was unfastened and folded away. But her body felt as if she had.

The curtains were open. Morning light spilled across the room, pale and relentless, painting every surface with a truth she wasn't ready to face.

Alice must have come and gone already, leaving the room in a state of gentle readiness. Her brushes were neatly aligned, tea steaming faintly on the tray, her slippers placed just so at the foot of the chaise.

Leticia sat up slowly, her fingers brushing the silk coverlet. Her hands trembled, though she wasn't cold. Everything inside her felt hollow, half-frozen, as if warmth had gone missing.

Across the room, a note from her aunt rested against the teapot. A soft envelope. Pale lavender paper with her aunt's unmistakable handwriting.

*My dearest,*

*I've accepted an invitation from Mrs. Bainbridge. She'd like us to join her for tea and wedding flowers, yours as well as hers. Say you'll come. We'll sit beside her garden and pretend everything blooms as it should.*

*Your loving Aunt Margaret.*

Leticia exhaled through her nose and set the note aside. She reached for her cup, then stopped. The newspaper next to it caught her eye.

The morning edition. Still folded. Still untouched.

She set it aside. Instead, she stood and crossed to the washbasin, her feet bare against the carpet. The air held a faint chill. Everything in the room was tidy, composed, unshaken. She was not. She poured water into the basin and dipped a cloth, pressing it against her face until the coolness chased back the heat blooming behind her eyes.

Dressing took longer than usual. Alice had laid out a soft blue walking dress with pearl buttons and a shawl the color of quiet seafoam. Leticia stared at it for a moment, then chose a different one, a deep gray silk with a higher neckline and no ornament at all. She brushed out her own hair, each stroke an act of control.

By the time she descended the stairs, her aunt was already waiting by the carriage in a tailored pelisse and her traveling gloves.

They did not speak as they rode. Leticia kept her hands folded in her lap, watching the gray morning drift past the window. Her body moved with the motion of the carriage. Her thoughts refused to follow.

Her aunt's silence was the kind that asked no questions, offered no comfort, only presence. Leticia was grateful for it.

The Bainbridge residence was bright with blooms, the garden already spilling into its spring colors despite the lingering chill. A footman opened the door with a bow, and they were shown through to the morning room.

Mrs. Bainbridge stood at the table, surrounded by ribbon samples, lace swatches, and three teacups that had already begun to steam, and an entire bouquet of anemones sat in a vase, as if watching. She turned with a smile that was only slightly too bright.

"There you are. I was beginning to think you'd both abandoned me to hydrangeas and indecision."

Leticia curtsied with more grace than she felt. "Thank you for including us."

"Of course I did." Mrs. Bainbridge waved them toward chairs with a gesture both elegant and conspiratorial. "You're the talk of the morning, my dear. I suspect if you opened the paper, you'd find yourself described as *luminous*."

A hundred eyes had seen her say yes. That made it true, even if she hadn't meant it. Leticia's fingers curled beneath the edge of the chair, out of sight, as if the truth had nothing to do with her at all.

Lady Eastbury raised a brow. "We prefer to leave the papers until after tea."

"A wise choice," Mrs. Bainbridge said lightly. "The news of the engagement is quite official. It seems everyone is preparing to congratulate you."

Leticia did not correct her.

She stared at the tea in front of her, watching steam curl up and vanish into the air. The scent of orange blossom and honey should have been comforting. Instead, it was a mask, lovely, and entirely false.

She had said yes. Danced. Smiled. And now the world believed what she had only dared to imagine for a moment.

She wondered what Ash would say if he saw her now. Would he call her radiant again? Would he say her name?

Mrs. Bainbridge reached for a spoon to stir her tea, but did not look up. "Lord Ashcombe left rather late last night, with Lord Barrington, I believe. He looked, well, not like a man recently engaged."

Leticia stilled.

"I daresay it had to do with that awful incident," Mrs. Bainbridge went on. "Theft at a masquerade? It makes one wonder who else was masked last night, doesn't it?"

Lady Eastbury said nothing, but Leticia could feel the glance she offered over the rim of her cup. She hadn't forgotten the scream or the missing necklace. But her mind wasn't ready for mystery, not yet.

Mrs. Bainbridge's smile softened. "Of course, no one will ask too many questions. Not now. The papers won't allow it."

Leticia nodded slowly, unsure whether that was a relief or another layer of which she'd never be free.

She lifted her cup, lowered it again. "I didn't mean for any of this to happen," she said quietly.

Both women looked at her.

Mrs. Bainbridge was the first to respond. "Most things worth remembering begin that way."

Leticia's gaze dropped to the tea. "It's just that he didn't, he doesn't know…"

Lady Eastbury reached over and gently touched her hand. "You are not obligated to explain yourself. Not to us."

"I know," Leticia said. "But I think I need to say it out loud. Just once." She paused. Breathed. Then, with great care: "He thought I was someone else."

Mrs. Bainbridge said nothing for a long moment. "That's the problem with masks. They only hide what people already refuse to see."

⟫⟫⟩⟨⟨⟨

ASH STOOD IN Barrington's study, one hand braced on the map table, the other curled loosely by his side. The windows were closed against the damp, and the fire was unlit, leaving the room cool and heavy with pipe smoke.

Barrington handed him a slim folio. "The second theft was discovered not long after the first. Retiring room. Jewels, again. No forced entry."

Ash flipped through the brief report. "Another high-value item. Whoever this is, they're not picking at random."

"No. They're escalating." Barrington crossed to the window, the fog dulling the light against the pane. "They want attention. But not discovery."

"This isn't petty theft. These targets are deliberate. I want to know if the Order's resurfacing, and if they've changed tactics."

Ash exhaled slowly. He had dragged her into this. A mistake, yes, but one now printed in headlines and whispered across parlors. And if the Order had truly resurfaced, she wouldn't just be the subject of idle gossip. She'd be a target.

"I need to speak with Lady Salisbury."

Barrington looked over his shoulder. "Now?"

Ash didn't answer. Not with words.

"Leticia's likely already surrounded. And your name is print- ed beside hers in every drawing room across the city."

"I know what I said," Ash replied. "And I meant it."

"You meant it in public," Barrington said, more gently. "But I'd wager she's waiting for you to say it in private."

Ash turned away, the folio still open in his hand.

He hadn't seen her since the garden, since her silence hadn't matched the softness in her eyes. He had asked her to stay. She had. And now, with every thread pulling tighter, he wasn't sure if he'd simply protected her or drawn her into something far more dangerous.

LETICIA SAT ALONE in the quiet after the carriage returned her home.

The house was hushed, as though holding its breath. Even Alice had the good sense not to ask any questions when she brought in the afternoon tea tray.

The paper was still there. Unfolded. Waiting.

Leticia picked it up.

Her name stared back at her from the third column, neatly

printed beneath a headline that included Ash's. No speculation. No rumor. Just a quiet declaration of fact. The Baron of Ashcombe is engaged to Lady Leticia Salisbury.

Her fingers tightened slightly at the sight of her name, so familiar and so foreign in print. The ink didn't blur. The news didn't stammer. The story didn't care who she truly was.

It was done.

Leticia read it again. And once more. Not because she couldn't believe it, but because this was the version the world had chosen to remember. She just wasn't certain if it was the one she could live with.

# Chapter Ten

L ETICIA HAD NOT expected to enjoy herself.

She had attended enough gatherings as her aunt's shadow to know how quickly conversation among ladies of the ton could turn sharp, particularly toward the unfamiliar. But Lady Marchmont's parlor, airy and scented with lavender, had a gentler rhythm to it. The circle of women gathered that morning were not cruel, merely interested. And in Sommer-by-the-Sea, curiosity wore civility like lace gloves.

Before leaving, Leticia had braced herself for a gauntlet of veiled scrutiny.

Her aunt met her in the front drawing room, offering no comment on Leticia's choice of gown but watching with a faint smile as she adjusted her gloves.

"Lady Marchmont's teas are not known for their heat, but for their precision," Lady Eastbury murmured. "You'll find the company more mannered than merry."

Leticia glanced over. "And what role am I meant to play? The curiosity. The scandal."

"The newcomer," her aunt said. "Which, in this village, is all three."

She moved to fasten Leticia's locket, her mother's, worn for luck, and rested her hand lightly on her shoulder.

"You'll manage. Just remember who you are. And whose house you return to."

There was no unkindness in it. No comfort either. It was a

warning disguised as care. Sommer-by-the-Sea might not rival London in grandeur, but the women here had their own hierarchies, their own customs, and quiet codes. Her aunt had offered little guidance beyond a thin smile and a perfectly timed squeeze of the hand.

She had chosen a gown in soft blue, neither too fine nor too plain. Let them talk, she had thought. But now, seated among them, she found the atmosphere less combative than she expected.

Leticia sat with her gloves folded neatly in her lap, answering polite questions about her time abroad, the suddenness of her engagement, and whether she had any interest in joining the village's charitable society. She gave mild, agreeable answers and learned far more by listening than speaking.

They were more curious than critical. Lady Marchmont presided gently, keeping the conversation flowing. Mrs. Dennington had a ready laugh and a fondness for embellishing even the smallest local scandal. A younger woman, Miss Elwood, asked Leticia whether the proposal had taken place in public or private. Leticia offered the mildest version of the truth, omitting mention of masks, confusion, and unexpected kisses. She watched as their eyes lit with delight, eager to embroider her story into something finer than the reality. They spoke of the proposal as if it had been orchestrated. It had, of course, just not in the way they imagined.

It wasn't until the third round of tea that the conversation shifted.

"Have you heard about Lady Tewksbury's theft?" asked Mrs. Dennington, her voice pitched just above genteel astonishment. "Brazen, really. Right out of her sitting room."

"Her ruby ring, wasn't it?" said another. "I would've thought they'd go for her sapphires. Those are heirlooms."

"No, not the ring," Mrs. Dennington corrected. "It was that old garnet brooch. The one she rarely wore."

A flutter of conversation followed. Leticia kept her expression politely neutral, but her attention sharpened. A garnet brooch over heirloom sapphires? That was no random choice. She made no remark, but her mind turned over the oddity like a stone she could not set down.

Lady Marchmont shook her head. "We haven't had anything like this in years. Not since the silver was lifted from the vicarage."

Mrs. Dennington laughed. "That was a fox, not a thief."

"It snatched the entire fork from the windowsill and vanished into the hedgerow like a phantom."

Miss Ashford let out a peal of laughter. "Ah, but what had the fork speared? A fine piece of mutton, I suppose!"

Laughter rippled through the room. Even Lady Marchmont allowed a rare chuckle. "It took the vicar a week to stop blaming the curate."

"Regardless," Lady Marchmont replied, "this is altogether unsettling. One can't help but feel watched."

Leticia glanced toward the window. The street beyond was calm, shaded by trees, as ordinary as any other. She reached for her teacup again just as the parlor door opened and Erica entered, cheeks flushed from the morning air. Watched. Yes. That was precisely how it felt.

"Forgive me, ladies," Erica said with easy charm, pulling off her gloves. "I was delayed at the milliners. The shop was quite lively today."

She took the empty seat beside Lady Marchmont and cast Leticia a pleasant glance. "It seems all anyone can talk about is your engagement. I'm beginning to feel unfashionably out of date for arriving without a question or a theory."

A ripple of soft laughter passed through the room, and the conversation turned, predictably, to the proposal once more.

THE GATHERING HAD begun to thin when Leticia made her

farewells, offering practiced smiles and half-promises to call again soon. By the time she reached home, the afternoon light had turned golden across the garden walls, and her thoughts, so carefully ordered during tea, had begun to drift. Not toward the theft. Not even toward the laughter. But toward a man whose silence she understood more than she cared to admit.

She had not meant to write him.

She'd meant to forget the softness in his eyes, the precision of his dance, the way he'd asked her to remain, not as an obligation, but an invitation. Yet after a night spent listening to the stillness of her chamber, counting shadows instead of sheep, she'd folded a sheet of foolscap and begun.

She kept the letter brief, with three carefully chosen questions, none of them simple. They weren't meant to trap him. Just reveal the spaces where silence too often lived.

She wrote slowly, pausing between lines to think, not only about what she wanted to know, but about what it might cost to ask. She could have asked about politics or duty. But she didn't want the baron. She wanted the man beneath the title. When she finished, she folded the paper once, then again, and held it against her lips.

"Alice," she said quietly. "Would you see this safely to Lord Ashcombe?"

"Should I wait for a response?" she asked.

"If he chooses to respond, he will. If not…" Leticia shrugged. "I've preserved my dignity and left the matter in his hands."

Her maid blinked, nodded. "Of course, miss."

After trying to read Camilla and not making much progress, she went to walk the gravel path between the espaliered pears and the trimmed hedgerow. She regretted only the silk slippers. The dew had not yet dried, and she'd not asked permission to use the orchard path. But solitude mattered more than propriety this morning.

She hadn't expected to see him, not so soon. Not here. Seeing him so at ease, a half-eaten apple in one hand and the sunlight catching in his hair, made her heart beat faster. She didn't know what she had expected, certainly not this.

He was there. Not near the stables or the terrace, but just beyond the orchard wall, where the south lawn dipped toward the rose garden. His coat was folded neatly across the wall, his sleeves rolled. He took another bite of the apple in his hand, the motion unhurried, his gaze already tracking her approach.

Leticia slowed. "I wasn't aware you were here, my lord."

He turned. Not startled, not smiling, simply aware. He tilted his head. "My lord?"

"Gabriel," she corrected herself.

"Good afternoon, Leticia. I went for a walk and found myself here. I hope I'm not unwelcome."

"You are always welcome here… Gabriel."

He retrieved his coat and stepped toward her. "I received your letter."

Leticia drew the shawl tighter. "You know I expect an answer."

"Do you want them all at once?"

"No," she said. "But I expect one today."

He nodded, slipping the coat over one arm. "Walk with me?"

They took the path toward the smaller garden enclosure, where the air smelled of thyme and damp brick, and the sundial sat half-shadowed beneath climbing roses. Leticia paced slowly, her hands folded before her, expression unreadable.

Ash broke the silence first. "You asked if I've ever lied to protect someone."

She looked over.

"The answer is yes," he said. "I lied to a man I respected. To shield someone who deserved neither protection nor loyalty. It cost me that man's trust."

"Did he ever learn the truth?"

"Not from me."

Leticia considered that. The garden held its breath. Or perhaps it was only her. Something softened behind her eyes, a flicker of understanding or regret.

A breeze tugged at the edge of her shawl. She clutched it tighter, unsure if the chill came from the air or from his reply. They passed under a bower of roses, petals scattered at their feet like soft punctuation.

"I have the response to your letter here." He reached into his coat pocket and withdrew a folded paper. "I added a note."

She took it but didn't open it. Not yet. Her fingers pressed against the crease, holding it more tightly than she meant to.

"I have a question for you. I think it's only fair," he said, a hint of amusement brightening his eyes. "Three questions, actually."

"You have questions for me?"

"I do," he said. "But I wasn't prepared to write them this morning."

Her lips curved, just slightly. "Next time, then."

He studied her. "You're taking this seriously."

"We agreed to be honest with each other."

His voice dropped a degree. "I didn't expect it to be so direct."

Leticia looked toward the sundial. "We've two weeks. If this engagement is to mean anything, to you, to your work, to my reputation, we must act with precision. As you do when you dance."

He stepped closer. Not enough to crowd her, but enough to change the air. Her pulse quickened, but she held her ground.

"You meant what you said. About clarity."

She nodded. "And you?"

Gabriel reached out, not to touch, but to offer an open hand between them.

Leticia didn't take it. Not yet.

Instead, she turned the letter over in her hand. "Your questions had best be good, Gabriel. I'm not in the habit of entertaining dull suitors."

He lowered his hand and smiled, slightly, unhurried. "Neither am I."

They parted near the rose arbor, the letter folded in her fingers, and the early afternoon just beginning to warm.

Leticia waited until she reached her chamber before she unfolded the paper.

He'd remembered so much: her shawl, her quietness, her willingness to stay. But not her name. He hadn't asked. She didn't know why that mattered, but it did.

She didn't read the note immediately. She let it rest on the writing desk, her fingers pressed to the edge as if holding something fragile.

Then, slowly, she opened it, hope pooling low and quiet like sunlight beneath the surface of still water.

Her eyes widened. She drew in a soft gasp, her breath catching before her lips curved upward, not with amusement, but with something warmer, brighter.

She smiled, wicked and wondering all at once.

# Chapter Eleven

I T HAD BEEN two days since the masquerade, yet the aftershocks still lingered. The unspoken glances, hesitant words, and the memory of a dance that had changed everything.

Sommer Castle still held the scent of stone and silence. The air inside was cool and dry, laced with the faint sweetness of ivy and something older than dust, perhaps memory itself. Sunlight slanted through tall, narrow windows, striping the floor in gold and shadow. Far below the cliffs, the North Sea surged and receded, its distant rhythm a reminder of the castle's perch above the world.

A hush lingered, the kind that made footsteps feel like an interruption. Somewhere beyond the walls, birds called. But inside the chapel, there was only the breath of stillness and the quiet echo of forgotten prayers. Sunlight streamed through mullioned glass, warming the worn flagstones. Ivy crept in through the broken mortar along the southern wall, and a scattering of dust motes danced in the air like fading ghosts of vows once spoken.

Leticia stepped into the cool shadows and let the hush fold around her. She walked slowly past the pews, trailing her gloved fingers along the edge of the smooth wood. The quiet did not unnerve her. It made her feel full, each breath carried meaning.

She paused in the center aisle, facing the modest altar, and tried to picture it draped in lilies and lace, filled with guests instead of dust. A wedding at Sommer Castle.

Her own?

The very thought startled her. The notion was foreign, even in silence. And yet, hadn't she made a kind of promise?

She drew a breath and let it out slowly. The air smelled of salt and stone.

The idea struck like a bell, too loud for the silence.

Mrs. Bainbridge's voice cut across it. "I can see the appeal," she said, tilting her head as she examined the carved altar. "It's private, it's dignified, and it doesn't smell of mildew. What more could a bride want?"

"An aisle long enough to make my mother feel important," Barrington muttered, stepping past a half-rotted pew.

Leticia stifled a smile.

Mrs. Bainbridge turned to him, one brow arching with wry precision. "We'll give her a good seat. Front and center."

"She wants a choir. And a trumpeter," he said, not facing her.

"She can bring them. I'll be the one walking down the aisle."

Barrington said nothing, though his expression suggested retreat.

Behind them, Kenworth entered, bearing a leather folio so stuffed it looked ready to burst. "Latest update on the guest list, sir. There've been twelve additions and four subtractions. Your mother decided the cousins from Surrey ought not be over-looked. Again."

"How many cousins are there in Surrey?" Mrs. Bainbridge asked.

"No one knows," Kenworth said grimly. "They breed in pairs and travel in battalions."

Leticia laughed, startled by the ease of it, delighted by the sudden lift in mood. The sound rang too brightly in the chapel's hush, but it felt welcome all the same.

Mrs. Bainbridge glanced at her and grinned. "You see? Even Lady Salisbury agrees."

"Only because I fear I may be seated beside one," Leticia said, glancing at Barrington, who was trying not to smile and losing.

"You'll be seated with the wedding party," Mrs. Bainbridge said. "If your intended hasn't scared you off by then."

The warmth rose in her cheeks, but she didn't look away. "I doubt he's easily rid of."

From the other side of the chapel, the man himself appeared, brushing dust from his coat sleeve as he ducked beneath a leaning arch. His cravat slightly askew. Sunlight lit the curve of his jaw.

She hadn't expected to see him. Not so soon. Not here. And certainly not looking so at ease. Her pulse quickened.

"Rid of what?" Gabriel asked, his tone mild.

"Surrey cousins," Leticia said smoothly.

Gabriel glanced at Kenworth, who looked deeply affronted. "I assure you, sir. They're a menace."

He smiled, but Leticia saw the flicker of something beneath the ease, a quiet intent. He had come for more than banter.

Kenworth cleared his throat with the gravity of a diplomat. "Might I suggest a compromise? A simple fruit sponge. No creams, no custards, and certainly no lemon curd."

Mrs. Bainbridge made a face. "You'll upset the lemon growers."

"We shall write them a letter," Kenworth replied, utterly serious.

Leticia stepped toward the window again, pausing in the warm shaft of light. Something brushed her skirts, a draft, or a memory. She let her gaze drift back toward Gabriel, who stood with one hand in his coat pocket.

He withdrew something small and folded.

Her breath caught.

Her letter.

He looked at it for a moment, his expression unreadable. Then tucked it back into his pocket, gently, deliberately.

Her fingertips pressed lightly against her palm, steadying herself.

"Honoria, have you seen enough?" Barrington's voice broke through the quiet. He turned to Mrs. Bainbridge with an air of finality. "You and I have walked through the ceremony, examined the rooms. There is little more to be decided."

Mrs. Bainbridge tilted her head, eyes lingering on the altar. "I suppose." Her tone carried resignation…and a flicker of satisfaction. "It will do."

Gabriel glanced at Leticia. "My coach is waiting. May I take you to Eastbury Manor?"

Mrs. Bainbridge waved a hand, her voice brisk but warm. "Go on, Leticia. We're finished here."

Gabriel offered his arm, his words gentle, deliberate. "After you, my lady."

The carriage ride from Sommer Castle was quiet, companionable. Outside, the sun began its descent over the hedgerows, casting the countryside in a golden hush.

When they reached her aunt's house, Gabriel stepped down first and offered his hand.

"Thank you for today," Leticia said softly, placing her hand in his.

He paused, still holding her hand. "It won't always be light-hearted. I hope you know that."

"I do." She hesitated. "But that doesn't mean it can't be meaningful."

"No," he said. "It doesn't."

They stood looking at each other for several heartbeats. Then Gabriel lifted her hand and kissed the inside of her wrist.

Leticia watched him go, her fingers brushing the edge of her sleeve where his touch lingered.

Erica would have known how to field the attention. How to make it hers. Leticia only borrowed it, and feared what price she might yet pay.

# Chapter Twelve

I T WAS RIDICULOUS, really. She had known he was coming. Had even selected her gown with that in mind. Yet when his voice reached her, deep, certain, and impossibly close, the world narrowed to a single sound. Her breath caught, and her fingers fidgeted with the hem of her sleeve. It was nerves, or the weight of what they were building. Yet beneath her ribs, something restless unfurled, a flutter she couldn't quiet.

It had seemed like nothing. A note written in her aunt's hand, sealed with the family crest, passed to the footman with quiet instruction. "For Lord Ashcombe," Lady Eastbury had said. Nothing more. No wink. No smile. Just the tone she used when she had an extra place set at the breakfast table.

Now it was clear. Her aunt had not left this meeting to chance. Relief rose at not having to navigate this uncertain courtship alone. And yet a flicker of wariness threaded through it. Was this her choice, or had her aunt quietly taken the reins again? Still, a part of her was grateful. It meant Gabriel was here, not by accident, but by intention.

And he had accepted.

The morning sun slanted across the floor of the Eastbury drawing room, painting long gold lines across the Aubusson carpet. Leticia sat straight-backed on the settee, her posture immaculate, while inside a low hum of anticipation stirred. She had chosen the soft lavender gown her aunt once complimented, and taken extra time with her hair, subtle acts that were habit, not hope. Yet now her gaze flickered toward the clock more than once. Would he look at her as he had in the garden, with recognition, rather than mistake?

Her aunt, as ever, was composed. Not distant but quietly observant, a thread of cool steel beneath the civility.

When the butler announced Lord Ashcombe, Lady Eastbury did not flinch. Instead, she poured the tea.

"Cream, my lord?" she asked, as though this were any ordinary call.

Gabriel entered with a slight bow. "No, thank you."

Leticia rose and curtsied, catching her breath at the sight of him, impeccably dressed, composed, and reserved. Yet beneath the polish, she saw the man who had stood in the garden and kissed her not with charm, but with feeling.

"Lady Eastbury," he said. "Lady Salisbury."

Aunt Margaret gestured for them to sit. "I'm glad you see the value in spending time together," she said, stirring her tea. "If this engagement is to proceed smoothly, it will require careful coordination."

Leticia said nothing. Gabriel inclined his head.

It was like a treaty between two nations, except she was both the prize and the problem. She bit the inside of her cheek to keep from smiling. Absurd, and yet… oddly comforting.

Aunt Margaret adjusted her spectacles, her fingers as precise as her tone. Even her teacup had been placed back on its saucer with exacting care. She reached for a small notepad and turned over a page.

Her breath hitched. What now? Was her aunt about to declare a list of unacceptable behaviors? Expectations? A prickle of unease touched her spine, even as a flicker of gratitude bloomed. At least there would be no guessing. No mixed messages. Just the rules. Whatever they were.

"I have outlined the expectations. There will be no further surprises." She glanced at him over her wire glasses. "The proposal was scandal enough."

Gabriel's stillness wasn't passivity but precision. He listened like a man trained to hear nuance, one who had sat at negotiation tables far more treacherous than this. He wasn't merely accommodating her aunt. He was evaluating the terms, and he did not flinch.

Her aunt continued, "You may see each other under the following conditions. You may walk in the garden after supper. You may call twice per week for tea, and on Sunday after services if you attend with the family. A chaperone will be nearby. If you wish to write letters, they are to be sent through me."

Gabriel gave a faint nod. "Understood."

"You may send modest gifts," Lady Eastbury added, "Nothing inappropriate, nothing lavish. Anything that draws further attention will be returned without comment."

Gabriel's lips twitched faintly. "I shall attempt restraint."

"I should hope so." She turned to Leticia. "And you will not wander into gardens without your gloves or your sense."

Leticia managed a prim smile. "Yes, Aunt."

"There are to be no more rumors. No whispers. No ambiguities. Sommer-by-the-Sea thrives on gossip, but it wearies of it just as quickly. Let someone else provide a better scandal."

Gabriel inclined his head. "It won't come from us."

"See that it doesn't."

Lady Eastbury stood. "You may walk in the garden. I'll remain here with my embroidery. If I stand at the window, you'll know the conversation has gone on long enough."

They rose together. Gabriel offered his arm. Leticia took it.

⤜⟫⟫⟫⟪⟪⟪⤛

THE GARDEN WAS drenched in sunlight and honeysuckle. Gravel crunched underfoot, and skirts brushed the clipped box hedges. The air smelled of warm stone and flowering vines.

"You accepted all that rather easily," she said.

"Did I have a choice?"

"No."

He smiled. "I did the wisest thing a man can do. I agreed with the woman in charge."

Leticia's lips curved. "You'll make a fine husband yet."

"Only if you'll make a forgiving wife."

The words were spoken in jest, but something about the ease of his voice and the curve of his smile unsettled her. Not in fear, but in the way fantasy starts to feel like memory. As though she'd always known him. As though she might trust him, if she weren't careful.

They turned the corner by the espaliered pear trees that grew on the far wall. He slowed his step to match hers. Could something true begin in the middle of a false engagement? She could not be certain. But she wanted to find out.

"It was honest."

"But difficult."

"Truth usually is."

They walked a few more paces. Leticia stopped near the arbor, her hand resting lightly on the trellis. "I've asked myself something since the masquerade."

"What's that?"

"Is it me or the mission?"

Gabriel didn't answer right away. "At first, it was the mission. Now… it's less clear."

She looked up at him. "I don't want illusions."

"You deserve more than that."

He reached for her hand. This time, she let him take it.

"I wasn't planning this," he said. "Not the proposal, not the investigation, and certainly not you."

"And yet, here we are."

"Yes," he said. "Here we are."

He leaned in, giving her a chance to step back. She didn't. For a single heartbeat, the world stilled, and only the whisper of the breeze and the nearness of him remained. Something in her braced, then broke. The wall she hadn't realized she'd built. The kiss, when it came, was gentle and sure, a declaration made in silence. It wasn't merely the feel of his lips or the warmth of his hand. It was the startling ease of it. As if she'd been waiting for that moment longer than she dared admit.

Her fingers curled against the sleeve of his coat. His hand cupped her cheek. They didn't rush.

When they parted, she stayed close.

"That changes things," she whispered.

"It already has."

They walked back toward the house, slower this time. Leticia's heart was a careful tangle of hope and confusion. Each step with him was both grounding and unsteady. She wanted him to say something that would reveal what he truly saw when he looked at her.

But he said nothing. And she was too afraid to ask.

At the threshold, Gabriel paused. "I should say goodbye to your aunt."

Leticia opened the door. "Of course."

Lady Eastbury met them in the drawing room. Her needle paused over her embroidery hoop.

"I trust the garden air did you both some good."

Gabriel inclined his head. "It did, ma'am. Thank you for the invitation and your guidance."

"You will need both," she replied, with the barest smile, "Do take care on your return. And do send word of your next visit."

Something unfamiliar flickered in her aunt's expression. There was a softness, a warmth she couldn't place. It vanished quickly, but it stayed with her.

"I will."

Leticia followed him to the door.

At the threshold, she paused. "Tomorrow after supper, then?"

He gave a half smile. "Tomorrow."

She watched him walk away.

Lady Eastbury stood near the drawing room door, her embroidery set neatly aside. She crossed to Leticia, her expression unreadable until she reached her side.

"You're blushing, my dear," she said, looping her arm through Leticia's with surprising tenderness.

Leticia started to deny it, but her words caught somewhere between a smile and a sigh.

"Come," Lady Eastbury said, steering her gently back toward the parlor.

Leticia glanced toward the door, but he was already gone. The garden beyond shimmered in sunlight, unchanged. And yet, nothing in her life was as it had been only days ago. The kiss had unsettled more than her heart. It had rearranged her expectations.

"Let's finish our tea," her aunt said lightly, though her eyes lingered on Leticia a moment longer. "There's more to discuss than ribbons and reputation."

# Chapter Thirteen

T HE CARRIAGE TURNED up the gravel drive toward Ashcombe Hall, its wheels crunching a rhythmic welcome as the great house came into view. Gabriel waited at the top of the stairs, not as a soldier or distant aristocrat, but as a man receiving guests. His presence, steady and watchful, made Leticia's pulse leap.

The carriage drew to a stop. Gabriel descended the steps and reached the carriage just as the butler opened the door.

"Lady Eastbury. Lady Salisbury. Welcome to Ashcombe Hall." He offered his hand to Lady Eastbury, but she waved him off with a familiar smile.

"Help my niece first, Lord Ashcombe. I'm perfectly steady."

Leticia accepted his hand, her fingers curling against his palm. A moment of stillness caught her. It was absurd, how something so formal could feel so intimate.

"Lady Salisbury," he said softly.

"My lord."

Lady Eastbury stepped down behind her and gave Gabriel a keen look. "That tea you sent was perfectly chosen. A fine blend of jasmine and oolong, my favorite, though I haven't found it in years."

Gabriel turned to Fenton. "I believe I have my butler to thank for that."

Fenton bowed. "It was my pleasure, my lady."

Leticia's cheeks warmed. The bouquet of cream roses he had sent, without any note, only his seal, lingered in her senses. They were graceful, restrained like him. She had pressed one bloom between the pages of *Camilla*, as though she could pin down the memory.

As they crossed the threshold into Ashcombe Hall, sunlight poured through arched windows, warming the stone floors. The faint scent of polish and lavender wrapped around her. For a heartbeat, she felt as if the house itself had taken a breath.

They were shown into a drawing room, where a tea tray sat already prepared. Lady Eastbury thanked Gabriel for the invitation and the thoughtful gifts.

"You're too kind," she added, eyeing the porcelain teapot. "This tea is a favorite of mine."

Gabriel cast a look at Fenton. "Entirely his recommendation."

Lady Eastbury smiled. "Well played, Mr. Fenton."

Leticia's gaze lingered on Gabriel. "You've made the place warm."

He tilted his head. "It remembers laughter. I'm only coaxing it back."

The words tugged at her, as though he spoke not only of the house but of himself.

Lady Eastbury settled into a high-backed chair. "And doing it well, I daresay. My sister and I visited Ashcombe Hall often in our younger days."

Leticia turned, startled. "I don't recall you mentioning that."

"I imagine I didn't," her aunt replied with a wistful smile. "Your mother was far better at managing memories."

A ripple of curiosity rose in Leticia. Her mother and Ashcombe Hall. What else had been left unsaid?

Gabriel crossed to the window. "Would you care to see the portrait gallery?"

"Lead on," Lady Eastbury said. "Though I warn you, I may correct the footmen if they get any names wrong."

As they rose, Lady Eastbury glanced toward the hallway. "Has Professor Tresham sent his notes on the Vienna acquisition yet?"

Gabriel paused, shook his head. "Not yet. He mentioned needing to consult a private collection. Something about provenance and mistranslation."

Lady Eastbury's voice softened. "He does love a contradiction. But the man knows his history."

The gallery was long and stately, with windows spilling light across polished floors. Portraits lined the opposite wall, a silent parade of Ashcombes past. Leticia slowed, caught by the hush that deepened with each step.

Halfway down, she stopped. Her gaze fixed on a portrait.

Three figures. Two women and a man. Her mother, unmistakable with her dark hair and serene smile. Lady Eastbury, younger and vibrant, was the other woman. And between them, a tall man with a mischievous gleam in his eye.

"Robbie Ashcombe," Lady Eastbury said softly, stepping closer. Her voice carried the echo of memory and surprise, drawing a glance from Leticia and Gabriel.

She added gently, "I hadn't expected to see this picture again. He was your uncle, Gabriel."

Leticia turned, startled. "You knew him well?"

"Well enough. We were all very close then." She said no more, but her tone suggested there was more beneath the silence.

Gabriel joined them. "I'd never noticed the resemblance until now."

"You didn't know?" Leticia asked.

"I wasn't certain who they were. The names on the brass plates have faded."

Lady Eastbury's eyes softened. "Your mother loved that brooch."

Leticia's gaze caught on the gem painted at her mother's throat, a teardrop stone that shimmered even in oil and pigment. A chill settled beneath her ribs. The same brooch now rested in her jewelry box.

"She always did like sparkle," she murmured.

Lady Eastbury smiled. "We found that piece in Vienna. Robbie called it a trinket, but your mother adored it."

Leticia swallowed, keeping her voice light. "I remember how some of Mama's jewelry twinkled like stars." Yet unease curled at the edges of memory, a shadow she could not name.

"You were forever rearranging my pearls," her aunt added fondly. "You wound them round her wrist once and snapped the thread. Took a week to find all the beads."

Gabriel placed a hand on the frame. "Shall we return to the drawing room? The fire might be welcome."

With tea replenished and a warm fire crackling, the mood lightened. Gabriel, sensing the shift, glanced toward the sideboard.

"If I may be bold, would either of you care for a game?"

Leticia arched a brow. "Cards?"

"Not precisely," he replied, lips twitching. "A game I learned in the officers' mess. 'Two Truths and a Dare.'"

Lady Eastbury's eyes twinkled. "Oh, I like the sound of that."

Leticia laughed. "You would."

Gabriel inclined his head. "I shall begin, then."

He lifted a hand. "I once lost a duel of words with Lady Marchmont. I've never danced the quadrille without stepping on a partner's toes. And I once climbed the library shelves at Eton to retrieve a contraband volume of *Ars Amatoria*."

Lady Eastbury lifted a brow. "The duel is true, obviously."

Leticia grinned. "You stepped on a partner's toes."

"Incorrect. I did climb the library shelves. The rest, alas, are embellishments."

Leticia's smile tilted. "My turn. I once escaped a persistent suitor by locking myself in a chapel. I speak conversational Italian. And I've never lost at whist."

Gabriel leaned forward. "The suitor story is real."

Leticia offered no answer, simply sipped her tea.

Lady Eastbury gave her niece a sideways glance. "She's blushing. It's true. And I know she speaks conversational Italian about as well as she does conversational English."

Gabriel's mouth curved. "Remind me never to have Lady Salisbury as my whist partner." He turned to Leticia's aunt. "Lady Eastbury, I believe it's your turn."

Lady Eastbury chuckled. "Very well. I once drove a phaeton through Hyde Park at dawn. I once beat a bishop at chess in under ten minutes. And I once turned down a marriage proposal from a duke."

Leticia gasped. "A duke?"

Gabriel leaned back. "The phaeton is too specific. That one's true."

Lady Eastbury gave a mysterious smile. "Correct on the phaeton. But it was the bishop who won the chess match."

Leticia stared. "You turned down a duke?"

"I did. But that's a story for another day."

The game continued for several rounds, laughter softening the shadows of the past.

Eventually, the hour grew late. Lady Eastbury stood and collected her gloves.

Leticia turned to Gabriel, her heart caught between gratitude and unease. "I wasn't sure what to expect today. Now I have more questions than answers."

Gabriel's expression remained unreadable. "You're not alone in that."

She hesitated. "I thought perhaps this visit was about us. But it's about the past."

He reached for her hand. "It's both. But more than that, I wanted you to see where I live. How I live."

Her pulse fluttered. "And the future?"

"That's not just my question," he said quietly. "It's ours. And we have two weeks to answer it."

She leaned in and brushed a kiss against his cheek. "I shall have my answer in two weeks."

Lady Eastbury's voice called from the room beyond. "It's time, my dears."

Gabriel offered his arm. "Shall I walk you to the carriage?"

Leticia nodded.

They descended the steps in silence, the air thick with possibility.

At the base of the steps, Leticia paused. "Thank you for today. For showing us the gallery, for sharing those memories, even if they raised more questions than answers. I hadn't expected so much."

"For what part?"

"All of it."

He smiled. "You're welcome. For all of it."

She stepped into the carriage and turned to watch him as the door closed. He waited as the wheels began to turn before moving. The sight settled somewhere deep inside her, equal parts promise and uncertainty.

Lady Eastbury studied her niece as they settled in. "You're blushing again."

Leticia pressed her lips together, unwilling to give the truth away.

Lady Eastbury smiled and took her hand. "Come. Let's finish our tea when we get home. I daresay I rather like this Lord Ashcombe."

# Chapter Fourteen

L ETICIA TURNED SLIGHTLY, adjusting the fall of her gown as she studied her reflection.

On the vanity before her, the brooch lay in a shallow dish, a teardrop stone in an aging silver setting, crooked in the clasp as though someone had tried to mend it and failed.

She had picked it up twice that morning, her thumb brushing the bent edge. Twice, she had thought to pin it in place.

And twice, she had put it down again.

Her aunt had once called it "a piece of paste," but Leticia had loved it because it was hers. Because it had been her mother's. Because sometimes value wasn't measured in gold or worn for others to see.

A knock at the door pulled her from the moment.

"Come in," she called.

The door opened to reveal Erica Notley, perfectly composed in a pale lilac day dress trimmed in velvet. Her gloved hands held a flat parcel tied with satin ribbon.

"I hope I'm not intruding," Erica said, her smile just short of warm. "Lady Pembroke asked me to deliver this, some updated fabric samples. She's in a frenzy of decisions and asked your aunt for help. I offered to deliver them on my way."

Leticia accepted the parcel with a polite nod. "Thank you. I've just come from Ashcombe Hall myself."

Erica blinked. "How lovely. I haven't been in ages."

"It was... more welcoming than I expected." Leticia paused,

then added, "I saw a portrait there, of my aunt, my mother, and the previous Lord Ashcombe."

Erica's smile shifted, almost imperceptibly. "A rare piece. I remember that one. Your mother? I didn't know she was part of the Ashcombe family's history."

"I was just as surprised as you are," Leticia said evenly.

Erica said nothing for a breath too long. Then, with practiced ease: "I imagine the tea was excellent, too."

Before Leticia could respond, another knock interrupted them. Gabriel stepped into the doorway, Lady Eastbury just behind him.

"My apologies," he said. "I hoped to steal Lady Salisbury for a walk, if she's amenable."

Erica turned with practiced ease. "Gabriel," she said, almost fondly. "Still punctual. I was about to trouble your Lady Salisbury myself, but it seems I've been outmatched."

Gabriel smiled faintly. "You'll forgive me for the interruption?"

"Of course."

Lady Eastbury crossed to Leticia's side and took the parcel. "We'll look these over after tea, shall we?"

Erica's smile returned. To Leticia, it was cool and polished rather than warm.

Gabriel glanced toward the hallway. "I'll leave you ladies to it."

"If you're stepping out, I'll join you," Erica offered quickly, her tone light.

Lady Eastbury's voice interrupted, light but firm. "Miss Notley, you haven't forgotten why you came?"

Erica blinked. "The samples. Of course."

Lady Eastbury tilted her head. "It won't take long."

Something passed between them, sharp as flint. Erica's posture shifted, chin lifted as if to object. But her gaze met Lady Eastbury's, and she reconsidered.

"Of course," she said again, with a different smile. "We'll do that first."

They moved into the small sitting room, where Lady Eastbury had already laid out a swatch book and a half-dozen folded fabrics beside the tea tray. Erica sat gracefully, smoothing her skirt as though she were preparing to be painted. Her tone was pleasant, but Leticia heard the faint hollowness beneath it.

Lady Eastbury lifted the first sample, a rich cream silk with a faint gold embroidery.

"For the Bainbridge wedding," she said aloud, more for Leticia than Erica. "Lady Pembroke wasn't satisfied with the original selection. Too stiff."

Erica nodded as if she agreed, though she hadn't been present. "It's a fussy fabric. Never sits right on the shoulder."

Leticia made a polite sound, but her attention kept drifting. Erica's eyes flicked between the tea tray and the door.

Halfway through the samples, another voice called down the hall.

"Anyone home? I've brought cake and scandal."

Mrs. Bainbridge swept in, cheeks flushed, curls rebelliously escaping her bonnet. She carried a small box tied with twine, eyes sparkling with mischief. Lady Eastbury raised an eyebrow. Leticia sat straighter, braced for something unexpected.

"Perfect timing," Lady Eastbury said smoothly.

"Oh, good, I thought for a moment I'd be crashing a duel," Mrs. Bainbridge said brightly, then noticed Erica. "Oh. Hello, Miss Notley. Don't let me interrupt."

She crossed to Leticia and handed her the box. "Lemon cake. I bribed the cook. It's not for sharing, mind you, unless you're feeling generous."

Lady Eastbury arched a brow. "You've arrived at just the right time."

"I always do," Mrs. Bainbridge said, then looked to Erica, her tone feather-light. "Of course, if I've interrupted important conversations about questionable fabric or even more questionable intentions, I shall simply hover and glean."

Erica rose, her smile tighter now. "I was just going."

"You'll take something sweet before you do?" Lady Eastbury asked.

"No, thank you." Erica gathered her gloves. "Another time."

Leticia watched the door close, a faint chill prickling her spine.

Mrs. Bainbridge was already helping herself to a second cup of tea and examining the discarded fabric samples.

"I've never seen a woman make cream silk look like mourning garb," she muttered, flicking one edge. "Honestly, who sends Erica Notley to deliver anything delicate?"

Leticia gave a weak laugh. "She's … composed."

"So is a marble statue," Mrs. Bainbridge replied. "But at least statues don't try to listen through doorframes."

Lady Eastbury offered no contradiction. Her silence spoke enough.

They remained in companionable silence as the fire crackled softly. A faint breeze stirred the curtains.

"Do you like her?" Leticia asked.

Lady Eastbury poured herself a fresh cup of tea. "I trust her to behave as she always has. And I watch closely, just in case."

Leticia almost laughed. "A diplomatic answer." Yet beneath her smile, a knot of unease coiled tighter.

"My favorite kind."

There was another knock. Gabriel returned alone, hair slightly tousled by the wind. His expression was pleasant, but his eyes settled on Leticia.

"She's off, isn't she?" he said after a moment.

Leticia tilted her head. "Erica?"

He nodded. "She talks in circles. I never noticed before."

"Because you trusted her?"

Gabriel's jaw tightened. He didn't answer.

"I'll call tomorrow," he said instead. "If you're free."

Leticia hesitated, gave a faint nod. "I'll be here." The words cost her more than she expected.

He took her hand and bowed over it. A kiss to her knuckles,

warm and brief, left her heart unsettled. She watched him go, as though the air he displaced lingered in the room long after.

When the door closed, Lady Eastbury crossed the room and sat beside her.

"You're sharper than you let on."

Leticia leaned back in her chair, pulse still unsteady. "I didn't know what I saw. I only knew I didn't like it."

"A good instinct. Will you see him tomorrow?" her aunt asked.

"Yes." She paused. "I want to believe in him. In us."

Lady Eastbury was quiet for a moment. "And if you change your mind?"

Leticia smiled. "I'll know better than to wear borrowed hope."

Her aunt reached over, took her hand, and gave it a gentle squeeze.

"Your hope isn't borrowed. You're simply learning where to plant it."

The firelight threw shadows across the carpet. Curtains shifted with the night breeze, whispering against the casement. The house seemed to listen.

Leticia went to her room after she and Mrs. Bainbridge left. She walked to her writing desk and opened the small drawer where she kept letters and small treasures. The sight of them stole her breath. Silvered edges glimmered in the lamplight, and the air was heavier, as though memory itself pressed close.

Some things didn't glitter. Some things didn't need to. That, she realized, was what made them dangerous. Especially when they were hers.

# Chapter Fifteen

T HE WIND OFF the North Sea rattled the panes in Barrington's study, carrying a tang of salt that sharpened his focus. He scanned the morning's correspondence, pausing at the echo of boot heels in the hall. At first steady, uneven, as though the visitor carried weight or favored one leg.

Kenworth stood in the doorway. "A caller for you, Colonel. An old friend, I'm sure you'll be glad to see."

Barrington rose, brows lifting as a tall man stepped inside, road dust dulling his coat, the hitch in his stride telling its own story.

"Townsend?"

"Colonel." Felix Townsend's grin was quick and warm. "I could hardly ride past without calling."

Barrington chuckled. "If by 'riding past' you mean three days' hard ride from London."

"Closer to four with this leg," Townsend admitted. "Your brother sends his regards and this." He produced a leather packet from inside his coat.

Barrington ran his thumb over the Whitehall seal before breaking it, his gaze narrowing on Townsend.

"Not exactly. Edward's orders were to put this directly into Ash's hands. Said he'd know what to do with it."

"You've come to the right place. He's in Sommer-by-the-Sea. Likely at Lady Eastbury's just now." Barrington's eyes narrowed. "And you? Between assignments?"

Townsend's mouth twitched, as if suppressing an answer. "Something like that."

Barrington let the silence stretch before clapping his old comrade on the shoulder. "Come, then. We'll ride. You can tell me what mischief you've been in since we last crossed paths."

The two men left the study, the rhythm of their steps uneven but companionable, a long friendship filling the silences between words. Outside, gulls wheeled against a silver sky as they set out toward Eastbury Manor.

⟫⟫⟫⟪⟪⟪

LETICIA HEARD THE knock and glanced at her aunt, seated beside her in the parlor, darning gloves that had seen better seasons.

"That will be Gabriel." She rose. "Or a messenger bearing a letter saying he cannot come."

Lady Eastbury didn't look up. "You'll know which by the tone of the knock."

But when the butler returned, it was not just Gabriel who followed.

"Barrington?" Leticia blinked in surprise as the colonel stepped inside, followed by a tall man in a travel-stained coat.

"Lady Salisbury. Lady Eastbury." Barrington bowed, stepped aside as Gabriel entered behind them, brows raised. "Ashcombe, this is Felix Townsend. I believe you two met in London."

"We did," Gabriel said, offering his hand. His gaze dropped briefly to the man's leg, assessing. "Are you well?"

Townsend grinned. "Well enough to travel, at least."

Lady Eastbury's eyes sharpened as she stepped forward. "A war wound, Mr. Townsend?"

He hesitated, cleared his throat. "I got through that arena unscathed. Unfortunately, my lady... this is not a tale for polite company."

Her brows arched, but she let the matter rest, though the

glance promised she would return to the matter later.

"And you're far from London."

"On behalf of Edward," Townsend said, pulling a leather satchel from beneath his coat. "He received word of the thefts. Thought you might find this useful."

Gabriel took the packet, thumb resting on the seal a heartbeat longer than needed before he broke it.

Leticia saw the soldier in him then, evaluating the importance of the information as if it were a weapon.

Lady Eastbury rose, setting her mending aside. "I'll see to some refreshments. Leticia, show the gentlemen to the library." She turned to the men. "You will have some privacy there."

She left the room, and the gentlemen followed Leticia through the hall. The library opened before them in afternoon light, lace curtains softening the glow, the air faint with polish and old paper. It was the kind of room built for secrets.

The documents inside were auction ledgers, six in total, and several copied entries with names underlined in a familiar hand.

Leticia leaned over them, the ink-smudged columns blurring for a moment before her focus sharpened. "These are from the recent society auctions."

Gabriel nodded slowly as he glanced up at Townsend. "Edward asked you to analyze them?"

"Actually," Townsend said, settling into a chair with a grateful sigh, "he asked you to analyze them. My only instruction was to deliver them and stay out of the way."

Leticia caught Gabriel's glance and tilted her head, wordlessly requesting the ledgers. He slid them toward her. Her fingertip traced the names, the paper brittle beneath her touch. Several women had purchased from the same seller. Several names repeated: Lady Enfield, Mrs. Greyson, and… she lifted her head and turned toward him.

"One of the buyers was Erica Notley," Leticia said aloud, her brow furrowing as she traced the line.

Gabriel looked up. "What did she buy?"

"Brooches. Necklaces. Minor pieces. All claimed to be from the estate of a former ambassador's widow."

Townsend reached into his coat and drew out another sheet. "The estate in question sold several lots, one as recently as this year, and another nearly thirty years earlier."

Gabriel stilled. Leticia's fingers hesitated on the page. "That's a long time span."

"Edward found it curious enough to include the document," Townsend said. "The same estate manager handled sales nearly thirty years apart. He thought the trail was worth following. The first lot included seemingly unrelated items, a silver teapot, a beaded reticule with a broken clasp, and a porcelain doll."

Leticia exchanged a glance with Gabriel. Her voice became quieter. "People collect odd things." Yet unease coiled in her stomach.

"True," Townsend said. "But sometimes oddities connect more than they appear to."

He leaned back in his chair, watching them all with the ease of a man who had seen a great deal and still found the company more interesting than the problem.

Gabriel straightened in his chair. "Same estate manager every time."

"Which means," Leticia said, eyes narrowing in thought, "he might know who owned the pieces before they were sold."

"Or," Gabriel added, "how they came to be in the widow's collection in the first place."

Barrington folded his arms, regarding her with interest. "That's a long memory to keep."

"Some men keep meticulous ledgers," Townsend said. "Edward thought it worth noting. Said if anyone could give you a trail to follow, it would be this fellow."

Leticia skimmed the papers again, her focus steadied. "Then he is our next step. One conversation could tie these threads together."

Gabriel glanced at her, one brow arched. "If he's inclined to share what he knows."

"That," she said with a faint smile, "is what charm is for."

Barrington chuckled. "If you're volunteering, Lady Salisbury, I imagine the poor man won't stand a chance."

"Nor will you," Gabriel murmured, though his tone was so mild it could have been mistaken for agreement.

Townsend smirked at the interplay, clearly entertained. "You two always work like this?"

"We're not working together," Gabriel said at once.

Leticia tilted her head toward him. "Aren't we?"

The flicker of a smile faded across his mouth before he bent again to the ledgers. "If we ride out tomorrow, we can be there before luncheon."

"Tomorrow?" Barrington gave a low whistle. "Eager."

"The longer we wait," Gabriel said, "the more likely the trail will fade."

"And the sooner," Leticia added, "the thief has time to act again."

Townsend gave her a full look. "Your instincts are good, Lady Salisbury."

"They have to be," she replied. "No one listens until it's nearly too late."

Silence pressed in, broken only by the cry of gulls outside the window.

Barrington slapped his hands against his knees. "Right, then. The estate manager it is. I'll send a note ahead."

"Don't," Gabriel said. "If he's part of this…"

"He isn't," Barrington said.

"…a warning will only give him time to decide what not to tell us," Gabriel finished.

Leticia lifted the top ledger again, letting her fingers skim the brittle edges. "What if he doesn't remember? Thirty years is a long time."

"Some things," Gabriel said quietly, "are worth remembering."

Her gaze locked with his, the unspoken pressing between them heavier than the paper in her hand. "Let us hope he agrees with you."

A knock came at the door, and Kenworth showed with a tea tray. The pot steamed fragrantly, but the cups remained untouched as the conversation swirled on.

Townsend leaned forward. "There's a chance we're chasing a shadow here. But if we're right, the estate manager could put a name to whoever gathered these pieces before they went to auction. Once we have that…"

"We follow the chain," Gabriel said.

"And when we reach the end?" Leticia asked.

He held her gaze. "We'll know."

"Or we'll have to start all over," Barrington said dryly. "And you'll wish you'd let me send that note."

Townsend laughed under his breath. "If nothing else, it will be an entertaining ride."

Gabriel gathered the papers into a precise stack, soldier's order in every motion. "We ride at first light."

Leticia's eyes softened, though her voice stayed brisk. "I'll see that we have the proper maps."

"We?" Gabriel asked again, a hint of amusement threading the word.

She held his gaze, heat sparking in her chest. "You didn't think I'd let you chase ghosts while I stayed home to pour the tea, did you?"

Something flickered in his eyes. She wasn't certain if it was wariness, desire, or recognition. For the first time since they'd met, a reluctant smile tugged at his mouth.

"No. I didn't."

# Chapter Sixteen

THE LONG GALLERY of the Sommer-by-the-Sea Historical Society was not yet visible from the vestibule, but Leticia could already hear the low murmur of voices and the occasional ring of polite laughter. The mingled scents of beeswax and champagne rode the crisp breath of early autumn, slipping through the high windows to brush her awareness. The afternoon promised the pleasure of fine company and remarkable displays, though she never trusted first impressions, not at gatherings like this.

The receiving room ahead glowed with lamplight and polished wood. Sir Albert Westcott stood just inside, offering bows and handshakes with the precision of a man long trained in Parliament. His once-dark hair was silver now, but his stance remained soldier-straight. Beside him, Lady Westcott, tall and elegant in pale blue silk, greeted each arrival with an appraising glance and a smile that warmed or cooled according to her estimation.

Gabriel inclined his head. "Sir Albert, it has been some time. The last occasion was Lady Stanhope's musicale."

Sir Albert's eyes softened. "Ashcombe. Yes, though my ears never fully recovered from the violins."

Lady Westcott's laugh was light but controlled, as though amusement were a form of courtesy.

Sir Albert turned to Leticia, studying her with a statesman's thoroughness. "And this young lady?"

Introductions were made. Lady Westcott's smile deepened by a fraction. "Lady Salisbury, how pleasant. I have heard of your aunt's work with the reading society. Do convey my regards."

"I will," Leticia said, her voice steady though her awareness sharpened. Lady Westcott's approval might set doors swinging wide. Her favor could open doors, or quietly keep them closed.

Before she could say more, Lady Westcott's gaze shifted past them. "Colonel Barrington. Mrs. Bainbridge. We were just speaking of you."

The couple stepped forward. It was Barrington with the quiet authority of a man accustomed to command, Mrs. Bainbridge with a smile warm enough to coax confidences from strangers.

"You must be deep in preparations," Lady Westcott continued. "Two weddings in such close succession will be the talk of the county."

Mrs. Bainbridge's eyes sparkled. "Preparations, yes. Agreement on the guest list, not yet."

Barrington's mouth curved. "We are narrowing the options."

"Or expanding them, depending on whom you ask," she countered, drawing a ripple of polite laughter from those nearby.

Lady Westcott's attention returned to Leticia, her eyes bright with interest. "And for you, my dear, congratulations are in order. Such a romantic proposal. It made my heart flutter."

Heat touched Leticia's cheeks. "It was… rather unexpected."

Gabriel's gaze met hers for a moment, steady, unreadable, before drifting over her shoulder to a tall, neatly dressed man standing a discreet pace behind Lady Westcott. The fellow carried a leather folio and had the precise bearing of one accustomed to balancing accounts.

"Mr. Denholm," Gabriel murmured for her alone. "Her ladyship's affairs man."

Lady Westcott gestured toward the adjoining chamber. "Do take a glass before you view the collection. Sir Albert insists one sees everything more favorably with champagne in hand."

They entered the receiving room beyond, where conversation rose beneath the warm gleam of candle chandeliers. Footmen in livery threaded through the crowd, silver trays of crystal flutes catching the light. Perfume wove with beeswax and champagne until the air was velvet with scent.

Across the room, two ladies whispered behind their fans.

"…after the theft at the masquerade, she guards them like a dragon with its hoard," one murmured, her eyes darting toward a nearby case.

Leticia turned toward the display, unwilling to appear curious. The mention of the masquerade still scraped like flint beneath the surface. She might have lingered to hear more, but Miss Erica Notley arrived at her side, her expression bright and her gaze already sweeping the room. "Such a crush," she observed. "I imagine the noise becomes invisible once one is accustomed to it."

"It does," Leticia said, keeping her tone mild and her attention elsewhere.

They moved together toward the wide archway leading into the long gallery. To the right, an alcove displayed historical texts on loan from private collections. A figure stood there, bent over a glass-topped case, hands clasped behind his back.

"Professor Tresham," Leticia said, pleased to see him.

He looked up, his reserve easing a fraction. "Lady Salisbury. I did not expect to find you here among the relics."

"Professor, may I present Miss Erica Notley?"

"A pleasure, Miss Notley." His tone was courteous, his manner precise.

"The pleasure is mine, Professor," she replied, her smile even.

"These are remarkable," Leticia said, leaning closer to the display.

"Several from Lord Harrington's collection," Tresham told her. "This charter," he indicated a sheet of vellum, "is a sixteenth-century grant reaffirming Sommer-by-the-Sea's market rights. The seal is unusually well preserved."

Miss Notley tilted her head toward another. "The hand looks

different."

"Fifteenth-century copy of an older text," Tresham confirmed. "More rounded, as was common then."

Leticia smiled. "I envy your skill."

"Only practice," Tresham replied.

From the corner of her vision, Leticia noticed Gabriel a few paces away, his posture relaxed but his gaze trained on the far end of the gallery, where Mr. Denholm now conferred with a uniformed guard. He moved to join her with unhurried steps that belied his focus.

"If you will excuse us, Professor," Gabriel said smoothly. "Lady Salisbury, there is something I would like to show you."

Miss Notley's smile was pleasant, if faintly edged. "Enjoy the rest of the exhibition."

Gabriel guided Leticia toward the jewel cases. The gallery light caught on emeralds, rubies, and sapphires, each gem catching the light as guests shifted before the glass. The air was quieter, as though the jewels themselves demanded it.

"I never tire of these," Miss Notley said lightly, reappearing beside them with the ease of one accustomed to slipping into conversations. "One wonders what scandals their histories would tell."

Gabriel's eyes lingered on a necklace. "Morton estate. Acquired at auction."

Miss Notley's tone was almost idle. "I remember a brooch there once, diamonds forming a larger diamond, something dark at the center, onyx, perhaps. I never looked closely."

The casual remark struck like a pebble against glass, rippling through Leticia. Her mother's brooch, hidden away for years, shared the same arrangement.

Gabriel shifted subtly, his shoulder brushing hers. His fingers brushed hers, steady, deliberate, before falling away, a silent reassurance or warning.

Miss Notley's smile did not falter. "Funny how some things find their way back, even after all this time."

"Others are best left where they belong," Leticia returned, her reflection in the glass meeting Miss Notley's.

Gabriel straightened. "If you will excuse us, Miss Notley." His tone was courteous. The meaning final.

"Of course," she said lightly, though her eyes followed them as they turned away.

They moved toward the far end of the gallery, their steps unhurried. "There's a teahouse around the corner from here," Gabriel said quietly. "A pot of Darjeeling and a quiet table might suit after this crowd."

The suggestion was simple enough, yet it carried the undertone of something more, a small withdrawal from the public stage, and perhaps the chance to speak without so many ears nearby.

Lady Westcott intercepted them near the exit, her smile gracious. "I trust you have enjoyed the afternoon, Lady Salisbury. Lord Ashcombe."

Gabriel inclined his head. "An impressive collection."

They exchanged farewells and stepped outside. The air was cool with a salty scent from the harbor. Leticia took his arm, aware of the warmth of his earlier touch and of the questions crowding her thoughts about the brooch, Mr. Denholm, and the ease with which Miss Notley had threaded herself through the afternoon. Too many threads. All too neatly tied. And one of them, she was certain now, was Erica Notley.

# Chapter Seventeen

T HE ROSTOV TEAROOM was a study in polished comfort, mahogany paneling, tall windows draped in soft green, and the scent of fresh bread mingling with tea. The low hum of conversation wrapped the room like a warm shawl. Two women sat at the center table, speaking in low tones over plates of seed cake. A couple occupied a small table near the hearth, while in the back, Felix Townsend looked up from his tea and gave Gabriel a brief nod. By the door, a man sat with a newspaper held high, the print rustling now and then as he turned a page.

Gabriel guided Leticia toward a small table tucked in the corner, away from the main flow of the room. A server came over with a polite bow, leaving menus and promising to return with the day's selection.

"The Historical Society does draw a crowd," she observed, glancing around. "I suspect Lady Westcott would have been disappointed if it had not. Our presence, yours especially, will give her something to remark upon the next time the ladies gather for tea."

"She was especially pleased at meeting you," Gabriel said, his tone mild. "Tolliver also tells me the ladies of the houses are already speaking of a love match."

Her brows rose. "Are they?"

"It seems they enjoy imagining the shape of other people's futures."

She smiled faintly. "And do you?"

His gaze met hers, deliberate and steady, and her toes curled in her slippers before she could stop them.

"Only when the imagining is worth the time."

The server returned with the teapot and two delicate cups. As he poured, the fragrant steam curled upward, warm against her cheek. She lifted her cup, the warmth sinking into her hands. "Earlier, when we were in the gallery, what Miss Notley said about the brooch. It looked very much like one in a picture in your hall. My mother's brooch has the same arrangement of stones."

Gabriel's expression did not shift, but his eyes sharpened. "You remember it clearly."

"Only from childhood," she said lightly. "It is the sort of thing one notices without understanding why."

He studied her a moment longer, as though weighing what had been said—and what had not.

"Patterns like that are rarely accidental."

"No," she agreed. "They are usually chosen."

Gabriel leaned back, studying her with a gaze that measured more than her words. "And yet some pieces remain exactly where they should."

Her lips curved faintly. "Yes."

From the corner of her vision, Leticia noted Townsend glancing toward them again before returning to his tea. The man by the door lowered his paper briefly, revealing a neatly trimmed beard and the clean line of a collar. His eyes swept the room once before the paper lifted again.

Gabriel's gaze followed hers for a moment, "Observation," he said quietly. "It's the most useful skill in any investigation. Look at Felix. What do you see?"

She tilted her head. "He's having tea."

"Yes. Where is he sitting?"

"In the back of the room."

"How is he sitting?"

She cast him a sidelong glance, unsure what he wanted.

"Look again."

Her gaze returned to Felix. He lifted his cup, met her eyes briefly, and nodded in greeting. She turned back to Gabriel. "He's watching me."

"And do you think anyone could come up behind him unnoticed?"

Her expression shifted as she considered. "No… his back's to the wall."

"Exactly." He inclined his head, faint approval in his eyes. "Now the other gentleman."

She glanced toward the man with the paper. "He's looking at the people in the room."

"And?"

She studied him a moment longer before her brow arched. "He's sitting by the door. For a quick escape."

Gabriel sat back, satisfied. "You learn quickly."

The server returned with a plate of currant scones, their sugared tops catching the light. Gabriel broke one in half and passed her the portion with the most fruit.

"Thank you." She took a bite, the soft crumb melting on her tongue. "You are quiet."

"I was considering," he said slowly, "whether our visit to the Historical Society accomplished what I hoped."

"And did it?"

His mouth curved slightly. "It confirmed several things. Not all of them were in the exhibits."

She lifted her cup again, watching him over the rim. "You are a man who enjoys keeping his conclusions to himself."

"Until the moment is right," he agreed.

She set her cup down and rested her hands on the edge of the table, not touching his. "If I tell you something without asking for a conclusion, will you promise not to give me one?"

"I can attempt moderation," he said. "For the length of one pot of tea."

"Acceptable." She breathed in the citrus of her Earl Grey.

"When Lady Westcott congratulated me in the receiving room, I felt… exposed. It was kind, and yet every eye turned at once. I do not enjoy being looked at as if I am a character in a story."

"You are," he said. "Only most people do not realize they have any say in the plot."

That drew a quick laugh from her. "And you, Gabriel, always revise the ending."

His eyes warmed, the change so slight she would have missed it months ago. "Only when the first draft is poor."

"You are impossible," she said, still smiling. "And infuriatingly calm."

"Tolliver, my valet, says the same when I alter our departure by a quarter hour without warning."

She leaned in, conspiratorial. "He does more than say it. He arranges your boots an inch out of place as revenge."

Gabriel blinked. "You noticed that."

"I notice many things. He places the left pair just ahead of the right. I think he believes you will correct them and feel restored to order."

A low sound escaped him, not a laugh, not a sigh. "I have been managed."

"Expertly," she said. "And with affection."

They fell into an easy quiet. The two women at the center table traded plates. The couple by the hearth leaned closer, heads almost touching. Felix's cup remained steady in his hand, his posture careful, his attention turned inward. Thomas Wade turned another page, the paper rustling like a small wave.

"Tell me something I do not know about you," Gabriel said at last. "Something not in any report, not in any drawing room account."

She considered his question while looking at her hands. "I can tie a bowline with my eyes closed."

A small lift touched his brows. "You can."

"My father taught me at the summer races. He said there are knots that hold and knots that look as if they will. One should know the difference before trusting a sail, or a promise."

Gabriel's gaze steadied. "Wise advice."

"You did ask for something you did not know." She hesitated, added, softer, "When the wind is right, you can hear the bells from the outer harbor from our garden. I used to count them at night and try to make stories from the pattern. If there were three, it meant good fortune. If there were five, a letter would arrive."

"Did it?"

"Sometimes," she said, smiling at her own foolishness. "I decided the bells liked to keep their secrets."

He looked as if he might say something more, but he sat back and studied her, and the look was almost enough by itself.

"Your turn," she said, to break the intensity before it made speaking difficult. "Tell me something that is not in any report."

"I cannot abide boiled carrots," he said.

She blinked, surprised into another laugh. "That is your offering?"

"You asked for truth. I am giving it." He paused. "Also, when I was twelve, I tried to teach myself the violin. The house still bears the scars."

"Your uncle allowed that?"

"He was out. The butler did not wish to contradict an Ashcombe."

"And the violin?"

"Returned to its case," he said, "where it has done no harm since."

"A tragedy for music," she said. "A relief for the staff."

He tipped his head. "Do you see, Leticia, what you have done? You have coaxed a confession from me."

"I will be discreet," she said. "Except when it suits me to tease you."

This time he did laugh, a quiet, rich sound that startled them both. He looked immediately away, as if the laugh might escape again if not watched. She let the pleasure of it move through her, light as a breeze.

"About the brooch," he said after a moment, more gently than before. "You recognized the pattern because of the picture in the hall. You said your mother's brooch is the same."

"It looks like her."

"You remember it clearly," he said. "Enough to recognize the pattern."

"Perhaps," she said lightly.

The question settled between them like a coin on velvet. "If I had it, I might," she said, her voice even. "But my parents died in a carriage accident… the brooch wasn't among my mother's things."

He accepted that with a small nod. Outside, a cart rolled past, iron-rimmed wheels clattering over the street. Somewhere in the kitchen, a bell chimed once again. The teapot had cooled to a soft warmth. The scones were nearly gone.

"You asked where I would go if I could be anywhere," she said. "May I change my answer?"

"You may."

"I would still choose the cove," she said, "but only if you promised not to speak for the first five minutes."

"I can be silent for far longer than that," he said.

"Yes," she said, amused. "That is precisely why I would allow only five."

He considered her, and the look in his eyes was not quite a smile, not entirely a question. "Very well. Five minutes. After which I reserve the right to remark upon the superiority of your shell-collecting to mine."

"I am not competing," she said, fighting a grin. "I am winning."

"You have not yet seen my technique."

"You will tell me there is a report on it."

"There is not," he said. "There is only practice."

She reached for the last currant scone and broke it cleanly in two. "Half each."

"Half each," he agreed.

A quiet pride moved through her at the simple exchange. It was less like politeness, more like a fact. Half each. Contentment was not loud. It did not declare itself. It arrived, pulled out a chair, and made a place at the table.

They spoke of the town's autumn fair, the booths that showed overnight, the sweet smoke of roasted nuts that lingered long after the stalls closed. He admitted a fondness for the chessboard that old Mr. Hollis set by his door, a board that challenged any passerby to a move. She confessed she avoided it because she disliked losing in public, and he warned her that Mr. Hollis had the patience of a saint and the cunning of a fox.

"I would pay to see you lose a pawn," she said.

"I am certain you would," he said. "You would frame the moment and hang it by your bed."

"Only if it were signed."

"You drive a difficult bargain."

"So I have been told."

Across the room, Felix lifted his cup. The women at the center table stood to don their gloves. The couple by the hearth rose, paid, and stepped out into the light. Thomas Wade turned his page again, folded the paper once, and held it neatly on his knee.

Gabriel settled the bill. As they stood, Felix offered a small nod. Leticia returned it. The man with the newspaper lowered it just enough to watch them pass, angled it slightly toward the back tables. She noticed, tucked the image away, and said nothing.

Outside, the afternoon was brighter than the quiet of the room they had left behind. They walked without haste, the town unfolding around them. She was keenly aware of the comfort in his silence and of the questions they had both chosen not to voice. It was not avoidance. It was a promise that the time would come to say what mattered, when it mattered.

Gabriel glanced at her. "The tide will be fair tomorrow afternoon."

She understood him. Or thought she did. "Tomorrow will do."

They reached a corner where the street opened toward the green. Children chased a hoop past them, the ring humming over the cobbles. Leticia watched it roll along. Her spirits were lifted, and the cause had nothing to do with the weather.

"You laugh easily today," Gabriel said. He did not look at her when he said it, which made the words land more truly.

"Not always," she said. "But I like that you noticed."

"I like that I heard it," he said. "I find I would like to hear it again."

She did not answer at once. Finally, softly, she said, "You must give me a reason."

He considered that, and the corner of his mouth tipped, not in a smile, but more in an admission. "I will try."

They went on together, and the town seemed to draw back a little, as if giving them space.

# Chapter Eighteen

THEY LEFT THE tearoom and walked with the tide at their backs. The air was clear and bright, the kind of afternoon that made the town look freshly polished, set out for display. Their steps fell into an easy rhythm. Neither pressed the other for talk.

"Will you take a turn by the green," Gabriel asked, "or the longer way?"

"The longer way," Leticia said. "I'm in no hurry to be indoors."

They passed a baker's yard where warm air drifted out, sweet with sugar and spice. Somewhere nearby, a piano ran through scales without apology. They didn't speak about the man with the newspaper or Felix's careful nod. They'd said enough for one afternoon, and the quiet was chosen, not empty.

At the corner by St. Peter's, a small curricle pulled up, driven with neat hands by Mrs. Aurora Penstone. The ribbons on her bonnet were an unrepentant crimson. She smiled down with the air of a woman who never missed an opportunity and never had to repeat herself to be heard.

"My lord. Lady Salisbury." She inclined her head. "I owe you congratulations on your engagement. I should have said so that evening, but I was… distracted."

Gabriel stepped forward. "We understand. I had hoped to speak with you about the theft at the masquerade. At your convenience."

"Now," she said with a decisive nod. "Best to have it over and done."

Mrs. Penstone's townhouse stood two streets off the green, bright-windowed and orderly. They were shown to a morning room where the light spilled through pale curtains. On a covered stand near the hearth sat an empty velvet tray, a small relic of something already lost.

"I prefer the morning room," Mrs. Penstone said, following their glance. "I don't care for shadows after unpleasantness. Tea would have been offered, but I won't pretend calm. Sit, or not, as you like."

"Thank you," Leticia said. "We won't keep you long."

"It's no trouble," Mrs. Penstone said, folding her hands with a firmness that told its own story. "You'll want it from the beginning."

"If you please," Gabriel said.

"The necklace was borrowed," she said. "From a cousin with more patience than taste. Diamonds, rather severe, with a small charm at the clasp. I wore it to the dance and didn't remove it until I stepped into the retiring room for a rest. I didn't sleep, though I might have, given the hour and the violinist's lack of restraint. When I returned to the ballroom, the clasp was gone and the necklace with it. My maid swears she saw nothing, she's a treasure, and I believe her. I don't believe the quiet woman who managed to stand behind my screen while I adjusted my mask."

Leticia leaned forward. "Quiet woman?"

"Brown hair, fair skin, nothing remarkable. That was her strength. I'd pass her on High Street and think of gloves, not danger."

"What did she wear?" Leticia asked.

"A brown gown. Plain. Forgettable, unless you saw the wig pulled from her head." Mrs. Penstone tipped her head. "I know how ridiculous that sounds."

"It sounds like good memory," Gabriel said. "You mentioned a charm. A figure, or a letter?"

"A small diamond set inside a larger one," Mrs. Penstone said. "Not large enough to draw notice. If one looked closely, and I did when it arrived, there was the outline of a raven etched on the back of the stone. Barely there. I told myself it was the mark of a proud maker. Now I think I told myself anything that would let me wear it without feeling vain."

Gabriel's attention sharpened so suddenly, it startled Leticia.

"A raven," he said.

"Yes." Mrs. Penstone's mouth thinned. "I didn't mention it to anyone else. I don't enjoy being laughed at."

"Was it engraved on the metal," Leticia asked, "or cut into the stone?"

"In the stone," Mrs. Penstone said. "Hidden. You had to catch the light to see it."

Gabriel nodded. "One more question. Had the piece changed hands many times?"

"My cousin bought it at a private sale. A friend of a friend. I warned her about such dealings. She warned me about my tone. It hardly matters now."

"On the contrary," Gabriel said, calm as ever. "It may make all the difference."

Mrs. Penstone drew a breath that set her shoulders. "I'm content to have done my part. I shall wear seed pearls and nothing else for the rest of my life."

Leticia stood. "You'll make them look regal."

"You're kind," Mrs. Penstone said, her mouth softening. "If you see the woman I described, give her my compliments and tell her I hope her conscience is sharp. It's the only thing about her that might improve."

They left with thanks and the sense of a door closing on a story not yet finished.

On the pavement, Leticia looked up at Gabriel. "A raven in a diamond."

"Yes."

"I don't care for birds in jewelry," she said, as if this were a matter of taste and not a marker that might open a vault of questions. "They seem caged even when they're free."

He glanced at her, a hum of appreciation in his throat. "Astute."

They didn't push further. The town leaned toward the later hour. A barrel organ played down the street, a cheerful tune with nothing to do with ravens, diamonds, or a quiet woman in a brown gown.

They walked slowly back to Lady Eastbury's, letting the afternoon do the talking. When the house came into view, Leticia couldn't deny the tug of competing wishes. Sit with her aunt and say ordinary things. Stay outside with Gabriel and say nothing. Stand alone in her room and breathe.

"Will you come in?" she asked.

"For a moment."

Lady Eastbury received them with the contentment of a woman whose roses had finally done something right. She praised the small posy of asters on the hall table, teased Gabriel for paying without letting Leticia argue, and asked whether they meant to win every ribbon at the fair or leave some for the less determined.

"Not every ribbon," Leticia said.

"Only the important ones," Gabriel said, winning a spark of approval from her aunt.

They didn't linger. After a few minutes, Gabriel rose. "I'll send a line to Barrington. We should meet him early."

"I'll be ready," Leticia said.

He helped her aunt with a stubborn window latch, took her thanks, and turned to Leticia with a look that said more than his words. "Good evening."

"Good evening," she managed, her voice even though her chest was not.

At the door, he paused. "Leticia."

She met his gaze.

"Thank you for today."

She didn't ask which part. "You're welcome."

When he had gone, the house settled on its foundations in a way that was both safe and too quiet. Lady Eastbury sent her to rest, promising to send up a tray if dinner was late. Leticia kissed her aunt's cheek, comforted by the familiar scent of lavender, and went upstairs.

Her room took her in like a friend who required no performance. She set her gloves on the dressing table and paused, fingers resting on the polished wood. The afternoon lined itself in order: tea's steam, Felix's nod, the man with the paper, Mrs. Penstone's velvet tray, a brown gown, a tiny raven inside a diamond.

Her breath caught.

She opened the top drawer, the one for letters, bits of ribbon, and, wrapped in an old lawn handkerchief, her mother's brooch.

It looked harmless, memory made into metal. Diamonds in a tidy pattern, the small dark stone at the center like a drop of night.

She carried it to the window. The light there was honest. She eased the clasp open and held it in her palm, back facing up. At first, it was only smooth gold and careful setting. She tilted it. The shift of light revealed more.

There it was. A diamond inside a diamond, no bigger than her smallest fingernail. Inside it, faint and exact, the outline of a raven.

Her hand closed on its own. She set the brooch on the sill, bracing herself against the frame.

If the Order marked its pieces, and this was one, how had her mother come by it? Bought quietly, as Mrs. Penstone's cousin had done? Given knowingly? Passed in ignorance? Used to shelter a secret? If she told Gabriel now, would he hear the question behind the words and wonder not about a brooch, but about the woman who had worn it, and the daughter who kept it?

The truth cut clean.

She laid the brooch on its handkerchief and folded the cloth once over it. Not hidden. Not displayed. A promise to the past, a debt to the present.

Gabriel would listen without interruption. He wouldn't accuse. He'd measure the shape of her fear and weigh the Order against the woman who'd raised her without breaking either. The thought steadied her and troubled her equally.

Not yet. Not until she understood what she was asking him to carry.

Night gathered outside. She lifted the brooch again, holding it as she might hold a bird too small for the world. She didn't look at the engraving. She didn't need to. It was already fixed in her mind.

"I'll tell you," she said into the quiet, "when I know whether I'm asking you to doubt my mother, or me."

She wrapped it, slid it back into the drawer, and closed it to the stop. Her hand lingered at the knob.

She blew out the candle by the window and let the harbor's pale light take its place against the glass, a small silver promise that morning would come and with it, another chance to be brave.

# Chapter Nineteen

MORNING CAME QUICK and clean. Leticia woke with the shape of a raven still sharp behind her eyes and the weight of a brooch she had already put away. She dressed with steady hands, tied her bonnet, and checked herself in the glass as if checking a stitch. Plain enough to pass in a crowd. Ready.

In the hall, Lady Eastbury paused with a basket of notes and a smile that knew more than it asked. "You will not keep the town waiting, I see."

"Only the important parts," Leticia said.

"Take my carriage. Cotton squabs are better than aching feet." Her aunt kissed her cheek and pressed a small paper packet into her hand. "Lemon pastilles. Do not offer them to Colonel Barrington. He cannot be trusted with sweets."

Leticia laughed and tucked the packet away. The sound eased the tightness under her ribs.

Gabriel arrived within the hour. His hat was in his hand, and there was that careful look he wore when he meant to be both thorough and kind. They exchanged good mornings and the kind of glance that said the rest could wait until they were moving.

He hesitated on the steps. "I have word from Barrington."

"Now?"

He held it so she could read along with him. The hand was brisk. The message was not long.

*A plain brown gown and a brown wig were found in a cabinet in the retiring room. Left in haste. The porter swears the door was locked earlier. I will expect you both.*

The ground settled beneath her. "So, she planned for the disguise and planned to shed it."

"She also planned a key," Gabriel said. "Or had a helper."

They did not say Denholm. They did not say anyone. They climbed in and let the morning take them down High Street while the town opened its doors around them.

Barrington received them in his study with a cheerful complaint about the lack of decent coffee and the abundance of decent muffins in his house. Mrs. Bainbridge had sent the latter. He made a show of offering one and ate it himself, which Leticia suspected was the result he wanted from the start.

Felix Townsend stood at the mantel with a small stack of papers and the look of a man who had run since dawn and meant to keep running. He bowed. "Lady Salisbury. Lord Ashcombe."

"Felix," Gabriel said. "Your note."

Felix handed over a folded sheet and the key to a cabinet tagged on a string. "The porter swears he locked the door after the supper set. When he unlocked it to help a lady whose hem had caught on a splinter, he found these. Brown wig. Brown gown. No name. No maker stitched in the lining. The combs are common. The seam at the hem is new."

Leticia glanced at Barrington. "She changed in that room, stole in that room, and left the costume there."

"Neat work," Barrington said. "She could have walked past the front door with a glass of lemonade, and no one would have looked twice."

"Mrs. Penstone's necklace," Gabriel said. "You are certain we can tie it to the retiring room and not the floor."

"We can now," Felix said. "Her maid confirms she adjusted her mask behind a screen and noticed the clasp was a bit loose. When they returned to fetch her shawl, the screen had been shifted. She assumed a draft. I do not."

Leticia stepped closer to the table where Felix had set a small drawing of a clasp. "A diamond set inside a larger diamond. If the light holds still, a raven inside the stone." She did not touch the paper. She did not need to.

Barrington watched her with that open, soldier's gaze that took stock and kept counsel. "You have a theory."

"I have a path," Leticia said. "We keep chasing ghosts and chance encounters. I would like ledgers instead. Mrs. Penstone's cousin bought her necklace through a friend. That friend had a seller. Sellers leave trails when they want money. Auctions. Private rooms. Subscriptions. Society notices that pretend not to name names."

Felix's mouth tipped, quick with approval. "The papers."

"And the jeweler," Gabriel said. "Even if the piece did not pass through his hands, he will have seen similar work. Someone cut that tiny raven. It is a boast disguised as secrecy."

"Good," Barrington said. "Felix, take Lady Salisbury's lead. Assemble the notices tied to private sales of diamonds this past season, and any report of a necklace of severe style with a charm at the clasp. The Morton estate pieces make a useful comparison. We have those sketches."

"I know the archivist at the Gazette office," Felix said. "He owes me a favor and a lunch."

Gabriel set the found cabinet tag beside the drawing. "We also want a list of who had a key to that retiring room and when it was issued. There is planning here. Planning leaves hands."

"I will have it," Felix said. "Today."

Barrington nodded, glanced at Leticia. "You understand this makes you part of the team, Lady Salisbury."

"I am already part of it," she said. "I would prefer to be useful."

"Spoken like a woman I admire," Mrs. Bainbridge said from the doorway, bright as the sun, a basket on her arm. Leticia had not heard her enter. "I have brought more muffins because the colonel cannot be trusted with only one." She set the basket down and greeted them all with a smile that took the edge off the morning. "Shall I have tea sent in, or are you all determined to starve in the name of justice?"

"We will eat while plotting," Barrington said. "It improves the temper of men and investigations."

They took tea. They did not linger over it. When they rose, the plan was simple. Felix to the Gazette and the records office. Barrington to question the porter and anyone who managed keys. Gabriel and Leticia to the jeweler on Westgate Street, to ask polite questions and earn less polite answers.

Outside, the day had sharpened. A breeze off the water kept the sun from bullying the street. Leticia fell in beside Gabriel. "You did not say all of what you are thinking."

"I rarely do," he said, with a glance that held apology and something warmer.

"Say enough," she said.

"The raven is a mark. Marks belong to men who believe the world should remember them," he said. "Men like that do not trust many. They trust themselves and a few hands they think they own."

"Tresham studies the Order," Leticia said. "He would know the marks."

"He would," Gabriel said. "So would anyone who wants to raise the Order's ghost with a cache of glittering proofs."

They turned onto Westgate. The jeweler's window was clean and full of soft things that would make a dull day kinder. As they reached it, a figure stepped back from the glass and into the flow of foot traffic. Erica. She saw them, offered a bright nod that held nothing to apologize for, and was gone in the next breath, as if the town had swallowed her like a coin.

Leticia held her place at the window and studied a watch chain as if she meant to buy it. "Do we follow?"

"No," Gabriel said. "We ask our questions."

He pushed open the door and stood back to let her pass first. The shop smelled faintly of oil and lavender. It was quiet in the manner of a church. A man in a sober coat looked up from a tray of pins and smiled the way men smile when they are certain they will send you out lighter in the pocket and pleased with the exchange.

"Good morning," Leticia said. "We have a question about custom work. Small work. Precise."

"You have come to the right place," the jeweler said.

Leticia met Gabriel's eye. They did not speak the word raven. Not yet.

They would ask about cutters who could set a diamond within a diamond, the kind of work that demanded patience and pride. They would ask to see the books that named those hands. And if the books were tidy and dull, they would ask to see the drawer beneath the ledger, the one that held the orders a gentleman preferred not to advertise.

Outside, bells struck the quarter hour. Leticia thought of the brooch sitting enfolded in its cloth and felt the pull of two loyalties. She did not look away from it. She placed them side by side in her mind and found there was room.

"Shall we begin?" she said.

Gabriel nodded. "Please."

The jeweler lifted a loupe and invited them closer. The glass caught the light. The morning moved on.

They were halfway through questions about cutters who could set a diamond within a diamond when the bell over the shop door chimed. Felix stepped in, hat still in his hand, a thin sheaf of papers tucked under his arm.

"I knew I'd find you here," he said, low enough not to carry past the counter. He glanced once at the jeweler, back to Gabriel. "The Gazette archivist came through faster than I hoped."

Gabriel straightened. "And?"

Felix laid one folded sheet on the glass between them, the print faint from age. "A notice for a private sale held four years ago. Included a necklace of 'uncommon restraint, clasped with a token stone in diamond form.' The seller's name is obscured, intentionally, I think. But the buyer of record…"

He tapped the line. Leticia leaned closer.

"I know that name," she said.

"You should," Felix replied. "They were at the masquerade."

The jeweler returned with a tray, smiling as though nothing in the world could be urgent. Felix stepped back, letting the lead rest like a spark waiting for the right breath.

"Shall we wrap this up?" Gabriel said quietly.

Leticia nodded, her mind already reaching ahead to the next question.

# Chapter Twenty

T HE AIR OUTSIDE the jeweler's felt sharper, as though the sunlight had thinned while they were inside. Gabriel, Leticia, and Felix moved away from the shop front before speaking. Felix glanced over his shoulder once, then passed a folded sheet to Gabriel.

"The Gazette notice," he said. "Private sale in Bath, four years ago. Necklace described as 'uncommon restraint, clasped with a token stone in diamond form.' The buyer was Mrs. Celeste Harcourt."

Leticia stopped mid-step. "Mrs. Penstone's cousin."

"The same," Felix said. "It confirms her account. Harcourt bought it several years before lending it to Penstone for the masquerade."

They walked on, the street busy with late-morning errands. A fishmonger's boy hurried past with a basket, the tang of the sea clinging to him, while a woman with a string bag of apples stepped aside to let them pass. Leticia kept pace beside Gabriel, aware of his steady presence at her shoulder and the folded paper in his hand like a burden waiting to be set down.

"She must value Mrs. Penstone greatly to lend her such a piece," Leticia said. "Or trust her beyond reason."

"Trust can be misplaced," Gabriel replied. "We'll know more when we speak to her."

Felix gave a short, dry smile. "Finding the notice took longer than it should. The archivist at the Gazette keeps his shelves in order but hides half the drawers behind an 'Out to be Cleaned' sign. I bribed him with two muffins from Barrington's table."

Leticia raised a brow. "I thought you were running on official business."

"I was," Felix said. "It just happens that official business sometimes requires baked goods."

The exchange loosened the tightness in her chest, though only for a moment. The necklace, the clasp, the raven, each step forward drew them deeper into a story without an ending.

They turned into Lady Eastbury's drive. Her carriage waited at the curb, the groom dozing in the shade, hat tipped forward. Inside, the house smelled faintly of rosewater and beeswax. Lady Eastbury met them in the hall, a sealed note in her hand and her expression bright with curiosity.

"I wasn't expecting you back so soon," she said, catching the name on Gabriel's lips. "Celeste Harcourt? Why, of course, I know her. We've been on the same charity committees for years." She moved toward the drawing room, waving them in ahead of her. "I saw her not long ago at the Historical Society's autumn preview. She was in conversation with Erica Notley. It was quite animated, if I recall."

The words landed like a pebble in still water, creating ripples that spread. "Do you know what they spoke about?"

"Not a word," Lady Eastbury said, settling into her chair. "But I remember thinking it an odd pairing. Erica rarely leaves Sommer-by-the-Sea unless there's gossip to be had, and Celeste is more likely to be found at a card table than an exhibit." She tapped her finger on the armrest. "Why the sudden interest?"

Gabriel answered her with care. "We believe Mrs. Harcourt's necklace may be connected to other recent… disturbances."

Her brows lifted, but she didn't press. "Then you must meet her. I'll invite her for tea tomorrow. I'll say we're gathering ladies to discuss the floral exhibition. No one refuses tea when flowers are mentioned."

"Perfect," Gabriel said. "We'll keep it casual."

Felix rose. "I'll keep my attention on the others, Denholm, Erica. If they're in league with this thief, they may try to move the next piece before we get close."

When he'd gone, the quiet in the room felt deliberate, as though the walls themselves expected her to speak. Leticia turned to Gabriel. "You've told me almost nothing about the Order. Now's a good time to change that."

He studied her for a moment, weighing the request. "The Order of Shadows began as a network hidden inside scholarly circles of collectors, antiquarians, and patrons of the arts. They weren't after beauty. They were after leverage. Jewels, rare manuscripts, artworks, all kept quiet, all valuable enough to buy loyalty or threaten ruin. Each piece bore a mark so its history could be traced within the Order, whose symbol is a raven inside a diamond."

"Why jewels?" she asked.

"Portable. Untraceable once removed from a setting. And they can pass from hand to hand under the guise of sentiment," he said. "A necklace given to a bride might seal a political arrangement as effectively as any signed contract."

Leticia's voice was low. "And decades ago, the cache was broken up?"

"Yes," he said. "Some sold quietly through intermediaries. Some were given as 'gifts' that carried more obligation than affection. We believe someone is reclaiming them now, not to hide them again, but to reassert the Order's presence."

The idea unsettled her more than she expected. "If my mother's brooch has the raven engraving, it makes her brooch—"

"—part of the same history," he finished gently. "And a reason to be careful."

Lady Eastbury, who had been listening without pretending otherwise, added, "Celeste bought her necklace in Bath, four years ago. Private sale, I believe. She never named the seller, only said it came through an old family connection."

Gabriel made a note of it but didn't press. "That's useful.

We'll keep it in mind."

Leticia sat back, her gaze tracing the floral border of the carpet while her mind worked at the loose ends. Bath. Four years. An old family connection. She filed them away, not as a puzzle to solve today, but as threads she might pull when the time was right.

Lady Eastbury smiled faintly. "You'll have her here tomorrow at three. Until then, let us not wear the air thin with secrets. Stay for supper, or at least let me send you with a jar of my chutney."

They took their leave not long after. The sun had lowered toward the harbor, sending long bands of light across the paving stones. The wind carried the salt of the sea and the faint cry of gulls.

As they stepped outside, a boy in a blue cap crossed the street toward them, an envelope in hand. He slowed as he neared, glancing once behind him before offering it to Gabriel.

"For you, sir."

Gabriel reached for his pocket, but the boy shook his head and darted off down a side lane. Leticia's gaze followed him until he disappeared. The sound of his footsteps lingered longer than the sight, quick and light, as if he'd been told not to be caught.

Inside was a single slip of paper, the writing elegant, the ink fresh.

*Be careful what she learns.*

No signature. No address.

Gabriel folded it once, slid it into his pocket without comment.

"You're not going to tell me," she said quietly.

"Not until I know what it means," he replied.

Her eyes drifted to the lane where the boy had vanished. At its far end, she caught the barest suggestion of a figure, still, half-turned, watching. The moment she blinked, the figure was gone, leaving only the ordinary bustle of the street.

They walked on, the silence between them no longer easy, but sharpened and watchful. Whatever tomorrow's tea might bring, someone already knew more about their plans than they should and had taken the trouble to warn them.

# Chapter Twenty-One

THE DRAWING ROOM at Barrington's home carried the quiet hum of a house that had been busy all afternoon. Light slanted through the tall windows, warming the oak paneling. A long table had been cleared for the guest lists. Also a neat stacks of paper, swatches of silk ribbon, and pencil sketches of floral displays. The air held a mild mix of tea and beeswax, with the faint promise of something baking in the kitchens.

Kenworth stood at the head of the table with two lists in hand, his expression set with mock gravity. He raised the smaller sheet. "One from Mrs. Bainbridge." He lifted the other, three times as long and written in an elegant but crowded hand. "And one from your mother, Colonel. I shall need a miracle, or a fair wind to sail them all up the east coast."

Mrs. Bainbridge tried to look stern, though amusement tugged at her mouth. "It will be a small wedding."

"It will be a proper wedding," Barrington said, the pride in his voice unhidden though the words were quiet. "Mother has waited a long time for our wedding and wants all her friends to celebrate with us." The warmth in his tone set even the lists aside for a moment.

"Frankly, my lord," Kenworth remarked, "I think she wants repayment for all the wedding gifts she and your father have given over the years."

A pause, one heartbeat, two, before laughter broke out, the kind that came as much from shared history as from the jest itself.

"Yes, retribution. That does sound like my mother." Barrington raised his goblet. "To Mother."

Before the moment could turn back toward debate, Leticia leaned toward the lists. "If we direct your mother's guests toward the outer tables and the bride's closest friends to the center, it keeps the heart of the room for those who matter most."

"It gives everyone the place of honor they believe they deserve," Gabriel said evenly, though his glance toward her carried something unspoken.

Their eyes met over the paper, the sort of look that could pass for nothing unless you were the one inside it. The table fell into a moment's stillness, the kind born of quiet understanding. Mrs. Bainbridge lifted an eyebrow and said nothing. Barrington glanced between them before looking down at the lists. Kenworth set the long sheet aside as though nothing at all had happened.

Footsteps sounded in the hall. Sanderson stood in the doorway with the composure of a man who could deliver a message across a battlefield without ruffling a cuff.

"Lady Marchmont and Miss Erica Notley," he announced.

Lady Marchmont entered in a sweep of pale blue pelisse, light catching on the trim at her cuffs. Erica followed, her plume nodding, her gaze bright. The air seemed to make room for them, carrying in a breath of the afternoon and a thread of perfume like a quiet invitation.

"Mrs. Bainbridge," Lady Marchmont said warmly, offering her hand, "I hope you will forgive the interruption. We were speaking earlier, and Miss Notley reminded me of something you admired in my library during the masquerade. We decided it should come here at once."

At her nod, Erica set a cloth-wrapped parcel on the table, handling it with more care than needed, as though the attention belonged to the gathering as much as the parcel.

Mrs. Bainbridge rose. "The Sèvres vase." She unwrapped porcelain the color of a summer sky, roses painted in such fine detail they seemed close to moving. "It is lovelier than I remembered."

"It belonged to my grandmother," Lady Marchmont said. "She brought it home from Paris. It was broken once, years ago, but mended so neatly the join is almost a memory." Her fingertip traced the faint seam. "It would lend a touch of grace to your celebration."

Leticia stepped nearer. The brushwork around the flowers had a steadiness that spoke of patience and a sure hand. Erica smoothed the cloth's edge. "It deserves to be seen," she said lightly.

They spoke for a few moments about where the vase might be placed, the mantel in the dining room, perhaps, or a receiving table at the castle entry to welcome each guest as they arrived. The talk was comfortable, a piece of daytime business that belonged in any good house.

Lady Marchmont's gaze turned to Leticia and Gabriel, a glimmer of mischief in her eyes. "And when will we be celebrating your vows?" she asked without pressure.

Gabriel's answer came steady, unhurried. "We are still in discussion, but we have vowed to have an answer by the end of next week."

Lady Marchmont's brows lifted a fraction. She smiled as if the answer pleased her. "I shall keep my best gown pressed."

Sanderson returned with a footman carrying a tall arrangement of chrysanthemums and glossy leaves. It was handsome enough, but far too high for a table meant for conversation. The footman set it where Kenworth pointed and stepped back with the practiced neutrality of a man accustomed to many opinions.

"From the High Street florist, ma'am," Sanderson said.

Mrs. Bainbridge studied the arrangement. "This is not what we discussed. It will block the view of anyone who tries to talk over it."

Kenworth moved closer, regarding it with professional concern. "It will go back at once with a note. We are testing the hand, not building a wall."

Leticia leaned in to examine the stems. "The flowers are fine, but they need a low bowl with air between the blooms."

Gabriel drew a small card and wrote a short message. "Ask for a table piece, not a church display. Tell Mrs. Hale the bride would like to see the work, not the height."

Kenworth took the card with a short nod. "Very good, my lord."

The conversation turned to lighter matters. Lady Marchmont admired the ribbon swatches, Mrs. Bainbridge asked after Leticia's aunt. Barrington spoke of the wind off the water that morning, lifting the gulls like scraps of white paper.

Erica, lingering near the vase, remarked that she had heard the watch was out late the previous night. The words carried a soft ripple through the room. She smiled as though it were nothing more than gossip. Leticia set her teacup down with care. Gabriel said nothing, but his attention sharpened in a way that she could feel, like a faint tightening in the air between them.

The clock on the mantel chimed. Lady Marchmont turned toward the sound. "We must not keep the society waiting. I promised my voice for a cause that will take most of the afternoon if I am not careful."

"We would not have you late on our account," Mrs. Bainbridge said.

Erica reached for her gloves slowly, smoothing each finger, and glanced toward the vase again. She did not say she wished to stay, but some part of her was reluctant to leave.

"Come along, my dear," Lady Marchmont said with pleasant insistence. To Mrs. Bainbridge, "If the vase pleases you, keep it through the wedding, and send a note after. If I need it sooner, I will send a footman."

"Your kindness is more than I could ask," Mrs. Bainbridge said.

Pleasantries were exchanged. Sanderson opened the door. Lady Marchmont offered a last friendly nod before leaving. Erica followed, half turning back as if to speak, but only smiled faintly and went on. The door closed with a soft, well-bred thud.

The room eased into a quieter shape. Kenworth returned with a fresh pot of tea and sugared biscuits. Sanderson lifted the tall chrysanthemums and carried them away to wherever unsuitable displays went to be reborn.

Gabriel poured for Leticia. The cup was warm against her fingers. "We are no closer than we were last week," she said, steady rather than complaining.

"Townsend's report added little," Gabriel said. "The ledger is stubborn. It's filled with names we already know, the rest written by a cautious hand."

Barrington drew up a chair. "If the auction lists do not give us the seller, perhaps the carriers will give us the buyer. Sanderson knows the coachmen. We might learn who collected the items and where they went."

Gabriel nodded. "Two lines, then. The jeweler's quiet commissions, and the carriers' trails."

"Tomorrow," Leticia said. The rightness of the plan steadied her. "We divide the work and report at noon."

Mrs. Bainbridge's gaze softened. "Set it aside for today and enjoy our supper like sensible people."

"We agree," Barrington said, rising to offer her his hand. "We are outnumbered and overruled."

"You are neither," she said, though she took his hand. "Only well guided."

Sanderson entered the room. "Dinner is served."

They went through to the dining room with the cheerful ease of people long accustomed to one another. The scent of roasting meat and fresh bread mingled in the air. Candlelight picked up the gleam of polished wood and silver. The Sèvres vase had found the mantel here, the painted roses approving their new vantage point.

The first course was a clear soup, steam curling up with the bright scent of herbs. Spoons touched china in a gentle clink.

Barrington leaned back, one arm over his chair. "Reminds me of the first days of my commission. I was so determined to look the part that I wore the Major's spare boots without realizing it. They pinched so hard I had blisters the size of coins before we'd marched a mile."

Mrs. Bainbridge winced as she lifted her spoon. "Surely you changed them at the first opportunity."

"I did," Barrington said, "though the Major never saw his boots again."

Kenworth, serving with a perfectly straight face, murmured as he refilled Barrington's wine, "He claimed to the end of his days some scoundrel spirited them away."

Barrington grinned. "A scoundrel? Never. I merely ensured they were… unavailable."

"Which is a polite way of saying you hid them," Mrs. Bainbridge laughed, setting her spoon down with a light clatter.

"Exactly." He raised his glass in mock solemnity. "To the comfort of one's own boots."

Mrs. Bainbridge shook her head, still smiling. "That reminds me of a summer garden party years ago. It began in bright sunshine and ended with three ladies of great consequence huddled under a chestnut tree in the rain. Their feathers drooped so badly they looked like bedraggled hens."

"What happened?" Leticia asked, resting her elbow on the table as if leaning in for the answer.

"A gardener appeared with a tarpaulin and marched them, one by one, to the terrace as though he were leading a parade. They thanked him as if he had carried them across the Channel."

Kenworth, pausing mid-pour for Mrs. Bainbridge's wine, said dryly, "He was the hero of the house for a month. In the village, he never paid for his own drink again."

"Nor should he," Barrington said. "That was service above and beyond."

The footmen exchanged dishes for the next course, the low murmur of their movements blending with the silver's faint ring.

Barrington turned to Leticia. "Speaking of spectacles, how close did the musicians come to losing their place when half the guests lost their partners during the reel?"

"Barely," Leticia said, smiling over the rim of her glass. "I think the harpist stopped playing altogether just to see who would find their way back first."

Gabriel's mouth curved faintly as he reached for the wine, the stem of his glass glinting in the candlelight.

"I once led a line of cousins into a chair during a country dance," Leticia went on. "My aunt said it was the most orderly collision she had ever seen."

The table laughed, the sound rolling easily between the place settings.

Gabriel, who had been quiet, set down his fork. "When I first learned to sail, I tied the lines so cleverly the boat circled the same patch of water for an hour. A boy on the pier finally shouted I had made a fine pond."

Even Mrs. Bainbridge pressed a napkin to her mouth. "And what did you do?"

"I pretended I meant to stay there all along." His eyes met Leticia's, and for a heartbeat the laughter dimmed everywhere but between them.

Kenworth arrived with a tart fragrant with sugar and brown butter, setting it at the center of the table. "I'll return that tower of chrysanthemums tomorrow with a note so neat Mrs. Hale could use it to train her apprentices."

"If she becomes so good at training, she can have my soldiers," Barrington said, leaning back in his chair with obvious mischief.

Mrs. Bainbridge shook her head. "And if she sends them back well trained, I'll send you along so you finally learn how to identify your own boots."

Laughter rose again, warm and unforced, carrying the table into the softer hum that comes when plates are removed and the wine decanter makes one last round.

When they rose, Leticia set down her napkin. "I should be getting home."

Gabriel rose at once. "Allow me to see you there."

She hesitated, nodded. "The wind rises early on the cliff path. A steady arm would be kind."

"It is my pleasure."

They said their goodbyes and stepped into the night air, cool with the salt of the North Sea. The cliff path lay pale against the grass, the sea's patient sound below. They walked without hurry. The quiet was not a lack of words, but something complete in itself, like the hush before a prayer.

At her door, she turned to thank him. He was already close. His hand lifted, not to claim, but to touch her cheek as if it were the most natural thing in the world. The kiss was deliberate, warm, lingering, like a ribbon drawn slowly through the hand, leaving heat and a steadiness that surprised her.

When he drew back, his voice was low, edged with a quiet smile. "Something to think about over the next week."

He stepped away at once, as if he knew exactly what to give and what to leave. Halfway down the path, he glanced back. The look in his eyes stole her breath so completely she had to steady herself with the latch.

She stood in the doorway for a moment, the sky deepening above the roofline, the faint scent of salt still in the air. Behind her, the house was quiet. Ahead, the week stretched thin and bright. She touched her lips not to hold the kiss, but to promise herself she would not forget how it felt.

# Chapter Twenty-Two

A SOFT RAIN had fallen in the night, leaving the morning air cool and fresh as it drifted through Leticia's bedchamber. The scent of damp earth and lavender slipped through the muslin curtains. She sat at her dressing table with the small box unlocked before her, the brooch resting on its bed of velvet. The fabric's nap pressed lightly beneath her fingertips, a whisper of her mother's touch. Turning it in the light, she caught the faint etching inside the diamond, a raven, sharp as if the stone itself remembered.

Her breath caught the first time she'd seen it. Even now, unease beat against her ribs, quick as a trapped wing. For years, she believed it was only a keepsake from her mother, precious for sentiment alone. Now it was a piece in a game she had only begun to understand. A chill stole through her even as sunlight caught the edge of the mirror, cutting across her reflection.

She fastened it at her throat, just above the lace of her morning gown. In the mirror, the diamond caught the light and threw it back with a pale spark. Her mother would have approved. And yet… wearing it was like stepping beneath a lantern, exposed, as though the walls themselves might watch. She imagined Gabriel's face if he saw it. He would know at once she had kept it from him. Thinking about it brought heat to her cheeks and a quick sting of shame behind it.

The pin came free. She set the brooch back on the velvet. "Not today," she murmured, closing the lid and turning the key.

The small click sounded too loud, sealing more than metal. The burden in her chest was heavier than the jewel itself. Secrets were poor company, yet she could not let this one go. Not yet.

Downstairs, the household moved with its usual quiet order. Lady Eastbury had ordered fresh flowers for the morning room and tea for ten. By the time the longcase clock chimed the hour, Leticia was by the window, arranging roses, steadying her hands as she resisted the urge to watch the drive. Her fingertips were damp from the dew on the petals. She wiped them absently on her gown, the scent of crushed blooms rising around her.

When the Harcourt carriage rumbled to a stop, she smoothed her skirt and composed her expression. Her heart steadied on the third breath. She could face this. She had to.

Celeste Harcourt entered with the grace of a woman accustomed to deference. Her mahogany hair was drawn into a precise braid. Her dove-gray gown carried an elegance that softened its formality. The corners of her eyes creased when she smiled, the kind of smile that concealed as much as it offered.

"Lady Eastbury, Lady Salisbury," she said, inclining her head. "Thank you for the invitation."

"We are delighted you could come," Lady Eastbury replied, gesturing to the settee. "I hear Bath keeps you busy with committees and concerts."

"I try to keep occupied," Celeste said as she took her seat. "An idle widow is a danger to herself, I am told."

"You could never be idle," Leticia said warmly. "Please, allow me to pour." The steady rhythm of the tea, porcelain against porcelain, soothed her nerves. It was a fragile music of civility.

Gabriel entered as the tea was served, his thick auburn hair neatly combed, his cravat tied with military precision. The faint scent of starch and rain followed him. He bowed to Celeste, and she looked between him and Leticia with a knowing lift of her brows.

"I have heard a great deal about this unexpected engagement," she said. "From your Colonel's mother, no less."

Leticia's face grew warm, though not from guilt. "It was...quite unexpected," she said. Across from her, Gabriel's mouth curved, the smallest betrayal of amusement. The flicker of it drew her breath, steadying her more than she cared to admit.

Lady Eastbury asked after Celeste's charitable work. Leticia inquired about Bath, the hot springs she had never seen. Celeste spoke of the library her late husband had loved, and how she had struggled to care for it after his death.

"I am no scholar," she said with a rueful smile. "When I found a volume in a language I could not name, I called the Historical Society. Professor Tresham came himself. He turned each page with gloved hands, speaking of the paper as though it were a jewel."

Gabriel smiled. "Professor Tresham has rescued more manuscripts than I can count."

"Indeed. His visit reminded me of the necklace I had just purchased, a small indulgence, though the engraving on one stone seemed curious enough to make even the Professor pause when he saw it later at an exhibition."

Leticia leaned forward. "Was that the necklace Mrs. Penstone wore to the Marchmont masquerade? The one that was stolen?"

Celeste's eyes sharpened. "The same. I bought it at a private sale four years ago. The seller sent an intermediary. A young woman with golden hair and striking blue eyes. Barely eighteen, but with the manner of someone twice her years."

She glanced at Gabriel. "Within a month, men began calling. One I remember clearly. He was nervous, always spinning the ring on his finger. An intaglio seal, engraved with a bird. He offered to buy the necklace. I refused. Later, when roof repairs became urgent, I sold it quietly through a Bath solicitor I trusted. The sale drew more notice than keeping it ever did."

Leticia's glance met Gabriel's. A golden-haired woman. A raven seal. Professor Tresham's deft hands. The pattern shimmered, so close she could almost touch it like threads on a loom before the image appears.

"Did you ever meet this solicitor?" Gabriel asked.

"Twice," Celeste said. "A man of middle years. Efficient, unremarkable. He left Bath soon after."

They spoke a little longer about the auctions and the hazards of country houses. When Celeste rose, she clasped Leticia's hand in both of hers. Her fingers were cool, scented faintly of rosewater and loneliness.

"You are more than you believe, Lady Salisbury," she said softly. "Do not let anyone tell you otherwise."

Leticia smiled, touched. "Thank you." The words lingered, threading warmth through the chill that had followed Celeste's tale.

From the window, they watched her carriage pull away. The horses' hooves struck wet drive gravel and faded into the distance. The silence that followed was soft but heavy.

"Will you walk with me in the garden?" Gabriel asked, offering his arm before she could answer.

They strolled along the path, edging the lawn. Rain clung to the rose leaves like diamonds. Birds sang from the hawthorn hedge. The air smelled of wet earth and new beginnings. Leticia recited the points aloud, as if speaking them might settle them into place.

"A golden-haired woman conducts a private sale. A necklace with a raven-etched diamond. Many people admire it. A man with a raven signet offers to buy it. Celeste sells it to repair her roof. Years later, it is stolen at Lady Marchmont's masquerade."

Gabriel's mouth curved faintly. "Sounds like one of Barrington's mystery tales. But," his brow furrowed, "it is a chain worth following."

"What do you think of the intermediary?" Leticia asked, though she suspected she knew.

Gabriel hesitated. "Celeste's description fits Erica. But we must be certain. If she is involved, there may be reasons we do not yet see." His gaze lingered on her, steady and unreadable, and it made her pulse trip.

They had almost reached the terrace when Felix ran up to them, his boots striking the gravel in a rhythm of urgency, and his hair windswept.

"There you are," he said, catching his breath. "I've been to the Historical Society. Tresham gave me a list of Bath solicitors who handle estate clearances. One shows on Celeste's receipt: Jasper Pierce. He closed his practice last year. Rumor puts him at Lammer Cove."

"Lammer Cove?" Leticia repeated. "That's a mile from my aunt's seaside cottage."

Felix nodded. "He was seen at Lammer Inn two days ago."

Gabriel looked from her to Felix. "We could be there by nightfall. We'll tell Barrington on the way."

Plans moved quickly. Lady Eastbury sent word to her staff at the cottage and began her own preparations for the journey. Leticia packed with brisk hands, her mind fixed on the road ahead and on the place she had vowed not to see again, the little cottage where her parents had spent their last summer before the accident. She had not been back in two years. The thought tightened her throat.

When her trunk was closed, her gaze fell to the small box on her dressing table. She did not open it. She only rested her hand on the lid.

"Not yet," she whispered, and turned away.

Outside, the sky had cleared, clouds scudding over the blue. Leticia climbed into the carriage beside Gabriel, the space between them holding what neither had spoken. The wheels began to turn as the sunlight spilled across the drive. The road to the coast stretched ahead, and for now, it was enough that they faced it together.

# Chapter Twenty-Three

THEY REACHED LAMMER Cove at the hour when daylight thins and the sea begins to sound like a thought one cannot dismiss. The cottage stood a little above the road with its back to the wind, its slate roof dark with the promise of rain. Sea mist gathered in the hedgerows like smoke, and every gust carried salt and the faint cry of gulls. Lady Eastbury rapped on the door with the authority of an admiral returning to her ship.

It opened almost at once. Brian, the housekeeper's boy, stood there taller than she remembered, his hair darkened by the damp and a smudge of ash on his sleeve. He blinked, then grinned, the expression pure memory.

"Lady Eastbury. Miss Letty," he said, ducking his head. "We weren't certain you'd come before the weather turned."

"Still quicker than a London footman," Lady Eastbury said, handing him her gloves.

He bowed and ushered them into the low-ceilinged warmth of the front room, where his mother, Mrs. Benson, was setting the last of the china on the hearth table. Her round face brightened at the sight of them, and she dried her hands on her apron before bobbing a curtsey.

"Fire on, tea coming," Mrs. Benson declared. "Storm's rolling in fast, my lady. Best not to linger in it."

Leticia's throat tightened. The familiar scent of peat smoke and lavender polish carried her back to summers when she'd run through this very room with seaweed in her pockets and Mrs.

Benson chasing after her with a towel.

Leticia stepped aside to allow Gabriel through. He filled the doorway, rain darkening the shoulders of his coat, the scent of wet wool mingling with smoke. He paused in the threshold a moment longer than necessary, his gaze sweeping the lane, the stubbled fields, the curling path toward the beach. The air carried that metallic tang before a downpour, and below, waves leaned hard into rock and fell back with a mutter.

Lady Eastbury shook the damp from her gloves. "I should like a look at the garden before it's pummeled to bits," she said briskly. "Ten minutes, Leticia. No longer. Lord Ashcombe, you may scowl at the horizon from the path like a proper baron if it pleases you."

"It rarely does," he said, but his mouth tugged faintly.

They stepped out together, three dark shapes against the paling sky. The cottage garden, tidy in summer, now looked like a creature bristling for weather. Leticia breathed the salt and the damp and experienced that curious steadiness that sometimes came to her before a crisis, when the world narrowed and every unnecessary thought fell away.

At the lane, she glanced back. A man stood where the road bent toward the dunes. His hat was pulled low, his coat collar high. Recognition pricked. She had seen him once before at the Historical Society, near the jewel cases. Tonight, he tipped his brim and turned away as if admiring the clouds.

"Do you know him?" she asked lightly.

Gabriel's eyes flicked toward the bend and back. "No, but I know his type."

"Which is?"

"The observant sort." He offered his arm so Lady Eastbury could take the steadier portion of the path. "I prefer to let the observant feel unobserved."

Lady Eastbury sniffed. "I prefer my observers invited to tea and made to speak sensibly."

A spit of rain pricked Leticia's cheek. The path widened at the cliff's shoulder, and the cove opened below, a scooped arc of shingle and black rock cleft by a ribbon of violent white water. Farther out, the sea wore a hard new color, blue hammered with iron. Wind hissed through the grasses, flattening them in uneasy unison.

"There," Gabriel said quietly.

A figure moved swiftly across the lower stones, a dark smudge slipping behind a jut of rock. Even at this distance, she recognized the set of his shoulders, the same man from the bend, moving with deliberate urgency, as if late to an appointment.

"Fisherman?" Lady Eastbury offered.

"Perhaps," Gabriel said, though the word sat uneasily. His gaze lingered, measuring distance as if deciding which consequence to accept. "The tide will be high within the hour."

"And the storm sooner," Lady Eastbury said. "We are going in."

They turned back, wind pressing at their backs now, rain beginning in earnest. The cottage door closed on the weather with a grateful thud. Fire snapped in the grate. The housekeeper set tea and bread on the table, promising a hot stew if the chimney behaved. Lady Eastbury removed her bonnet with a decisive tug.

"Plans," she said, the word as practical as flint.

They took to the dining table like a council, Lady Eastbury at the head, Leticia and Gabriel opposite each other, a map of the coastline unrolled between them. Raindrops pattered on the slate above, a counterpoint to the crackle of fire. The cottage had seen a hundred such councils before, floods, harvests, and winter aid, and lent its confidence to this one.

"Tomorrow," Gabriel said, tracing a finger along the cliff line, "I'll take the upper path at first light and watch the cove from the ridge. Felix should reach us by midday if the roads hold. We'll speak to the innkeeper, and I'll see if Jasper Pierce's name loosens any tongues." He looked to Leticia. "You and your aunt will remain here. If anything stirs, send word by the housekeeper's boy and do not go down to the beach."

Leticia met his eyes evenly. "We will not go down to the beach."

He nodded, as if the repetition bound the promise.

Mrs. Benson entered to lay the cloth and set the spoons. Rain found a seam in the window and spattered the glass. The fire offered its ordinary cheer, but it did not settle Leticia. The storm's voice pressed close against the panes, and beneath it she felt the faint hum of purpose, a wheel beginning to turn.

Gabriel rose and crossed to the window, watching the black seam of the cliff. "He was down there for a reason," he murmured, more to himself than to them. "And if the storm covers his tracks, we'll lose them." He reached for his coat.

Leticia stood. "You mean to go after him now?"

"Not far. Just to see if he's still there." He took up a lantern. "If anyone is foolish enough to be on the cove in this, I'd like to know why."

Lady Eastbury's tone softened under its reprimand. "Take care. And if the wind shifts, you come back here."

"I will."

Leticia tightened her shawl, the words pressing against her teeth. She was not his wife, but they had an arrangement, a partnership neither named yet both honored. "Be quick," she managed.

He looked at her, truly looked, and it did something complicated to her lungs. "I will," he said again, and she had to let him go.

The door opened to noise and cold, and the peculiar brightness of a night that intends a spectacle. The lantern's glow faded into the dark like a swallowed star.

They listened. Waiting could be loud, the pop of a knot in the fire, the faint clatter of a spoon, the tick of the clock's brass rod. Outside, the storm gave the sea a voice, and the sea roared itself hoarse against the headland.

Ten minutes stretched into fifteen.

Lady Eastbury stood. "He is taking longer than a quick check."

"He is," Leticia said, and went to the door before deciding to.

They stepped onto the threshold together. The wind whipped the hem of Leticia's gown against her ankles and flung salt to her lips. Lightning split the eastern sky in a white-hot gasp, and in that instant, the cove became a stage for two figures struggling on the slick lip of rock, one driving the other back, both a slip from death.

The dark closed again. Thunder followed, late and outraged.

"Back," Lady Eastbury said, already moving. "We will not stand wringing our hands. Do something useful."

Leticia knew before her aunt spoke what that was. Her father's room, untouched by time, and the drawers as he'd left them. She had run across those boards as a child and knew exactly where the long case lay at the back of the wardrobe. The oiled cloth. The weight, heavier than a pistol, steadier than panic.

Her body remembered what her mind did not stop to consider. The measure of powder, the tamping of shot, the feel of a weapon balanced for the shoulder. Her father's voice echoed beside her. *You will not be an idiot about danger, Letty. If you must be near it, at least be clever.*

In the front room, Lady Eastbury had already set the lantern low to keep its light from betraying them.

Another flare. This one closer. Gabriel reeling as the other's fist caught his jaw, the cliff edge three steps away. The dark man raised a rock two-handed, taking aim.

Leticia stepped into the doorway, braced the butt to her shoulder, and let the world shrink to sight, breath, and the memory of her father's steady voice. *Squeeze. Don't pull.*

The shot cracked the storm clean in two.

The man jolted, the rock thudding to the shingle. He staggered, glanced up, his face a smear of angles and fear, and fled along the ledge, disappearing the way rats know the dark.

For a heartbeat, only the rifle's echo argued with the cliffs.

Gabriel stood very still, touched his jaw as if confirming it remained. He took two steps after the fleeing man, saw the water leap at the path like a dog at a gate, and chose the living over the chase. By the time he reached the cottage, rain had smudged his hair flat and turned his collar to paste.

Lady Eastbury caught the door before the wind could wrench it wide. "Inside," she ordered. "You will not bleed on the step."

Leticia lowered the rifle, her hands suddenly useless. Mrs. Benson brought towels, a bowl, and the old green bottle of spirits. Gabriel sat where Lady Eastbury pointed. Blood marked a bright line from chin to cravat; Leticia touched it with a cloth, careful as she had not been with the shot.

"You could have been killed," he said, not loud, not sharp, but enough to make the room smaller.

"So could you," she replied, without adding the rest, *and I can count the cost.*

His breath caught at the sting. "You fired cleanly."

"I fired," she said.

Lady Eastbury set a thimble of spirits near his hand. "Drink that, or I shall pour it over your head."

He obeyed.

"Hold a moment," Leticia murmured, angling the candle closer. "Aunt, the glass."

Lady Eastbury fetched the small looking glass. Leticia lifted Gabriel's chin, keeping her touch steady.

Under the cut, the bruise was blooming into the precise geometry of a diamond shape with a bird scratched within.

"Do you see?" she asked quietly.

Gabriel stilled, took the glass, and turned it so the candle spared no detail. The mark looked back at them, impertinent and clear.

"A raven in a diamond," Lady Eastbury said, as if naming a thief at a tea party.

"His ring," Leticia said. "He hit you with it."

Gabriel set the glass down, the anger in him a controlled line from problem to remedy. "He'll have the bruise to match. He wasn't there by chance."

"Who, then?" Lady Eastbury asked.

"A watcher," Gabriel said. "Paid to take note. Perhaps to intervene."

"Paid by whom?" Leticia asked.

His gaze met hers, words spared. "We will have to find out."

The wind eased, the lull sounding like an omen. Mrs. Benson set the stew on the trivet and asked whether anyone meant to eat like people intending to remain upright.

Lady Eastbury took the bloody cloth from Leticia and replaced it with a clean one. "Tomorrow," she said.

Gabriel nodded, including them both. "At first light."

Leticia set the glass back on the mantel. She could still feel the echo of the rifle in her shoulder, the shot in her bones. The mark on his skin would fade, but for tonight, the raven remained in the room.

She lifted her chin.

"Next time," Gabriel said, "you do not step into a doorway with a weapon when men are trying to kill each other."

"Then don't give me reason to," she answered calmly.

His mouth tilted, not quite a smile. "I will endeavor to be less foolish."

"That would be a welcome novelty," Lady Eastbury said briskly. "Now, I will eat, because storms are best met on a full stomach. Lord Ashcombe, you will sit until that bleeding stops. Leticia, bring another candle. The corners of this room have gone gloomier than I like."

Leticia lit a second taper. Rain drummed steadily on slate and sill. Beyond the glass, the cove waited, invisible but present, like an audience holding its breath.

She sank into the chair opposite Gabriel. "Tomorrow," she said again.

He inclined his head, the candle catching the faint outline on his jaw.

"Tomorrow," he said, and this time it sounded less like a promise and more like a vow.

# Chapter Twenty-Four

THE STORM HAD passed, but the sea moved heavily under its memory. A gray swell rolled in from the horizon, throwing brine into the wind and shoving the small fishing boats against their moorings. The air carried the remnants of thunder, salt and iron, restless and alive. The path to Lammer Cove dipped steeply toward the water, lined with scrub grass and gorse that rattled dry seed pods in each gust. Sea spray beaded on Leticia's lashes while the tang of it clung to her tongue. Below, gulls wheeled low over the tideline, their cries sharp against the steady boom of surf.

Leticia kept her skirts clear of the damp ground, one gloved hand on Lady Eastbury's arm. Gabriel walked slightly ahead, his coat collar turned up, the set of his shoulders sharp against the pale sky. He moved with that quiet readiness she had come to recognize—the tension of a man who expected danger but refused to name it. Every few steps, he glanced over his shoulder, whether to check the footing for the ladies or to see if anyone followed, she could not say. The habit steadied her. He noticed things. He always had.

"This is a ridiculous place to arrange a meeting," Lady Eastbury said. Her hat was pinned against the wind but still tilted. "One would think your Mr. Pierce might choose somewhere indoors. A tearoom, perhaps. With scones."

"Pierce does not take tea," Gabriel said without turning. "He's more comfortable in places where no one listens closely."

"Which is exactly why we brought Lady Eastbury," Leticia

said, giving her aunt a quick smile. "You can talk loud enough for all of Sommer-by-the-Sea to listen."

Her aunt's sniff was drowned by the crash of a wave.

They rounded a rock outcrop, and the cove came into view. The tide had drawn back, leaving slick ribbons of kelp along the sand. A single man stood near the waterline, cap low over his brow, coat flapping open in the wind. He looked worn into the shore, weather-worn, all angles and salt.

A crabber with a creel slung over one shoulder came stumping up the shingle. His boots left dark ovals where the water licked in and withdrew. He tipped his cap at Lady Eastbury, eyes flicking to Gabriel and back. "Storm's thrown odd things ashore this week," he said, as if to no one. "Odd folk, too. Strangers askin' after paths that aren't their business. Best keep to the upper track when the sea's got its temper."

"Sound advice," Lady Eastbury said crisply. "We brought our tempers with us, but we shall try not to let them meet."

The crabber's mouth curved, almost in a smile, as he trudged on. Leticia watched him go, a stitch of dark wool against the pale seam of shore. She had the distinct sense that the land itself was listening, holding its breath between gusts. A prickle lifted along her neck that wasn't from the wind.

Pierce turned as they approached. His eyes flicked to Gabriel first, narrowing, to Leticia and Lady Eastbury. "You brought company."

"They insisted," Gabriel said. "This is Lady Eastbury and her niece, Lady Salisbury."

Pierce gave a stiff nod. "I remember your father," he said to Leticia. "He could handle a boat."

"Do you remember my mother, too?" Leticia asked, searching his weathered face for recognition. "She loved the cove."

A brief pause. "Aye," he said at last.

The single word was like a stone dropped in deep water.

"I remember," he added.

"Reckless to bring a lady here in weather like this," Pierce muttered, as if speaking to himself.

The wind whipped her skirt, tugging at her shawl. She caught Gabriel watching her before he turned back to Pierce. "You've been in and out of town these past weeks," Gabriel said. "You've heard things."

Pierce hesitated. His gaze drifted toward the far end of the cove where black rock teeth bit into the sea. "Depends on who's asking."

Gabriel stepped closer. "The sort of man who doesn't have time for games."

Lady Eastbury clucked her tongue. "And the sort of lady who is cold enough to turn back if someone doesn't start talking."

Pierce's mouth twitched, almost a smile. "There's been movement. A man came through two nights ago. Stayed at the Fishman's Rest. Not his own name. Heavy coat though the evening was warm. Kept one hand covered. Carried something small. Valuable. Never took it out where anyone could see."

"What happened to him?" Gabriel asked.

Pierce shifted his weight. "Met with another man before dawn. Left by the cliff path. Didn't take the main road. Went north."

Leticia tucked that away. North, toward the Morton lands and the old auction house that kept appearing in her notes. The information brushed cold fingers down her spine. The shape of a pattern brushed her mind, then slipped away, gone, leaving a chill.

Pierce squinted at her. "You're not just here to listen."

"I'm here because this concerns my family," she said evenly. "Pieces of what you've said fit with what we already know."

He didn't ask how. "Careful with that sort of talk, Lady Salisbury. You'll find yourself with more trouble than you want."

Gabriel's voice was quiet but firm. "She already has."

For a moment, only wind and the hiss of the waves filled the space between them. Pierce looked past Gabriel to the curve of the bay. "If you're looking for where the man went after he left here, ask after a place called Dunmere Cross. Not much more than a marker stone and an old smuggler's shed. The right sort knows it."

"Why tell us?" Leticia asked.

Pierce's eyes hardened. "Because the men you're chasing don't belong here. They think they can use our coast for their dealings. They're wrong."

Lady Eastbury drew her shawl tighter. "Well. We've been suitably chilled by both the wind and our company. Perhaps we might take our leave?"

"Wait." Pierce tipped his head toward the bluff. "Guard on the upper path these days. Not a constable. Someone else. If you must climb, keep your heads down on the turn."

Gabriel's attention sharpened. "You saw him?"

"I saw enough." Pierce tipped his cap, already turning away. "Be careful on the climb back. Rocks are slick."

Gabriel waited until they'd walked out of earshot. "He gave us more than I expected."

"He gave us Dunmere Cross," Leticia said. "And a smuggler's shed."

"And a direction," Gabriel added.

They began the ascent toward the path. The sea boomed behind them, filling the silence. Halfway up, Leticia paused to look back. Pierce was gone, swallowed by the curve of the cove. She could feel the cliff's shoulder to her left, the drop to the rocks below on her right. Gabriel shifted to walk on the outside edge, always between the ladies and catastrophe. His presence there, wordless and deliberate, felt something like a vow. Lady Eastbury puffed slightly from the climb.

"If I'd known we were going to be trudging over rocks and through wind for a few scraps of gossip, I'd have sent a footman."

"It's not gossip," Leticia said. "It's a trail."

Gabriel met her gaze over his aunt's shoulder. "One we'll follow in Sommer-by-the-Sea."

They reached the turn where the path narrowed and stopped

for a breath. Leticia tasted the odd, metallic quiet that comes when a bird of prey passes overhead, and everything goes still. The stillness stretched so thin she could feel her pulse inside it. A gull shrieked, and the world resumed. Gabriel's shift to the outside edge without comment set something steady and low inside her, an answer to a question she had not dared put into words.

⫸⫷

BACK AT THE inn, the warmth of the fire made the salt-stiff air sharper in her lungs. Smoke curled lazily above the hearth, the scent of peat and ale settling around them like a shawl. Leticia loosened her shawl and sat near the hearth. Gabriel stood by the window, looking out at the lane as if the man from Pierce's story might walk past. The low murmur of voices from the bar blended with the pop of peat in the grate.

"Dunmere Cross," she said, trying the name aloud. "It sounds like something out of a smuggler's tale."

"It is," Gabriel said. "Old stories say it was where smugglers met to divide cargo. That shed's been empty for years, but if Pierce says someone's using it again, we'll find out who."

Lady Eastbury, unpinning her hat, glanced between them. "You'll do no such thing without me."

"We'll be going back to Sommer-by-the-Sea," Gabriel said. "The next step is there."

Leticia caught the faintest emphasis on we. "And what will you do with what Pierce gave us?"

"Start pulling the threads," Gabriel said. "See where they lead."

She thought of the man in the heavy coat, the hidden hand, the dawn departure. The image sat uneasily beside her mother's brooch, locked away in her drawer. Every thread she touched seemed to hum with the same dangerous promise: pull, and something will come undone.

The inn door opened with a slap of wind. Two fishermen stamped in, knocking mud from their boots. The landlord called a greeting, leaned on the counter as Gabriel approached. From the corner, Leticia watched the conversation in the ale mirror. The mirror warped their reflections, bending Gabriel's tall form into something caught between shadow and light. His calm mouth moved, the landlord's brows rose, and a thumb swung toward the coast. The landlord drew a mark on the wood with a damp finger, two lines crossing with a dot to one side, wiped it away with his cuff.

Meanwhile, Lady Eastbury had already gathered a small court near the hearth. She sat with a woman in a faded blue shawl and another with red hands and a laugh like a cart on gravel. "Prices have gone up dreadfully," her ladyship declared. "Tea, lace, even gossip. In my day, gossip was free."

"Still is if you buy a round," the blue shawl said.

Lady Eastbury produced a coin with a magician's air and placed it on the table. "Let us be extravagant. Tell me, what sort of people ask about sheds?"

"Quiet sort," the red hands said. "And always askin' the tide times twice."

"Twice?" Lady Eastbury tilted her head.

"So they can pretend they forgot," blue shawl said. "But they never forget. They just want to hear it from different mouths."

From the fishermen's corner came the low rumble of a conversation meant to stay private.

"…shed down by the Cross…"

"…wouldn't go near it after dark…"

"…man with the glove, asking after the tide times…"

Leticia let her gaze rest idly on the tabletop, her ears tilting toward their words. The glove. The tide. A meeting place shunned by locals. Each detail slid neatly into place beside Pierce's account. Together, they fit like fingers closing around the same small object. She did not yet know its shape, only that it fit the palm too well.

Gabriel returned, settling opposite her. "Nothing certain," he said softly, "but the name is known here. More than I'd like."

"Pierce was right," she said.

"Pierce was right about more than he said aloud."

The landlord brought out a plate of oatcakes, and Lady East-bury promptly declared them the best she'd ever had, though she admitted she couldn't remember the last time she'd eaten any. "The secret is lard," she confided to Leticia in a whisper that carried across the room. "All good things are scandalous."

When the driver came in to tell them the tide had dropped enough to cross, they rose, settling cloaks and gloves before stepping back into the wind.

⤐✖⟕

As THE CARRIAGE rolled toward Sommer-by-the-Sea, the landscape shifted from ragged shore to gentler fields. Leticia leaned her shoulder against the window frame, watching sheep dot the hillsides, their wool bright against the green. The air inside was warmer now, heavy with the faint scent of peat and salt clinging to their clothes.

The man with the glove returned to her thoughts, the whispered warnings about the shed, the crabber's caution, and Gabriel's watchfulness at the inn. The threads were drawing together her mother's brooch, the Order's shadow, and now this coastal meeting place. It all moved toward something she could sense, the feeling of a door half open in the dark. Tug the wrong one, and everything might come loose. Wait too long, and someone else might tug it for her.

She glanced at Gabriel and found him already looking at her. No challenge in it, only the steady question he carried for her alone. *Are you with me?* The answering warmth surprised her, quiet, certain, like a harbor found in hard weather.

"Sommer-by-the-Sea," he said quietly, as though promising both an answer and a reckoning.

"And seedcake," Lady Eastbury added, rousing from her corner with a decisive rustle. "I cannot be expected to face villains on an empty stomach."

Gabriel's mouth tugged. Leticia let her cheek rest against the cool glass and watched the road unspool ahead. For the first time since leaving the cove, she let herself believe the storm might be steering them toward the truth.

# Chapter Twenty-Five

THE CARRIAGE LEFT the cove road and settled into the smoother way toward Sommer-by-the-Sea. Wind off the water softened to a steady breeze through the open window, carrying the faint salt of drying kelp. Leticia sat opposite Gabriel, his hat beside him on the seat. He had the stillness he wore when thinking, not distant, but assured.

Lady Eastbury tapped her closed parasol once against the floor as if to signal the day to behave. "We shall stop in the square."

"For Beckett's?" Leticia asked.

"For seedcake," her aunt said. "If I send Peters, they will call it fresh and hope I do not know the difference. If I arrive in person, they will find their best and add a proper slice as a courtesy." Her lips curved. "I enjoy being served what I actually requested."

Gabriel's mouth eased. "Practical."

"Plain sense," Lady Eastbury said, looking toward the turn into town.

"We're off to speak to Barrington," Leticia said.

"Very well," her aunt said, pulling on her gloves. "I will be home within the hour."

The carriage drew up before Beckett's shop, the windows bright with glass trays. Warm spice and sugar drifted into the street. Lady Eastbury accepted Gabriel's hand, stepped down, and crossed the threshold with the calm assurance of a woman who did not beg favors and did not need to. She gave them a brief nod that meant she had everything in hand.

They set off toward Barrington's.

The square had taken on its late morning order. A delivery cart rattled toward the hotel. A pair of navy officers walked in conversation without lowering their voices. An elderly gentleman moved at a dignified pace, leaning on a cane polished by use rather than vanity. Shops wore their best faces. The baker's boy darted out with a paper twist for a waiting girl and received a grin that would set him up for the day.

They turned up the path to Barrington's house. Before Gabriel could lift the knocker, the door opened.

Kenworth stood as if expecting them at that very moment. "Welcome, my lady. Lord Ashcombe."

"Good morning, Kenworth," Leticia said. "Is Colonel Barrington at home?"

"Not just now. He left an hour ago with Mrs. Bainbridge. A short ride along the cliffs. They will return by the afternoon." Kenworth's tone shifted slightly, lowering the way one might when offering a morsel meant for the right ears. "Professor Tresham sent word this morning for the Colonel. Something about having found a document of interest."

"Would you give him a message?" Gabriel asked. "We wish to meet him tomorrow at Lady Eastbury's home at nine."

Kenworth inclined his head. "I will see to it."

"Thank you," Leticia said.

They left their card and turned back toward the square.

At the corner, a vendor called above the rattle of a dray. The warm smell of buns reached them. Gabriel paused, paid for two, and handed one to Leticia.

"You are very good at small rescues," she said.

"I like buns," he answered, trying not to smile.

They walked beneath the beech trees, where the air always carried a light scent of drying leaves and the faint sweetness of fallen ones crushed underfoot. She ate in small bites, more from habit than hunger, the sugar and spice steadying in their ordinary way.

Halfway down the lane, she sensed a faint pull at the back of her neck that meant attention. Not fear, just a prickle of notice. A boot scraped behind them. Another set of steps shifted, as if testing its pace. She glanced toward a bow-front window where a woman was polishing a glass. The reflection gave a narrow view of the street of a gentleman standing a little too still near the edge of the pavement. His hat set at a careful angle. Not close. Not far.

Gabriel did not change stride. He reached across without comment and brushed away the sugar at the corner of her mouth. The gesture was unhurried enough to look like affection and ordinary enough to be exactly that. The man near the window studied a sign he could not possibly read from where he stood, drifted on.

"Eat," Gabriel said.

She ate. When she was two bites from finished, he took the rest from her hand and finished it in one clean bite.

"That was mine," she said.

"I am uncommonly daring," he said.

"You are insufferable."

"Only when it saves time."

She laughed in spite of herself, the sound easing the tension and leaving space for her thoughts. One thought took hold. People were searching for the sixth gem, speaking of it now in low voices at the edges of rooms, as if it were a matter of record and not a story. What if it was hers? What if the brooch in the drawer was not only a memory? What if her mother had known? Not by accident, by choice. The idea did not fit with the woman who had tied a ribbon in her daughter's braid and told her she would grow into herself at her own pace. Yet the mind held two things well. It could love and doubt without losing either.

"You have gone quiet," Gabriel said. He did not press, only marked it as he marked so many things, with silence.

"Thinking," she said.

He nodded and let that be enough.

They reached her aunt's house. The small front garden sat in neat order, the privet hedge clipped the week before, and smelled green and clean. Peters opened the door before the knocker fell, with the air of making a door welcome rather than merely admitting them.

"My lady. Lord Ashcombe." His tone placed Leticia as one of the household, and Gabriel as expected. "Her ladyship has not yet returned. The garden is very pleasant. Shall I have tea laid in the morning room for when you come in?"

"Please," Leticia said.

They walked through to the back. The stone path warmed the soles of their shoes. Roses climbed the south wall with more ambition than discipline. The lavender held bees in honest work. Someone had left a cushion on the bench under the pear tree to catch the sun.

They took the path once without speaking. Gabriel stopped and faced her. "May I ask you something?"

"You may," she said.

"When you look at me, what do you see?"

She held his gaze. It was not an indulgence to answer properly. It was a responsibility. "I see a man who notices more than he says. I see steadiness that does not need to be admired. I see a mind that waits for all the pieces and still chooses when the picture is not yet complete. I see someone who is careful with other people's hearts." She drew a breath. "I see the man who stood between me and the edge of a cliff without making a speech of it."

He didn't answer at once. His gaze held hers until the air between them was taut. He stepped closer, his hand warm along her jaw, steadying her as if the ground itself might shift. She rose to meet him, the first brush of his mouth deliberate, not a question but a claim, deepening until the ache in her chest eased and something fiercer took its place. The kiss settled where it landed, easing something that had been tight for too long. When they parted, she kept his hand a moment longer than necessity asked, knowing the world was still the same, though she would never see it that way again.

"That was… good," she whispered, because anything more would have been too much.

"Yes," he said, which was as much as he needed to say.

The garden door creaked. A maid stood with her hands folded. "My lady. Her ladyship has returned."

"Thank you," Leticia said.

They went inside. The morning room was ready with tea. Lady Eastbury stood by the table with the air of a commander reviewing provisions. A paper-wrapped parcel rested beside the cups like a trophy.

"Two seedcakes," she said. "We will not be found wanting."

"You prevail where others falter," Gabriel said.

"Competence frightens the idle," Lady Eastbury replied, pleased. She seated herself and reached for the pot. "Tell me the plan. I am prepared to approve it if it suits me."

"We called at Barrington's," Leticia said. "Kenworth will tell him to come here tomorrow at nine."

"Very good. Nine gives you an hour and does not encourage dawdling." She poured, added, "I must send to Turnbull and Sons for a cleaner. I want my jewels ready for the soiree. You may as well take any of yours that need attention."

Leticia's mind went at once to her mother's brooch. "I will," she said. "It could use a fresh polish."

They spoke of small things while they ate a thin slice of cake. The crumb was warm and delicious. Lady Eastbury had found the words for it years ago. Cake should taste like comfort, not apology. This did. She asked after Mrs. Bainbridge and nodded, pleased to hear they had been out together and were at ease. She mentioned a note from the vicar about the chapel and looked as if she had strong opinions about the placement of runners.

"I am out for a short call," she said when the tray was cleared. "Mrs. Denholm's maid is unwell. I promised broth. I will return before four. If Peters tries to enlist either of you in the question of the pantry shelves, refuse him. He has decided that gentlemen have views about vinegar."

"I shall be firm," Leticia said.

Lady Eastbury touched her cheek, and Gabriel's hand as well. "You both look well," she said. It was a benediction offered as a remark. She was gone with the brisk step of a woman who kept promises by habit.

The house settled. The quiet that followed was not the quiet of emptiness, but of trust.

They returned to the morning room window. From there, the garden looked contained and well behaved. It was different to walk inside it and feel the work of bees and the drift of leaves. Leticia rested her palm against the wood, the paint smooth under her fingers.

"Barrington at nine," Gabriel said.

"Yes."

They sat a little longer. He told her a short story about Kenworth and a deliveryman that ended with three crates bowing to a set of steps. She laughed, and the knot in her middle loosened. He made things bearable without pretending they were easy.

By late afternoon, Lady Eastbury returned. They took another cup of tea to please her. She listened while they repeated the next day's order and approved the plan once more, adding a slight adjustment to remind them she could.

When it was time, Gabriel rose. He had an appointment of his own and the habit of keeping it. Lady Eastbury saw him to the door, told him she would expect him for breakfast at half past eight if he arrived early, and that he would get a plate even if he did not. He thanked her with his usual quiet courtesy.

Leticia walked with him to the front step. The air had cooled with the autumn afternoon. He looked out across the street as if testing the evening, turned back to her.

"Until tomorrow," he said.

"Tomorrow," she answered.

He did not reach for her hand in the open doorway. He did not need to. The look they exchanged held more promise than touch could have managed. He went down the steps and set off along the pavement with an easy stride. She stood where she was until he reached the corner. He paused there and lifted his hand the smallest degree. He went on and was lost to the turn.

She climbed the stairs to her room and crossed to the window. From there, she could see the corner and the bit of pavement beyond. She set her hand to the frame and leaned into the view. She had not meant to do it. She did it anyway. She watched the place where he had gone out of sight and felt her heart lean after him with more certainty than she had allowed herself before. She was close to an answer. Not a distant one, a near one.

She had only days left to give him that answer. Not many. Enough to be honest.

She let the curtain fall back into place and turned toward the dressing table. The late light struck the glass and threw a small gold square onto the wood. The box lay where she had left it, neat, ordinary, wrapped in soft cloth inside. Her mother's brooch belonged to a life that had once looked simple. It might belong to a different story than the one she had told herself. The thought came and stood its ground.

She pushed the idea aside, not banished, not settled, set aside so the rest of the evening could sit without wobbling. She sat at the table and smoothed the cloth there as if smoothing a page that had picked up a crease and would soon be read. The room sounded like itself: a small sound from the street, a faint clink from the kitchen below, the clock on the mantel keeping an even count.

Tomorrow would be full. There would be answers to ask for and questions to hold back. There would be Barrington at nine and the matter of polish at Turnbull and Sons. There would be the quiet place in the garden she could carry with her. There would be the memory of a kiss that did not ask twice.

She drew a breath that reached all the way down. She opened the latch.

# Chapter Twenty-Six

S HE SAT BEFORE she knew she had to. The bed gave beneath her, the box still open at her side, but all she saw was the brooch. All she could feel was its weight resting against her lifeline.

She had never asked where it came from. Her mother had pressed it into her hand on a summer afternoon after a fitting, no ceremony, no story. Only, "It suits you better than it ever suited me."

She'd kept it hidden. Not because she knew it was dangerous, not even because her aunt would disapprove, but because… because it had felt like a secret. And now she couldn't decide if that made her mother clever or cruel.

A raven in a diamond.

Her fingers closed around it. Not tightly. She didn't dare. She'd seen a sketch once in Gabriel's papers. She hadn't understood it then. She hadn't needed to.

She did now.

What if she'd been wearing it at the museum?

The thought landed like a blow. The air thinned. Her chest refused the next breath. She stood abruptly, carried the brooch to the small writing desk by the window, and set it down beneath the light. Her hands shook only a little, but it was enough to rattle the lid as she closed the box around it.

She didn't lock it.

She didn't dare.

A knock at her door would undo her. Her aunt's voice would crack the illusion she was still building, that this could be nothing and that the mark was a coincidence. That her mother…

She stowed the box in the back of her desk drawer as she pressed her hand to her brow.

Her mother must have known. She was too precise not to. Too careful. That brooch had been chosen. Given. Protected. Not by accident.

But if Aunt Margaret knew, she'd ask why it was given to Leticia. Why it had been kept quiet. Why Leticia had waited until now to even look for the truth.

And worse still, if Gabriel saw it. The panic rose without warning. Not fury. Not even shame.

Loss.

The sudden, suffocating terror that he would turn from her. That he would think she was part of it. That the kisses he'd given her, the ones she hadn't let herself dream about, would be the last.

She crossed to the bed, sat again, and tried to breathe in even rhythm.

It was still just a brooch.

It had not changed.

But dear god, she had.

SHE DIDN'T SLEEP. Not in the way that mattered.

At some point in the night, she lay down fully dressed, the brooch locked in its velvet box, the box sealed in the drawer beneath her stockings. But her thoughts never slowed. They circled. They clung.

Her mother's face would not come without the brooch. She tried to imagine what Gabriel might say. Would he demand answers, or worse, stop asking altogether?

The moonlight shifted across the floorboards. Once, she rose and stood at the window, as if she might find certainty in the darkness beyond the streetlamps.

But there was nothing to be done.

Until morning.

She remembered the errand her aunt had mentioned in passing, the clasp on her necklace, the need for a proper cleaner, the familiar name: Turnbull & Sons. The kind of shop that opened at dawn and closed before luncheon.

Leticia left a note with the maid just before six, her script tidy despite the tremor in her hand. She dressed plainly but carefully, choosing her simplest walking cloak and a wide-brimmed hat. If Aunt Margaret stirred and found her gone, she'd only think her prompt.

Not hiding or chasing something. Just a task, early and innocent.

By the time the street lamps dimmed, Leticia was already halfway to Cross Street.

⪥⪥⪥⪤⪤⪤

LETICIA ARRIVED JUST as he unlocked the front doors, her gloved hand tightening around the handle of her reticule.

"Lady Salisbury," Mr. Turnbull said with a deferential nod. "You're early."

"My aunt asked me to fetch some cleaner for her necklace," she replied, careful to keep her voice light. "She wants to wear it today, and the clasp has dulled."

He smiled and gestured her inside. "Of course. Just a moment. I keep it in the back. Please, make yourself comfortable while I fetch it."

The bell above the door gave a soft chime as it shut behind her. She moved past the display case of rings and came to a stand of brooches near the window. They were delicate pieces, many antique. She scanned them absently and abruptly paused.

Letica stared at a brooch nearly identical to hers.

A circle of diamonds. A dark stone in the center. Not exactly like hers, but close enough to steal her breath.

When Mr. Turnbull returned with a small bottle wrapped in paper, she stepped aside but didn't move away.

"That brooch," she said, nodding toward the case. "The one with the sapphire."

"Ah, yes. A fine piece," he said, stepping around the counter. "Would you like to see it?"

"If you don't mind."

He opened the case and lifted the brooch with a velvet cloth, holding it carefully. "There's a bit of a secret to this one," he said, eyes twinkling. "Hold it to the light just so, and you'll see."

He angled it toward the windowpane, letting the light strike the gold backing.

Leticia leaned in. There, glinting faintly beneath the clasp, was an engraving.

Not a raven. Not a diamond. A rose. Simple, unguarded, human.

"It was part of a set," Turnbull added.

Her breath caught. "A set?"

"It was part of a private estate sale. A lovely collection, though each piece was different. Most had hidden marks. A rose, a harp, a stag. Some romantic tradition, I imagine."

Leticia's lips parted, but no words came.

"Do you know which estate?" she asked, trying to keep her voice even and calm.

"Lady Templeton," he said with easy confidence. "She had an extensive collection of etched stones similar to this one. Her ladyship passed some years ago. Her solicitor handled the sale. That brooch came to me through a small auction, held just a week before the Morton estate's first dispersal, if memory serves. The rose caught attention for its beauty, that was all." He smiled faintly. "No secrets tucked behind that one."

She thanked him, took the cleaner, and stepped back into the street with the morning sun low behind her. The air was crisp, the town quiet. Her feet found the familiar rhythm homeward.

It was 8:06 when she stepped through the front door.

THE HOUSE WAS quiet, the kind of quiet that pressed in rather than settled. Ashcombe Hall did not sleep. It waited.

Gabriel moved through the corridor with his trousers tucked into worn boots, waistcoat unbuttoned, sleeves rolled. He'd been up since before the sky turned gray. Tea had gone cold beside him. The library fire had died sometime after four.

He hadn't meant to wander, but the silence had made him restless.

He passed the study, ignored the front drawing room, and found himself in the main hall, long and shadowed, lit only by the faint bleed of early morning through the high windows. The portraits lined the wall in silent procession.

His gaze swept over familiar faces. Lords and ladies of Ash's past. The uncle who'd raised him. And farther down, a canvas that had once meant little, a study of three young people in Vienna. It had been painted in haste, commissioned by someone who cared more for fashion than fidelity.

And yet.

He slowed.

His Uncle Robbie stood in the middle with Lady Margaret on one side. Her pearl necklace caught the light even in oils.

His gaze shifted.

Another, younger woman with darker hair and almond-shaped eyes stood on his uncle's other side. She wore no necklace. But the shape of her mouth was familiar.

A smile crept across his face, Leticia's mother.

And there, pinned to her gown, half-lost in the shadows of the paint, but glinting somehow despite it—

The brooch.

He stepped closer.

Even in oils, the center gem shimmered. The artist had rendered it too well, perhaps an indulgence. Gabriel leaned in, brow furrowed, following the way the light pooled around the diamonds, the subtle shading at the clasp.

He didn't see a mark. Of course, he didn't.

But something in him recoiled.

He stepped back. Crossed his arms. Tried to shrug it off.

It could be a coincidence. A family trinket. A resemblance. But instinct didn't work on evidence. Instinct worked on the skin, the breath, the way his gut drew tight when things didn't align.

And something didn't align.

He left the hall without looking back.

⋙✦⋘

LETICIA STEPPED INTO the morning room just after eight. The maid had taken her cloak as well as the bottle from Turnbull's. Aunt Margaret's voice filtered in from the dining room, cheerful and equally as sharp.

She hadn't meant to be so quick, but she hadn't lingered. She was home. On time. Composed.

At 8:14, the bell at the front gave a soft chime.

The door opened.

Leticia turned just as Gabriel entered the morning room, coat still unbuttoned, a hint of wind clinging to his hair.

"You're early," she said, her voice low.

"So are you."

He didn't ask where she'd been. She didn't offer.

He came closer.

"I wanted to see you before Barrington arrived," he said.

Leticia glanced around the room. "You have succeeded."

A silence followed, brief but full.

"I thought of you this morning," he said quietly. "I wondered if you'd slept."

"I didn't."

His eyes searched hers, but only for a moment. Slowly, carefully, he reached for her hand.

He lifted it to his lips, not rushed, not showy. His mouth brushed the inside of her wrist, just above the glove's edge.

Her breath faltered.

"I'll be at your side today," he murmured. "Whatever it brings."

Leticia didn't speak. But her fingers curled lightly around his, holding them there just a moment longer.

From the hallway, Aunt Margaret's voice rose. "Gabriel, do come in, we've just sat down!"

He released her hand with a last touch and stepped away, the moment closing shut behind him like a page turned.

Leticia followed.

# Chapter Twenty-Seven

THE CARRIAGE CRESTED a rise where the road narrowed into gravel and coarse grass, the sea opening beneath them like a forgotten map left out to the weather. Dunmere Cross sprawled below. It was not a village, not even a proper ruin. Just the bones of an old chapel, the faint line of a crumbled cloister, and farther off, a gray slant-roofed shed crouched near the cliffs, as if bracing against the wind.

Leticia leaned forward as Gabriel exchanged quiet words with the driver. Barrington stood down first, scanning the path toward the edge.

Beside her, Lady Margaret peered out. "That must be the smuggler's shed," she said lightly, fanning herself with one gloved hand. "Charming. If it collapses on us, I shall haunt you all with particularly inconvenient timing."

Gabriel turned to offer Leticia his hand. "There's an upper track," he said, his voice low enough to belong to the wind. "We'll walk the ridge, circle down. Fewer chances of being seen."

Leticia took his hand and felt the warmth through her glove as she stepped down. The steadiness of his grasp anchored her more than she wished to admit.

They weren't here for sightseeing.

She could feel it in Gabriel's stillness, in the way Barrington checked the angle of the sun. Even her aunt's carried purpose, sharp, deflecting, designed to fill silence before questions could.

As they moved down the track, Lady Margaret called out to a

man by the marker stone. He was broad-shouldered, wore a cap pulled low, and leaned on a walking stick. "Tell me, is that where the monks used to stand? Or is it just a dramatic fencepost?"

The man chuckled and launched into a story about smugglers and false blessings. Leticia smiled faintly but kept walking, her eyes forward.

Gabriel and Barrington broke off, heading toward the shed. The wind pressed against them, lifting strands of Leticia's hair beneath her hat. She kept to the narrow path, the stones shifting slightly beneath her boots.

A raven called once from the rocks below, a sound so clean and sudden it emptied the air, followed by silence.

Leticia paused near the remains of the cloister wall. Half-covered in moss, a flat stone jutted out like an old book left open. She might've passed it, except the sunlight hit it at just the right angle.

She stepped closer.

A carving. Rough but deliberate.

A diamond, uneven, and inside it, a single mark: a bird with outstretched wings.

Not a rose. Not a harp.

A raven.

Her breath caught. The chill that slid down her arm—recognition rather than surprise. She didn't call out to Gabriel. Not yet.

Instead, she let her gaze shift toward the shed.

The door hung slightly ajar. Gabriel stood just inside. Barrington knelt at the threshold, examining something on the ground.

Leticia drew a slow breath, turned her back to the stone, and brushed her gloves together as though she'd only brushed away dust.

She walked down the incline toward the others, wind tugging at her skirts like a warning she pretended not to hear.

No one stopped her.

The shed wasn't locked. It didn't need to be. The sea had

already claimed its toll: rusted hinges, half-sunken roof, salt-swollen boards that sighed with every gust.

Gabriel pushed the door open with his gloved hand and let it swing wide.

Inside, the shadows held still for a moment. Then, the scent reached him, damp rope, cold ash, and something fainter, oil, maybe, or wax.

Barrington followed, ducking slightly beneath the warped lintel.

Gabriel didn't speak. His eyes moved through the gloom, cataloguing absence, crates, coils of rope, old nets, ordinary until proven otherwise.

But the floor told a different story.

He crouched, brushing his fingers lightly over the dirt. Near the door, dust lay thick and undisturbed. Six feet in, the pattern broke, one sharp scuff, a heel turned too quickly. Someone had turned suddenly, unplanned.

The mark ended near a dark stain on the wall. Soot. A lantern had burned here. Recently.

Barrington crouched beside him. "He waited."

Gabriel nodded. "Or met someone. But not for long."

Barrington gestured toward the entrance. "And if someone was watching from the path?"

"They'd see a ruin." Gabriel rose, brushing off his hands. "But they'd hear voices. Footsteps. If the tide was low, maybe nothing at all."

He stepped to the far corner. A broken crate leaned against the wall, its slats loose. Gabriel nudged it aside and froze.

A scrap of gray cloth lay caught against the earth. Small. Torn clean.

He lifted it.

"Glove?" Barrington asked.

"Wrist lining," Gabriel said. "Wool. Torn, not cut. Caught on the edge when he moved too fast."

"You think he was nervous?"

"I think he was interrupted."

Outside, the wind shifted. A gull shrieked right before he heard the soft scrape of boots on gravel.

Gabriel looked toward the door and saw Leticia.

She walked carefully, as though not to disturb anything. Her eyes met his once. She didn't speak.

He didn't ask why she was alone.

Leticia stepped through the door, pausing just inside while her eyes adjusted. Light from the sea rimmed her in pale gold. Gabriel straightened, the scrap of cloth disappearing into his pocket.

She paused just inside the doorway, letting her eyes adjust to the dim light. Gabriel straightened from the corner, the bit of cloth still in his hand. He let it slip into his coat pocket as she approached.

She glanced toward Barrington, who offered a brief nod and turned his attention to the lintel with exaggerated courtesy.

Gabriel watched her carefully. "You came alone."

"There was too much breeze near the cloisters," she said. "And my aunt had questions for the guide."

His mouth tugged faintly. "And you decided the shed was the more pleasant company?"

A flicker of dry amusement touched her lips. "For the moment."

A pause stretched, deliberate, not awkward. He didn't press.

Leticia took a step forward, trailing her fingers along the edge of a splintered crate. The wood was damp beneath her glove. She withdrew her hand, flexing her fingers as if shaking off the cold.

"There's nothing much here," she said.

"Not anymore," Gabriel replied.

He watched her, but gently. Not as an investigator might a suspect, but as a man reads a map drawn in invisible ink.

She turned toward the open door again, letting the light brush across her shoulder.

"Someone used this place," she said. "Recently."

It wasn't a question.

Gabriel nodded. "A quick stop. A handoff, maybe. Or a signal that wasn't answered."

Leticia stayed where she was, back to him, eyes fixed on the ridge.

"There's a stone by the cloisters," she said at last. "Covered in moss. A bird, inside a diamond."

He stepped closer, slow and sure.

"Did you show anyone?"

"No." Her voice was soft. "Not yet."

He stood behind her now, not touching, but near. Close enough for her to feel steadiness where her own certainly trembled.

"You did the right thing," he said.

"I didn't say I was hiding it."

"You didn't have to."

Leticia turned then, facing him.

"There's something at work here," she said. "And I don't know if it's following us, or if we're chasing it."

Gabriel looked at her for a long moment. "Maybe both."

He didn't speak right away.

Would he ask her what it looked like? How certain was she? But he only said, "Show me."

She led him back up the ridge, her steps careful on the uneven stones. Barrington lingered behind, half in the doorway of the shed, watching the sea with polite disinterest.

The cloister wall curved into the slope like a jawbone left by time. Leticia stepped to the flat stone near its base and brushed the moss aside with the back of her glove.

The carving was still there, simple, shallow, but unmistakable.

A diamond.

And inside it, a raven.

Gabriel crouched beside her. He didn't touch it, only studied the way light caught in the grooves, the precision that ruled out accident. His gaze swept left, right, cataloguing what was missing, marking everything else that wasn't there.

When he stood, his voice was quiet. "It's deliberate."

Leticia nodded.

"You don't have to tell anyone," he said quietly. "But don't ignore what you saw."

She looked up at him, breath caught in her throat, words hovering and unsaid.

Behind them, a gull wheeled overhead, calling once before vanishing into the wind.

She turned from the stone. "Let's go before Aunt Margaret buys the guide's coat out from under him."

Gabriel's tone went dry. "He would be a poorer man for the bargain."

Leticia glanced up, her lips curving. "And she would still think it a victory."

# Chapter Twenty-Eight

THE MORNING BROKE gray and reluctant. Leticia stood at the drawing room window, the newspaper slack in her hand. The quiet in the house pressed close, not peace, but the hush before something declared itself. Her teacup cooled beside her, the porcelain gone pale with waiting. She should have been dressing. Instead, she stood anchored to the spot.

Upstairs, wrapped in linen and in a box in the back of her drawer, the brooch waited heavy with questions she no longer dared to ignore.

Leticia crossed to the writing desk and began sifting through her aunt's neatly stacked society pages. Announcements. Engagements. Auctions. Each line a trail she hadn't known to follow. At first, nothing stood out. Then, a rhythm emerged. Lady Vexley. Mrs. Denham, Mrs. Harcourt, names repeating like the tide, a pattern hidden in plain sight.

The door opened, and her aunt entered, quiet as always.

"You're up early."

"I couldn't sleep," Leticia said, eyes still on the papers. "Do you remember the Morton auctions?"

"A little. They sold the estate in parts, no heirs, no rush." Her aunt poured herself tea. "Why?"

"I think I've seen pieces that came from it. Erica mentioned one. I'm trying to trace the others."

Her aunt's expression shifted from mild interest to something sharper. "Lady Vexley would know. She never passes on a pedigree."

Leticia nodded, though her thoughts were elsewhere.

Six pieces. All gone.

Except hers.

She climbed the stairs and opened the drawer. The air felt heavier there, as if the drawer itself held its breath. She lifted the brooch. It nestled against her palm, the stones catching the gray light like an accusation.

Slowly, she turned it over.

A raven inside a diamond.

Not just a keepsake. A mark. A warning. A signature left to be found.

She pinned it briefly to her morning dress. It caught the light in the mirror, beautiful, cold, and entirely out of place. Her reflection gave nothing back. With deliberate care, she unpinned it again, wrapping it in cloth with deliberate care.

She remembered her mother wearing it to a musicale, her hair swept up, her laughter drawing every eye. Nothing dark, nothing secret. Just grace. That memory made it worse.

Her mind flicked back to the rose intaglio she'd seen at Turnbull & Sons, similar in design, though not in origin. The jeweler had traced its history with ease, Lady Templeton's estate. Auctioned the same year as her mother's brooch. A rose. A raven. One bought for beauty. The other, perhaps, for purpose.

She almost wished her mother had chosen the rose.

That afternoon, her aunt arranged a word with Lady Vexley. Leticia found the older woman in the garden, bent over a single bloom that had opened too soon. A sharp breeze stirred the petals. Lady Vexley's gloved hand steadied the stem.

Her aunt exchanged pleasantries and left with a graceful nod. Leticia didn't wait.

"Lady Vexley, did you attend the Morton auctions?"

Lady Vexley turned, faint amusement lifting her brow. "Of course. Everyone did."

"Do you remember any unusual brooches? Ones with engravings?"

"I do. I was outbid on one. Central dark stone. Diamonds around it." Her smile thinned. "Not to my taste. A piece that wanted to be remembered for the wrong reasons."

Leticia tilted her head. "The wrong reasons?"

Vexley's smile returned, brittle as frost. "A reputation for misfortune, my dear. Jewelry that keeps its own account of tragedy."

"Do you know who purchased it?"

"No. Word was that it was sold privately later on. Off the books."

Leticia studied her face. "Thank you."

Lady Vexley smiled, too knowingly. "Collecting stories, my lady?"

Leticia held her gaze. "Only the kind that come with shadows."

⁂

ASHCOMBE HALL HELD the sort of silence that had texture, not absence, but waiting. Gabriel moved down the corridor, one hand along the banister, the other curled tight around the study key.

He hadn't slept. Not truly.

Leticia's brooch. Her mother. Robbie. Threads of loyalty and suspicion tightening into one knot behind his ribs.

If she'd known, why hadn't she told him?

If she hadn't, what else had gone unseen?

The ledger waited where he'd left it, open to the page marked *Vienna*. His uncle's handwriting, neat, deliberate, columns of numbers, dates, and beneath them, a scrawl that didn't belong.

*For her. She loved the raven.*

No name. No initials. Just six words heavy enough to unbalance a man.

He closed the book and left the room.

The portrait gallery greeted him like a quiet congregation. Ancestors, benefactors, saints, and sinners, each watching with the indifference of paint.

Robbie. And beside him, the woman whose face Gabriel had memorized long before he ever knew her name. Anne Salisbury, Leticia's mother.

The same clear eyes. The same poised tilt of the head. And there, pinned to her gown, the brooch. The raven, sparkling even in oil and shadow.

He leaned closer. The artist had caught too much light on the gem, an indulgence perhaps, but not an accident.

His uncle had loved her. Or thought he had. Maybe it had never been spoken aloud. Maybe it hadn't needed to be.

Gabriel stepped back. The air in the gallery cooled.

Did Leticia know?

Would she protect her mother's secret if it meant hiding the truth from him?

He exhaled, slow and hard. No. He wouldn't ask that of her. Not yet.

"You don't have to tell anyone," he whispered, echoing his own promise from the cliffside. Only now, it sounded less like mercy and more like hope. "But don't ignore what you saw."

He wasn't sure whether he meant the portrait. Or the woman.

He only knew he loved her.

But love didn't silence doubt. And trust, once cracked, could take a lifetime to mend.

He would see her. He would listen. And if she met his eyes without flinching, he would believe her.

THAT EVENING, LETICIA sat at her desk, a fresh sheet of paper before her. Ink gathered like hesitation at the tip of her pen.

The first draft had been too distant. The second, too raw. The third betrayed what she hadn't dared to admit. The fourth, deliberate and composed, was the one she sealed.

She held the letter for a long time, turning it as if the verdict was in her palm.

*He'll understand,* she told herself. *He knows what this means. He'll see reason.*

Her hand hovered over the bellpull.

She recited the words she'd chosen. They sounded like armor, not a confession. She broke the seal.

"This may be the truth you need to hear," she read softly. "But it should come from me, not like this."

Her breath caught. She rose, crossed to the fireplace. The flame took the paper greedily, blistering the wax and curling the paper to ash. The truth reduced to ember.

Later, alone, she opened the drawer and lifted the brooch from its cloth. It lay in her palm, small and silent, terrible in its simplicity. No gleam now. No deception.

She held it to her chest.

No one else needed to know. Let the Order come. She was the next. And the last.

And she was ready.

# Chapter Twenty-Nine

THE GARDEN BEHIND Lady Eastbury's townhouse should have smelled like autumn roses, fading and sweet. Instead, it carried only the chill of earth and endings. Leticia stood beneath the arbor, hands folded at her waist, trying to quiet the unrest rising beneath her skin.

Gabriel had sent word.

Her aunt had passed along the message in the hall, her voice clipped and unreadable. "He's asked to see you in the garden." There was no look, no tone. Only the words.

Before she left, her aunt crossed to the escritoire, drew out a small sheet, and wrote a few quick lines. When she finished, she sealed the note and handed it to a waiting footman.

"Take this to the address written and wait for a reply," she said.

The man bowed and disappeared down the corridor.

Only then did she turn back to Leticia. "Don't keep him waiting."

Now, alone beneath the arbor, Leticia pressed her fingers to the edge of her skirt and exhaled slowly. She had nothing to fear. The brooch was hidden. She hadn't said anything. He couldn't know.

The gravel stirred with the sound of heavy, deliberate steps. She didn't turn. She knew his step.

Gabriel emerged from behind the hedge, coat collar turned against the wind, expression shadowed. Not angry. But close.

"I came as soon as your aunt said you were here." He stopped a pace away, giving her space.

Leticia inclined her head. "You said you needed to speak with me."

"I did." He stopped just out of reach. His gaze slid to the rosebushes beside her, back to her face. "I saw the portrait again. At Ashcombe Hall."

Her chest tightened. "Your uncle and my mother."

His eyes held hers. "And the brooch."

Leticia didn't move.

"I didn't recognize it at first. Not truly. But the artist, the way he captured the light, it's the same piece, isn't it?"

She hesitated. "Gabriel…"

"Do you have it?"

His voice wasn't unkind, but it carried consequences.

"Yes," she said at last. "I have it. It's safe."

"Safe." He said it as though the word itself were bitter. "Where?"

"No one knows where it is."

"Except you."

"And now you," she said softly.

His expression shifted, lips tightening. "That's not enough. You shouldn't have kept this from me."

Leticia stepped to the side, distancing herself more than she intended. Her hands went to her sleeves to comfort herself. "Do you think I wanted to?"

She drew her arms across her middle. "I didn't know what it was until the Historical Society. Someone pointed out a necklace. I looked more closely at the brooch that night. That's when I saw it. The raven."

She swallowed. "I didn't know what it meant, only that it could not be innocent."

He stood still, unreadable.

"I wanted to say something," she said. "But my mother warned me never to speak of it. Not to my aunt. Not to anyone."

She glanced toward the windows. "I didn't know if Aunt Margaret was involved. I didn't know who to trust."

She met his eyes again. "And you and I… we weren't what we are now. Maybe we still aren't."

She let the silence sit for a moment before adding, low, "I didn't hide it to deceive you. I was trying to decide what to do."

Still, he didn't speak.

"You don't trust me," she whispered. Even she heard the accusation in her throat. "Even now."

Gabriel's jaw ticked.

Leticia frowned. "What aren't you saying?"

He hesitated, exhaled hard. "A note came. The morning after Lammer Cove."

Leticia's brows knit. "A note?"

"They didn't name you. But it was clear. *Return what is ours. Or bury her with it.* Next time, they warned, we won't miss. Give us the brooch." He kept his voice steady as if he were reciting a fact.

She drew back as if struck. Her hand flew to her mouth, fell away. "You knew? All this time, and you didn't tell me?"

"I was trying to protect you."

"By keeping me blind?" Her voice broke. "You let me walk into danger without knowing."

He stepped closer. "I thought that if you did not know everything, you would not be targeted directly."

"You thought to spare me by leaving me helpless?" she snapped. "You let me face the cliff and the cove without knowing the full danger."

"I thought someone meant to kill us," he said, the confession raw at the edges. "I thought keeping the matter contained was the only way to manage it."

"You knew there was a threat," she said, heat rising. "And you told no one?"

"I told those who needed to know," he said. "I arranged watches. I—" His voice cracked. "I tried to keep you from seeing how dangerous it was."

"You received a threat against my life and told no one," she said, incredulous. "How could you think that was protecting me?"

"I was trying to protect you," he repeated, voice low, but the certainty had holes.

"And I was trying to protect you!" Her voice cut like wind over stone. "I've followed clues. I've spoken with people. You have no idea what I've done."

His brows pulled together. "You were alone?"

"I'm not a child. I am capable of taking care of myself."

"No," he said flatly. "You can't. Not against this."

Her chin rose. "I saved you at Lammer Cove."

That stopped him. For a heartbeat, something like shame crossed his face. He hadn't known.

"You said you were shielding me," she said, her voice trembling with restraint. "But I was already in it, Gabriel. I chose to be. I climbed that cliff with you. I risked just as much."

He said nothing.

"And yet you still kept the brooch," he said finally, almost accusing. "What else are you hiding, Leticia? Are you sure you aren't in deeper than you admit?"

She stared at him. Her hand curled into a fist at her side. "If you truly believe that, if you actually think I could be part of something so dark, then you don't know me at all."

The wind shifted. Leaves rattled like applause for a performance long finished.

"You should never have come here," she said.

She turned and walked toward the house, unhurried, though her chest felt hollow. Behind her, she heard the quiet crunch of gravel as he turned and walked away.

Neither of them looked back.

LETICIA STEPPED INSIDE and stopped short. Her aunt stood at the hearth, her arms crossed. The fire burned low, but her expression radiated heat.

"You heard," Leticia said.

"I did." Her aunt's voice was as flat as the embers.

"I'm sorry."

Her aunt didn't blink. "What brooch?"

Leticia looked down. "My mother's."

"The one with the raven."

Leticia's head jerked up. "You know it?"

"I begged her to get rid of it years ago. She wouldn't listen." Her hand braced against the mantel, fingers whitening on the carved edge. "I never," Her voice broke. "I never thought she'd give it to you. That cursed thing has haunted us for decades."

Leticia swayed. "I didn't know. To me, it was a keepsake. Something from Vienna. A kindness." Her voice dropped. "She told me never to speak of it. Not to you. Not to anyone. I didn't know she was leaving me with a burden."

Her aunt's eyes softened. "She didn't know what it was," she said quietly. "She gave you what she thought was hers to give. Love, and something beautiful to remember her by. She couldn't have known the cost."

Leticia dropped onto the settee. "Why didn't anyone tell me?"

Her aunt's voice was quiet now. "Because we were afraid it would matter again."

"And now it does."

Her aunt nodded once. "Now it does."

Leticia bent forward, elbows on her knees. Her hands shook. "I...I could fix it. I...I could hold it long enough to learn its secrets, and then..."

Her voice trailed off. The sob came suddenly and without warning, rising before she could stop it.

Her aunt moved at once, wrapping her arms around her, holding her close, smoothing her hair with the same rhythm as years past. The steadiness of it calmed her.

"We'll face it, child," she whispered. "Whatever comes."

⟫⟫⟫✦⟪⟪⟪

THE STUDY AT Ashcombe Hall smelled of smoke and stillness.

Gabriel hadn't lit the lamps. Shadows stretched across the floor, broken only by the hearth's red glow. He stood beside the fire, the untouched glass of brandy heavy in his hand.

Leticia's words haunted him. *I was already in it. I chose to be.* She'd risked her life beside him, and he'd turned on her.

A sound broke the stillness, a knock, deliberate and too polite for the hour. The butler entered with a silver tray. "Colonel Barrington's man delivered this, sir." He placed a folded note on the tray.

Gabriel took the note. The paper was creased, the edges damp.

"There was an incident at Lady Eastbury's," the butler added. "A man was seen at the servants' entrance. He fled, but left this."

Gabriel set down his brandy and opened the note.

*Return what is ours. Or bury her with it.*

He froze.

"When?" he asked, waving the note at Kenworth. "When did this happen?"

"Half past six, sir."

That was just before he'd arrived. The muscles in his jaw locked. His hand tightened.

"She knew," he said quietly. "She knew when I was standing in front of her." Barrington's note slipped out of his hand. He picked up his brandy again and stared into the hearth.

Something broke in his expression. Fury, shame, fear braided together.

"She looked me in the eye," he whispered, "and still said

nothing."

He hurled the brandy glass into the hearth, shattering it against the stone, the liquid hissing as it met the flame.

His butler flinched but said nothing.

Gabriel stood breathing hard, the note crushed in his fist.

"Leave me," he said.

The butler bowed and left.

Alone again, Gabriel stared into the fire. If they came for her again, he would be ready.

And so help him, he would have the truth.

# Chapter Thirty

THE WEST WING of Sommer Castle smelled faintly of beeswax, rain-damp stone, and the lingering sharpness of dried lavender. Though much of the grand estate remained shuttered and silent, one sun-drenched chamber had been coaxed into life.

A long table stretched beneath the tall, mullioned windows, its surface hidden beneath bolts of ribbon, ledgers, sealed envelopes, and a precarious stack of plate samples long since declared unsuitable and forgotten.

Leticia stood near the hearth, her gloves tucked into one hand, the other resting against a stack of guest lists she had already reviewed twice. She did not belong, and this room offered no answer.

Across from her, Lady Eastbury sat with the poise of a woman who had once overseen the seating of three dukes and a bishop at a christening breakfast. She made notations in a small book, spectacles low on her nose, her pen gliding in firm, efficient strokes. At the head of the table, Mrs. Bainbridge swept into motion like a small but determined storm cloud, opening boxes and lifting lids with theatrical flair.

"Three cakes," Mrs. Bainbridge declared. "And I refuse to be told I can't have all three. If Barrington has opinions, he may air them to the almond torte."

Leticia glanced over, lips twitching.

Lady Eastbury didn't look up. "He does object to almonds. Says they remind him of barracks soap."

"Then he's eating the apricot," Mrs. Bainbridge said. "But I am choosing the almond."

She carved neat slices from each and passed the forks with decisive intent. Leticia tasted the apricot first. It was warm, soft, with a jam-like sweetness that made her smile. The taste took her back to late summer afternoons, before the world had shifted underfoot.

"The apricot," she said quietly.

"The almond," said her aunt as she dabbed at the corner of her mouth.

Mrs. Bainbridge grinned in triumph. "Almond it is. And pears in claret jelly for Lady Northwood, Barrington's mother. She claims they aid digestion."

"She also says they repel scandal," Lady Eastbury added dryly.

Leticia looked up then, her smile thin but genuine. "We should serve them in buckets."

Laughter softened the edges of the room. They moved on to flowers. A cloth-bound book of pressed samples was laid open between them, fragile petals preserved beside penciled sketches. Mrs. Bainbridge leaned over Leticia's shoulder, rattling off names with delight: autumn roses, sprigs of yew, orange-tipped leaves, something oddly labeled *spiked foxbrush*.

Leticia reached for a tiny myrtle blossom before she realized her hand had moved.

"Your mother's favorite," Lady Eastbury said softly.

Leticia nodded, turned the page. "It suited her."

Silence followed, the hush of remembered things, broken only by the rustle of skirts and the arrival of Mrs. Pembroke, the seamstress, her arms full of silk.

"Final fitting," she announced.

"Now we shall see if I can still breathe in silk," Mrs. Bainbridge said, vanishing behind the screen with an energy that bordered on dangerous.

Leticia stepped in to help when called, tightening the back laces, adjusting the neckline, and folding the hem slightly at the edge. When Mrs. Bainbridge emerged, the room stilled.

The gown shimmered pearl-gray, the embroidery catching the sunlight in quiet defiance. It was elegant, poised, and entirely *her*.

Leticia stared.

Mrs. Bainbridge turned, hands on her hips. "Well?"

Leticia's throat ached. "It's perfect."

Mrs. Pembroke smiled. "A dress should suit the heart of the woman who wears it. This one does."

Leticia turned away before her expression could betray her.

They returned to the table, that last round of names waiting. Mrs. Bainbridge sifted through the envelopes, Leticia read the names aloud, and her aunt made elegant ticks beside each one with tidy precision.

"Lady Lennox and the Duke."

"Marvelous," Mrs. Bainbridge said. "If she behaves, she'll only insult three people. Four if the music offends her."

"Lord Ellington and Lady Edythe."

"Lovely woman. She has such kind eyes."

Leticia continued. "The Baron and Baroness of Grenville. The Viscount and Viscountess Hollingsworth. Lord and Lady Rockford. Oh, and here is the response from Marquess and Marchioness of Glenraven."

Lady Eastbury looked up. "Barrington's entire brigade will be present."

"And the ladies graduates from the Sommer-by-the-Sea Female Seminary," Mrs. Bainbridge said. "All of them. I'm absurdly proud."

Leticia managed a faint nod. Each name fell with quiet finality. These were women she had once met in bright rooms scented with ink and tea. The days then had felt hopeful rather than fragile. Now they would be guests at a wedding.

"And the Duchess of Herridge?" Lady Eastbury asked.

"Regrets," Mrs. Bainbridge said. "Gout."

Leticia murmured, "She's consistent."

Gentle laughter fluttered through the room. Then Mrs. Bainbridge's tone softened. "And what will you wear to this evening's soiree, my dear?"

Leticia straightened the ledgers, fingertips resting on the paper's edge. "I'm not attending."

Silence fell, not sharp, but heavy.

Lady Eastbury looked up. "No?"

"I've made plans to visit friends in Alnwick."

Mrs. Bainbridge stilled. Not abruptly, but with that careful sort of stillness that comes when hope is put on hold. "I see. I wish you a peaceful visit."

Leticia nodded, though the motion was brittle. She excused herself with polite phrases and collected the fabric samples from the end of the table, tying them with a loose ribbon. The conversation behind her drifted onto menus, music, and seating arrangements she would no longer be part of.

Among the papers she gathered, one envelope lay apart from the rest. No seal, only her name in Gabriel's familiar hand. She had broken it quickly. The words had burned into her more sharply than any threat the Order had sent.

*"If silence is what you choose, I will match it. But know this…silence does not mean absence. You have my eyes, my thoughts, my loyalty. Whether you claim them or not."*

She folded it once, twice, and tucked it beneath the ribbon with the fabric swatches. And she walked out into the corridor, not so much leaving as slipping away, drawn by the quiet rather than any clear destination.

The corridor beyond was cool and dim, steeped in the scent of old polish and rain. Her shoes echoed lightly on the stone, each step carrying both resolve and regret.

At the far end of the hall, Gabriel stood.

How long had he been there? He didn't move, only watched her as if he had been watching longer than the moment allowed. Lamplight caught the line of his jaw. He stood in the lamplight, unmistakably real.

Her breath hitched. The bundle in her arms felt suddenly heavy.

He did not step toward her, and she did not speak his name. Her heart beat fast, fast enough she was certain he could hear it. She gave the smallest nod and turned away.

She heard no movement behind her, but she *felt* his gaze, the sense of a presence that never reached her.

Her aunt appeared from the adjoining passage and fell into step beside her.

"I must prepare for Alnwick," Leticia said, her voice even, her hands trembling beneath the folded swatches.

They passed beneath an arched stone lintel. Leticia went on. Her aunt stood watching her as Mrs. Bainbridge came to her side.

"Leticia hasn't any friends in Alnwick."

"I know," Mrs. Bainbridge said.

# Chapter Thirty-One

GABRIEL STOOD AT his desk at Ashcombe Hall, dressed for the soiree, but unmoving. The polished surface beneath his palms was scattered with records and sketches, his uncle's notes folded and unfolded so many times the paper had grown soft. A decanter of brandy stood untouched.

The brooch. He could not get it out of his mind since she had walked away. Since she'd chosen not to look back.

But it wasn't Leticia who haunted him now. It was the burden she carried, and the knowledge that she did not yet understand it.

Six pieces, his uncle had written. Six. Each with diamonds arranged to mimic the symbol the Order held sacred, angles cut so precisely they formed a diamond within a diamond. At its heart, the dark gem. Always the dark one.

He turned toward the painting propped against the armchair. His uncle's hand, rendered in oil and shadow, had captured more than just likeness. The woman's gaze held that same luminous clarity Leticia wore when she was determined not to cry. And there, at her shoulder, glimmered the brooch. Too precise to be a coincidence. Too familiar to be anything but fact.

He leaned in. Even in oils, the jewel sparkled, as though it would not be subdued. And it matched the sketches exactly.

He drew a breath, slow and sharp, his fingers curling against the desk. Leticia's brooch hadn't just been a keepsake. It was a relic tied to the Order, tied to danger. And someone would come to reclaim it.

He carefully wrapped the painting with linen, slipping it under one arm. He folded the notes into a folio and secured it with twine. He didn't call for his butler, nor wait for the carriage, nor pause to explain. He walked out the door with purpose in every stride.

Because there were answers now. And someone needed to hear them.

THE LAMPS INSIDE Barrington's house burned low, the kind of light that invited secrets. Sanderson showed Gabriel to the study without delay. Mrs. Bainbridge sat curled on the fainting couch, a porcelain cup of chocolate balanced on her knee. Barrington stood by the hearth, the flicker of firelight sharpening the furrow between his brows.

"I didn't expect you until later," he said. But his gaze had already landed on the bundle in Gabriel's arm. "What is it?"

Gabriel set the portrait carefully against the chair and passed the folio to him. "The last piece of the Morton estate. It was never missing. It was here. With Leticia."

Barrington's brow furrowed deeper as he flipped through the pages. Mrs. Bainbridge leaned over his shoulder, taking each page as he passed it. With each sheet, her expression shifted further into disbelief.

Gabriel loosened the linen slowly, as though even this required care. He set it upright, and the brooch gleamed back at him, painted, and yet too real.

"Leticia's mother," he said quietly. "The brooch. It's there. Same as in the sketches. Same as in the Morton records. My uncle Robbie purchased it for her mother. She passed it to Leticia."

His gaze didn't leave the canvas.

"That," he said, pointing to the glint at the woman's shoulder, "is the sixth piece."

Barrington muttered a low curse. "So it wasn't missing."

Gabriel shook his head once, but his jaw had tightened. He moved to the mantel, bracing himself with one hand.

"She told me her mother always wore it. I went back through the ledgers. The sketches. I had hoped it wouldn't be true."

Barrington looked up. "So you'll tell her tonight?"

A shadow crossed Gabriel's eyes. "She's gone. To Alnwick. I don't think she's coming back."

A silence settled, heavy and unforgiving.

Mrs. Bainbridge spoke, low, but steady. "You know why you have to be there. Not just for answers. For her."

He stared at the brooch in the painting. The light no longer touched it.

"Let them come," he said.

⟫⟪

THE AIR IN the salon held the perfume of lilacs and burning beeswax. Champagne shimmered on silver trays. Candles reflected in mirrored sconces. Every surface glowed, but none of it reached Gabriel's mind.

He stood inside the entrance, scanning the room as though assessing a field of engagement. He had told Barrington she wouldn't come.

Leticia's silence hadn't been a test. It was a verdict. One he hadn't wanted to hear. Even so, he could not stop watching the door.

He murmured greetings. Accepted a flute of champagne, he would not drink. Colonel Rutherford passed with a nod, mentioning something about the ledgers, the auction house, the pattern emerging from beneath the surface.

But without her, the answers were thin. He was tracing a shadow that refused to resolve into form.

He drifted toward the edge of the room, where the candlelight pooled thickest and conversation slowed to murmurs. A few women wore unusual pieces of jewelry, chokers with antique clasps, brooches glinting with stones that caught the light wrong. Pieces like those had already been stolen, worn now by women who didn't know they might be next.

Two women who'd worn similar jewels had already been attacked. One refused to leave her home after dusk. The other now traveled with a manservant trained in defense, under the pretense of needing assistance on the stairs.

Only one remained. Leticia. His fingers tightened around the stem of the glass. She was the next target, and he still didn't know who the thief was.

The air changed. Not the music. Not the lighting. The atmosphere shifted as the far doors opened.

She stood in the doorway. Leticia.

Every inch of her was poised, each step deliberate. She wore the same green gown from the masquerade. Silk with silver threads. But this time, no mask. No anonymity. Only resolve.

And at her shoulder, glistening like a mark of fate, rested the brooch.

The room exhaled, murmurs rising through the room. Not about the party. Not about the ball. About her. About it.

Gabriel did not move. He couldn't.

She greeted her aunt, turned toward the heart of the room, drawing every eye with her. The crowd parted for her like the tide.

Not with bravado, but with certainty. She hadn't come to be bait. She had come to set the terms.

Gabriel's pulse pounded in his ears. He handed his champagne to the nearest footman and crossed the room.

SHE STOOD BENEATH the candlelight near the pianoforte, her chin lifted, her shoulders relaxed, the brooch catching the flicker of flame like it had a mind of its own. She held a glass of champagne, which she had no intention of drinking.

Gabriel approached without haste. He had imagined what he might say, what he might do if she were here. He had not expected to find himself silent.

"You wore it," he said, though the words carried to the room as much as to her.

Leticia turned, slowly, as if judging the moment. "It was the only way to test a theory."

She stood composed, unyielding. Radiant, untouchable. And his. Except she wasn't.

"I wasn't certain you'd return," he admitted.

"I didn't," she said. Her gaze scanned the crowd. "I came for this."

Gabriel moved closer, close enough that his next words would not carry. "You're sure?"

"I've compared the sketches. The flaw in the center stone. The engraving." Her eyes lifted to his. "It's the sixth piece. And it's mine."

His throat worked. "You're making yourself a target."

"I know." Her voice didn't waver, the words carrying the conviction of someone who had already accepted the consequence.

"Let them look," she said. "Let them wonder. Let them try."

His mouth twitched. "You sound like Barrington."

"I sound like myself." She paused. "This isn't about my safety. It's about my mother's name. My aunt's. And yes, yours."

He studied her. She had always been like this. It simply took him too long to see it.

"I've spoken with Barrington," he said. "And Mrs. Bainbridge. The house is secure."

Leticia nodded. "Then we play the part they expect. Until they show their hand."

He offered her his arm. He imagined this was when he'd step in, the moment she would need him. But she had never needed him to stand in front of her. Only beside.

She rested her hand against his sleeve, not as a plea, but a choice.

She wasn't alone. Not in that salon. Not in danger. Not now. She had her aunt at her back. Barrington and Mrs. Bainbridge holding the line. And Gabriel, even though he hadn't yet known how to stand with her.

He took her arm, gently. Their steps matched in perfect rhythm. They crossed the floor together, past whispers, glances, and candlelight.

And behind them, the soiree swirled on.

But ahead, somewhere in the circle of polite conversation and too-sweet champagne, was the one who believed the brooch still belonged to the Order.

Leticia scanned the crowd.

There was Erica, chin dipped, smile too practiced. Professor Tresham, at ease, unreadable. Townsend, near the window, sipping his drink with the careless grace of a man watching everything. Maybe it was none of them.

Gabriel's hand rested lightly at her back. She didn't speak. Neither did he. They stood together in the hum of music and polished civility.

And if the Order meant to take her brooch, they would have to go through both of them.

# Chapter Thirty-Two

THE MUSIC FROM the quartet curled beneath the chandeliers, graceful and measured, never still in Lady Eastbury's salon. Guests clustered in conversational knots beneath glittering sconces, the hush of silk and the clink of porcelain weaving a pattern of civility over the tension rising beneath it all.

She moved with deliberate ease, Gabriel a quiet presence beside her. They played the part well. A recently engaged couple basking in polite attention. She inclined her head to those who offered congratulations, accepted compliments on her gown and smile, and allowed the glances at her shoulder to speak for themselves.

The brooch glittered high on her bodice. In any other light, it might have passed as ordinary. Here, among crystal chandeliers and social scrutiny, it sparked like flint against stone.

The hum of conversation thickened with curiosity. Smiles were too bright, laughter a note too sharp. "Every gaze in the room is focused on you," Gabriel murmured, offering her a fresh glass of champagne.

Leticia accepted the glass but didn't drink. "That was the idea."

He gave the faintest nod, his gaze drifting to the periphery where footmen moved with mechanical precision. The crowd had grown, but not by much. There were only a few unfamiliar faces.

Gabriel inspected the edges of the room as if measuring the

room for movement. The posture, the stillness of some guests, the way one man near the terrace doors kept glancing at Leticia without ever approaching. It all built a pattern. He wasn't certain what he was looking for, only that he'd know when something slipped out of place.

One man leaned against a column near the musicians. Nondescript, but too observant. Gabriel recognized him, Barrington's man. One of three embedded in the crowd. Leticia was being watched by more than the Order tonight.

"Anyone of concern?" she asked softly.

"Not yet," he said. "But I don't think we'll have to wait long."

Leticia turned to acknowledge Lady Marchmont, who swept over with a smile and an assessing gaze.

"My dear, your engagement is the topic of the evening," she said. "And that brooch, how bold. It catches the light magnificently."

Leticia offered a soft smile. "It belonged to my mother."

"And looks as if it was meant for you," Lady Marchmont replied, her tone kind but curious. "I daresay you'll start a fashion."

She moved on before Leticia could answer.

Gabriel leaned slightly closer. "That was subtle. For her."

"She's deciding whether I'm reckless or fashionable."

Leticia felt the eyes. Dozens. Not all unfriendly. Not all known. Her pulse skated beneath her skin. If she faltered, even slightly, it would be noticed.

Erica emerged from a knot of people near the west wall, a flute of champagne in one hand and a smile polished to brightness.

"Letty, darling," she sang, arriving with practiced delight. "You're a vision. That brooch is amazing, the way it catches the light."

Leticia met her gaze. "It was my mother's."

"Of course," Erica said, voice light. "It's just that it reminds me so much of a piece I nearly bid on at the Morton auction. But

I'm sure I'm mistaken."

Her eyes lingered a second too long. She turned to Gabriel, offering a nod. "And Lord Ashcombe. You do cut a fine figure beside her."

"The effect is entirely hers," he replied.

Erica laughed, too brightly. "What a charming answer."

She drifted away, but Leticia felt the burn of her glance long after.

"She knows," she whispered.

"She suspects," Gabriel replied. "Or she's testing how much you know."

Leticia scanned the room. The footmen. The open doors to the garden. The shadows near the pianoforte.

Gabriel stiffened. "Denholm just slipped through the side corridor."

Leticia's heart kicked once. "Follow him?"

He shook his head. "Not yet. Whoever he's meeting is still here."

A moment later, Lord Westcott stood near the garden doors, his gaze sweeping the room with a soldier's wariness. He moved to Denholm's former post near the pianoforte, nodded once, and turned back the way he came.

"That's her husband," Gabriel murmured. "It may be nothing."

But Leticia had already seen the glance Westcott cast toward his wife. Protective. Sharp.

"Not a thief, then," Gabriel said quietly. "Likely placed to watch over her."

Leticia let out a slow breath. "So he's a guard."

Gabriel nodded. "And not ours. Which means someone else is also worried."

They drifted toward the east corner, away from the press of guests. Gabriel spotted Barrington near the refreshment table and nodded once. A signal. Barrington adjusted his stance and slipped through the opposite corridor.

Leticia reached for her champagne and brought the glass to her lips, lowered it again without drinking. Her hand was steady, but there was a thrum beneath her skin, the tension of being observed, hunted, displayed.

She and Gabriel moved to the edge of the room, standing for a moment near the arched window that opened to the garden. She didn't look out. She only let the cooler air brush against her cheek. It gave her an excuse to breathe.

Behind them, the music faltered. A glass shattered. Someone laughed to cover it.

This was the eye of the storm. From here, she could see everything, the movement, the music, the tension dressed in silk and civility. But the reflection in the glass caught her breath. Not because it showed fear. Because it didn't.

Calm. Poised. A woman who looked as if she belonged at the center of all this. But the truth pressed beneath her skin like a pulse. She was the lure. And she had agreed to it.

What would her mother say now? Not the memory, but the imagined voice. Real enough to whisper in her mind: *You're making yourself a target.*

She could almost hear the answer rise beneath it, fierce and quiet. *I shall aim true.*

Gabriel was here. So were Barrington and Mrs. Bainbridge. But this moment, the risk, the decision, was hers. If they came for her, she wouldn't run. She wouldn't flinch. She would be the spark that lit their unraveling. Whatever came tonight, exposure, betrayal, danger, she would meet it on her terms.

Leticia turned. Gabriel was already watching. He shook his head slightly. *Not yet.*

Professor Tresham approached, hands clasped behind his back.

"Lady Salisbury, Ashcombe," he greeted. "A fascinating piece you wear this evening. The diamond pattern is rather reminiscent of a Prussian setting from the late eighteenth century."

"It was my mother's," Leticia replied evenly.

"Ah. Sentimental value, then. Still, one might argue pieces belong in preservation, not circulation."

Gabriel stepped forward. "Some heirlooms were meant to be worn."

Tresham inclined his head. "Of course. I only meant to admire it. Enjoy your evening."

He disappeared before she could respond.

"He's deflecting," Leticia said quietly.

"Or collecting information," Gabriel answered just as quietly.

They began to move again, weaving back into the flow of guests. Gabriel caught sight of another familiar face, another of Barrington's guards, subtly redirecting a footman from the western hallway. The net was drawing in.

Erica returned.

She caught Leticia just as she turned toward the refreshments.

"Letty," she said with a sly smile. "Forgive me. I didn't mean to pry earlier. But I must say, you wear that piece so well. Especially given all the stories lately."

Leticia raised an eyebrow. "Stories?"

"You were at Lady Marchmont's masquerade. Bits of jewelry have gone missing. Odd, isn't it? Pieces without pedigree, but suddenly sought-after." She sipped. "Just the sort of thing that makes a soirée sparkle."

Leticia met her eyes. "Rumors have a way of starting somewhere."

"Yes," Erica said sweetly. "But they never end where you expect."

She moved on.

Leticia watched her disappear into the crowd. She exhaled slow and steady. That wasn't a conversation. It was a warning. Erica had revealed too much in just a few words. Not to implicate herself, but to rattle Leticia's grip.

Gabriel returned to her side. "What did she want?"

"To remind me I'm not the only one who knows the stories."

He offered her his arm. She took it.

"We have enough," she said. "Don't we?"

"We have motive. We have an opportunity. But we don't have proof." He gently patted her hand.

"We must draw them out."

Gabriel looked out over the crowd. "Barrington is posted at the corridor. His men are in place. The exits are covered."

Leticia nodded. She moved toward the heart of the salon, where the candlelight was brightest. Not by accident. By choice.

And in that moment, she became something more than a woman in satin and diamonds. She stepped into the candlelight with intent. She became the center of gravity, the point every gaze tilted toward, whether they knew it or not.

Gabriel couldn't breathe. His gaze swept instinctively to the walls, three men in position, good men, but not fast enough if someone made a move.

Leticia didn't glance back. Didn't look for him. She didn't need to.

She had always been like this. Unshakable. Fierce. And for too long, he had tried to shield her from the storm, not realizing she *was* the storm.

If anyone reached for her, he would cross the room in a heartbeat. Protocol be damned. This was no longer about the plan.

She wasn't his to protect. She was his to stand beside.

The quartet played on. Laughter spilled around them. And somewhere nearby, a decision was being made.

Leticia let her breath settle, slow and measured.

If the Order wanted the brooch, and if Erica was ready to make her move, it would not be in shadow. It would be here, in the light. The first move was no longer hers. But the final one might be.

The snare had been laid. And the game had begun.

# Chapter Thirty-Three

THE AIR SHATTERED with a scream, a high, ragged wail that split the music and froze conversation mid-word.

A bowstring snapped against a violin, releasing a discordant screech that hung in the air. Someone gasped. A chair scraped backward. Silver clattered against porcelain. A delicate chime of crystal hitting marble rang out, followed by a glass that toppled and broke.

Silence followed for a single heartbeat.

Murmurs rose, soft at first, scattered across the room. "Did you hear that?" "Who screamed?" "Did someone fall?"

The musicians faltered, fingers hovering just above their strings. The conductor turned, searching for guidance. Near the head of the room, the hostess was already on her feet. Somewhere near the card tables, a servant dropped a tray. The second crash was louder, clumsier. The scent of spilled wine joined the perfume-laced air as liquid spread like blood across the polished floor.

Chairs scraped. Fans snapped shut. Every sound after struck too loud.

Leticia's fingers gripped Gabriel's arm more tightly. Beneath her hand, his muscles had gone taut. He scanned the room, surveying exits, gauging expressions, estimating distance. He was not alarmed, but alert.

At the far end of the ballroom, another gasp rippled through the guests. A footman hurried past, calling for fresh linens.

Someone sobbed, the sound too raw for theatrics.

From the open terrace doors, a draft swept in, sharp with night air. One candle flickered. Followed by another. Half the room shifted their attention toward the source of the cold, toward the open doors and the garden beyond.

Gabriel leaned down, his voice low against her ear. "Stay close."

She nodded once. Her lips pressed into a line, but her jaw did not tremble. The weight of the brooch at her throat was suddenly heavier and warmer, as though it knew what it had drawn. She had agreed to this. To be the spark. To lure the Order into the open. She had accepted the risk.

But she hadn't expected it to be like this, as though the rules had shifted before the first move had been made.

They moved with the crowd, edging toward the terrace. The surge of guests pressed in from all sides. Shoulders jostled her, perfume mixed with cologne, and the air grew thick with murmurs and heat. A heel caught the toe of her slipper. Her breath caught. Her balance tipped for a moment before Gabriel steadied her.

Ahead, the garden flickered with lantern lights, but shadows stretched long between them. Too many lanterns remained unlit. The night was uneven, too quiet in places, too loud in others.

She didn't look away. Not from the garden. Not from the press of shadows beyond the terrace. Something in the air had turned.

It wasn't fear. Not yet. But her skin prickled with awareness, and the back of her neck tightened in warning.

"Leticia!"

A hand brushed hers.

Erica.

Her voice trembled with urgency. She looked flushed, breathless, dark strands of hair loosened from their twist, clinging to her cheeks.

"Your aunt, Lady Eastbury, she's in the garden. She slipped."

Leticia blinked. "What? Where?"

"Near the arbor. Come quickly." Erica's eyes shone with insistence. "No one can lift her."

"I didn't see her go out."

"She didn't want to make a scene. Please, she's asking for you."

It sounded exactly like her aunt. *Avoid disruption. Avoid attention.* The words struck a note of truth.

Leticia turned, expecting to find Gabriel beside her. He was gone. She looked again, searching the crowd, her pulse rising. The crowd closed in. Her view was gone. She could see no broad shoulders, no dark hair.

Her heart lodged in her throat.

Erica's grip found her hand. "Hurry."

Leticia hesitated before she stepped onto the terrace.

⋙⋘

NIGHT AIR STRUCK her cheeks, cool and damp, heavy with the scent of trampled grass and woodsmoke. Somewhere closer, a sharp note of something sweeter, roses, bruised and fading, twined through the breeze. The terrace stones gave way to the path, where gravel crunched beneath each step, loud in the hush.

Behind them, the faint strains of music still drifted from the ballroom. It sounded warped now. Slower. Disconnected. Like a melody out of time.

Ahead, the gardens opened into soft pools of lamplight and long swathes of shadow. A couple strolled past in awkward silence, arms linked, eyes darting. Lanterns bobbed above their heads. Their nervous laughter faded as quickly as it had sparked.

Leticia followed Erica, drawn past the edge of the terrace into darker paths. Her slipper slid slightly on loose stone, and her balance wavered again. She lifted her skirts just enough to walk faster.

Here, there was no cluster of guests. No flash of lilac silk. No cry for assistance. And no sign of Gabriel.

Her heart slowed, not with calm, but with stillness. Dangerous stillness settled. The kind that warned of something lying in wait.

She stopped walking.

Her foot ground deliberately against the gravel, once again, dragging a rough sound from the stones. A warning. A marker.

She didn't know if anyone would hear. She didn't know if it mattered.

The brooch at her throat was like a stone fresh from the hearth, too hot, too solid. Her chest ached beneath it.

Gabriel had asked, but she had said yes. Even now, even with Erica's fingers tightening just slightly around her wrist, she didn't regret it.

But her fear had shape now. Weight. Teeth.

Would her mother have called her brave? Or foolhardy?

She could almost hear the voice, dry and fond. *My brave, darling, choosing not to let fear drive your decisions.*

The breeze stirred her hem and carried the imagined voice away.

Leticia turned slightly, meaning to look back toward the ballroom, toward Gabriel. No familiar figure met her gaze.

Behind her, Erica's voice changed. "Come. She's behind the arbor." Not pleading. Not rushed. Flat.

Leticia's spine stiffened. "I should get Gabriel."

Erica's grip clamped down. "No time."

The shift was subtle, but she felt it. Too late. Not a mistake. Not an accident. She had stepped into it.

The words struck clean. The shadows near the hedges stirred. Two men stepped forward. They didn't wear evening coats. One wore boots crusted with road-dust. The other had a scar running from his temple into the collar of his shirt. Neither looked like they had been invited.

She stilled, measuring, not yielding but not resisting. Rough palms. Smoke on their sleeves. Hands seized her arms. Not violent, but certain.

"You're making a scene," Erica said.

Leticia turned toward her. The other woman's face was calm, too calm. Her tone lacked all urgency now, all pretense.

"I had hoped you would come quietly."

Leticia held her gaze.

The garden drew in around them, the lantern light thinning, the path narrowing to a line she had already crossed.

She did not speak again.

GABRIEL SEARCHED THE ballroom. The terrace. The garden. No Leticia. No Erica.

He pushed through the guests, faster now. Elbows brushed him. Voices murmured. Nervous, oblivious laughter sprang up in pockets. Some guests had already begun returning to their seats. The scream had already turned to curiosity, a tale to be embellished by morning.

But not for him.

His jaw locked. "Leticia?" The word was low. Controlled. No answer. He strode across the threshold into the garden. Cool air closed around him like a glove.

His boots hit the terrace stone, gravel, loud, deliberate, unmistakable. The sound grated, deliberate, meant to be heard.

He paused. Turned his head. Had someone else walked this path? There, drag marks. Disruption. A scattering of stone that hadn't settled yet. The faintest scrape across the gravel where someone had moved sideways, not forward. Gabriel followed it.

"Ashcombe."

He turned at the voice. Professor Tresham stood near the edge of the terrace, wineglass in hand, his silhouette framed in soft lanternlight. Impeccably calm. Not a wrinkle in his coat. No sweat on his brow. No breath visible in the cool night air. And no dirt on his boots.

Gabriel froze. A beat too long.

Tresham lifted his hand. "I need a word."

Gabriel didn't break stride. "Not now."

"I believe you'll want to hear."

"I said not now."

He passed him without another glance. But the timing lingered. The direction. Tresham had come from the hedgerow. The same direction as the hoofbeats. The same path that led to the back gate.

A fraction too precise. Too well placed to be chance.

Gabriel's pace quickened.

The farther he moved from the lanterns, the more his instincts took over. His eyes swept the edges of the hedge line. He searched for silver silk. For a pale ribbon. For anything that did not belong.

He passed the arbor. Nothing. A chill coiled in his gut.

The scent of roses lingered faintly, but it was mingled now with something else. Horse sweat. Damp leather. Earth, freshly gouged.

He broke into a run.

The gravel roared beneath his boots. A part of his mind registered the sound, not just loud, but uneven. Disturbed.

At the curve of the garden path, he found it.

The edge of the hedge bore two wide arcs, grass pressed flat. Ruts cut deep into the ground. Mud clung to the rim of the path.

A carriage had been here. And recently. He crouched. Reached. Something pale caught the light.

A ribbon. Green. Frayed at one end, where it had caught on a branch or buckle. His fingers curled around it.

Leticia's.

His breath caught. She had trusted him. He had promised she wouldn't face this danger alone. And they had taken her. He stood slowly, the ribbon still clutched in his hand. His grip tightened until his knuckles blanched.

He turned sharply toward the house. "Barrington's men, to the garden gate!" His voice rang out like a shot, cutting across the garden.

He didn't wait.

And then he ran.

# Chapter Thirty-Four

THE BALLROOM HAD already begun to forget.

The music had faltered but not stopped. Conversation had dipped, only to resume, hushed and eager. Guests circled in curious clusters, exchanging theories about the scream, the spill, the drama. The incident, such as it had been, now served as the evening's diversion.

But Gabriel wasn't listening. He moved through the room with purpose, Leticia's ribbon clenched in his hand, his focus fixed and unyielding, and the crowd parted before him.

He found Barrington near the French doors, flanked by Mrs. Bainbridge and two of his men. Gabriel didn't slow. He pressed the length of green silk into Barrington's palm.

"She's gone."

Barrington stiffened. "What?"

"Erica and two men took her. There was a coach waiting past the garden wall." Gabriel's voice was flat but not calm. He didn't bother with ceremony. There wasn't time.

"I saw no coach," Mrs. Bainbridge said, already turning toward the door.

"It didn't wait at the front. It came through the side access. I suspect there was no crest and no lanterns. The gravel is fresh with track ruts. Gate guards missed it or were distracted. Either way, they're gone."

He turned to Barrington's men. "You. To the hedge. Confirm the direction and depth of the carriage tracks. Look for fresh hoof prints. Any wax drips from the lanterns. Anything dropped in the scramble."

The men scattered.

Gabriel turned toward the ballroom again, scanning faces, searching for any flicker of guilt or retreat. He wanted to see someone run. He wanted to catch them mid-turn.

Instead, he saw Lady Eastbury.

She stood at the edge of the hall, skirts brushing the marble, head high, but her eyes sharp. She moved toward him.

"Where is my niece?"

Gabriel met her gaze. "Taken."

The word landed without a cushion. Her lips parted, but she didn't gasp. Her chin lifted by a fraction.

"For the brooch?"

"No," he said. "For her."

For a moment, nothing moved between them. Not air. Not breath.

"I let her out of my sight," Lady Eastbury said, her voice too even.

Gabriel shook his head. "She made the choice. She knew the risk."

She looked away, but only for a breath. When she looked back, her composure had returned, but not untouched. "We must act quickly."

"We are."

A young footman approached, pale and stammering. "M-my lord, someone said they saw a dark carriage leave the side path less than ten minutes ago. It headed west, toward the old toll road."

"We're behind," Gabriel said. "But not by much."

He turned to Barrington. "I'm not waiting for a coach. I'll take a horse."

Barrington nodded. "We'll follow in carriages. Give me a direction."

Gabriel didn't answer. Not yet. He turned on his heel and

strode out of the ballroom, boots ringing sharply on stone. He needed space. He needed air. He needed a map in his head and silence to trace the route.

Behind him, the music resumed, faint, awkward, and completely irrelevant.

Leticia had trusted him. And they'd taken her.

But he wasn't going to follow their path. He was going to intercept it.

THE COACH SWAYED hard with the road.

Leticia sat with her wrists bound and her ankles pressed tight together, the leather straps not painful, but firm. A loop ran through a hook bolted into the floor, tethering her with the quiet certainty.

They hadn't blindfolded her. They hadn't gagged her. They didn't think she'd scream. They had not needed to force her silence.

Erica sat opposite her, unbothered by the ruts and jolts. She looked entirely at ease, legs crossed, gloved fingers tugging at a loose thread on her cuff. The oil lamp hanging from the ceiling creaked with every jostle, throwing dim golden arcs across the wood-paneled cabin.

Leticia stared at the knot binding her wrists, and at the gap between shutter slats. The road outside blurred past in bursts, gravel, hedgerow, black sky. They weren't going slowly, but they weren't galloping either. Leticia tracked the movement of the coach, counting turns, marking distance by sound and rhythm.

Gabriel would have seen the tracks. He would have heard the gravel when she dragged her foot. He would.

She pushed the fear down, pressed it hard against the place where panic wanted to root. Her throat tightened, but she locked her jaw against it.

The man beside Erica dozed with his chin tucked, and his hat slouched low. Another drove the coach. She could hear him shift with the motion of the wheels, the creak of leather, the soft metallic clink of something at his hip.

None of them had spoken since they left the garden, none except Erica. And even now, she wore silence with ease.

Leticia turned her head. "Is this your plan then? Kidnap me in full view of a ballroom and hope no one notices?"

Erica's lips twitched. "You give yourself too much credit. No one notices what they don't understand. You walked into the garden with me. You followed. You disappeared." She shrugged lightly. "They'll assume you stepped out for air. Or that you and your aunt went to her room. People see what they expect."

"My aunt doesn't leave parties early."

"No," Erica said softly. "But you do. For him."

Leticia held her gaze, but something in her stomach dipped.

Erica leaned forward slightly, resting her arms on her knees. Her voice was low, coaxing. "He can't save you this time, Leticia. He's too proud to ask for help. Too used to being right. Men like him don't lead rescues. They walk into traps."

Leticia flinched before she could stop herself. Not visibly, not enough for Erica to gloat, but it was there. The crack. The breath that caught.

"That's what you're counting on?" Leticia asked. "Gabriel making a mistake?" Leticia held her gaze. Not arguing. Not conceding. Listening.

"I'm counting on men like him thinking they're the ones who set the rules."

Leticia glanced again at the shutter slit. Trees passed. A low wall. Gravel again, louder this time. The road was bending, narrowing. Closer to fields now. Country.

She shifted in her seat to ease the stiffness in her shoulders, the tightness in her throat.

"You've told me this much," she said. "Why not more?"

Erica sat back, lips curving. "I don't need to frighten you.

Just… distract you. Long enough."

Then she was meant to listen. "Long enough for what?"

"For us to get where we're going." She smiled faintly. "And for him to take the wrong path."

Leticia looked down at her wrists again. Her hands were tingling. Not numb, alive. Still hers. She closed her eyes briefly and breathed in through her nose.

Gabriel would follow. Not the road, but the trail. He was trained for that.

He'd see the hedge, the broken stones. He'd notice the smell of horse sweat and oil. He'd hear the silence behind the noise. She just had to last long enough.

Leticia lifted her chin. "Whatever you're part of, whatever this is, it's temporary."

"Oh?" Erica's brows lifted.

"Yes," she said simply. "Because Gabriel Ashcombe does not miss."

Erica studied her for a long moment. She laughed, a soft, musical sound with no warmth behind it.

"We'll see."

⋙⋘

THE STABLE SMELLED of sweat, damp straw, and saddle soap. The air was thick with heat and motion.

Gabriel's coat was off, his sleeves rolled, his gloves in his teeth as he cinched the girth strap tight on the bay gelding pawing the straw beneath him. The horse tossed its head, sensing his urgency. Good. He wanted an animal that matched his pace.

"Where are you going?" Barrington asked behind him, breath short from keeping up.

"West. The old toll road. Carriage prints veer in that direction."

Barrington grabbed a bridle from the wall, tossing it to Mrs.

Bainbridge. "Too obvious, isn't it?"

Gabriel nodded once. "They'll leave the road. The coach will divert into cover soon, less speed, more secrecy. That gives me an advantage."

"You're not following them?"

"I'm intercepting."

He fastened the final buckle and stepped back, the map clear in his mind with the terrain and the possibilities of paths not traveled often, fields unguarded, and old stone markers in wild hedges.

"We know the direction," he said. "We know the time. And we know what they think we'll do, chase them. But we don't need to chase. We need to arrive first."

Barrington frowned. "How?"

Gabriel turned, voice steady now. "Dunmere Cross."

Bainbridge froze. "That old smuggler's pass?"

"It connects the toll road to the coastal fields beyond the Hawthorn rise. No one watches it. Most assume it's overgrown. But the paths are still there." He tightened the reins. "If I cut across from Mill Meadow, I'll reach the back fields before the coach ever slows for the turn."

"And if you're wrong?"

"I'm not."

Barrington gave a slow nod. "We'll bring carriages behind. Armed."

Gabriel swung into the saddle. "No more delays. If they've taken her for the brooch, they'll want time. But they won't waste it."

The gelding stamped once, restless beneath him.

Barrington stepped forward, gripping the saddle's edge. "You're not thinking clearly."

"I'm thinking very clearly. I know how they move. I know how she moves. And I know what time I lost."

He turned the horse.

"Gabriel."

Lady Eastbury stood just outside the stable arch, the lantern-light catching on the trim of her cloak. She was alone. Wind tugged at her hood, but her spine was straight, her hands unshaking.

"I need a word."

Gabriel didn't dismount, but he turned the horse toward her.

She stepped forward. "There's something you don't know. About the brooch."

"I assumed as much," he said.

"It wasn't just her mother's." Her voice was tight, clipped. "It came from a set. Six pieces. All from Vienna. They were part of a cache her uncle brought back with him. I told myself they were sold. Lost. But that was a lie."

"Why?"

"Because some secrets are more useful if you pretend they're forgotten."

She met his eyes.

"Someone is collecting those pieces again. Someone who knows where they scattered. And if your suspicions are right, that the brooch marked her, they're not just reclaiming heirlooms. They're reclaiming power."

Gabriel's breath stilled.

Lady Eastbury stepped closer, her voice low. "You must find her. Before they decide she's served her purpose."

"I will."

A beat passed.

She did something unexpected, something that struck him harder than any plea. She reached up and pressed her hand once, briefly, to the horse's shoulder. A silent blessing. A benediction for the road. And she stepped back.

Gabriel didn't look at the others. He turned the horse toward the gate, heels light against the gelding's flank. And he rode.

THE CLATTER OF hooves faded into the dark.

Barrington stood at the edge of the stable yard, arms crossed, face set. Lady Eastbury hadn't moved. Her gaze followed the road, as if she could force her vision farther than the lanterns allowed.

A few stable hands hovered nearby, uncertain whether to retreat or offer aid.

A rider approached from the east. Hard and fast. One of the guards reached for his weapon, but Barrington lifted a hand.

"Townsend," he said.

Felix reined in hard, throwing dust as he dismounted. "Report for you, urgent. Direct from Edward." He handed over a folded packet. "It's the records. From the auction house. Ledger pages. And…" He broke off, looking around. "Where's Ash?"

"Gone," Barrington said. "Minutes ago. He's headed west. Dunmere Cross."

Townsend looked stunned. "He went alone?"

Lady Eastbury spoke, her tone even. "Because no one else knew where to look."

Barrington opened the packet, flipping through the top page. Names. Circled. Erica among them. Two others beneath.

His gaze narrowed.

The seller: Morton Hall Estates.

He passed the page to Mrs. Bainbridge. "It wasn't just about what they bought. It was about who sold it."

Lady Eastbury said nothing. Her eyes were closed.

THE MOON BROKE through the cloud cover just long enough to silver the hedgerow and cast pale light across the fields.

Gabriel crouched low in the saddle, his coat snapping in the wind. The gelding moved beneath him like a creature with the same intent as his, fast, relentless, focused.

Each hoofbeat was a heartbeat. Each gust of wind against his face was a warning.

He leaned lower, eyes fixed ahead.

The road forked just beyond the hawthorn rise. One way dipped toward the toll road, the other climbed the incline to the pass above the cliffs.

He didn't hesitate.

He took the rise.

# Chapter Thirty-Five

THE LANES MET in a shallow dip where the earth looked worn by years of decisions. To the east, the ground fell toward a dark glint of sea. To the west, the track bled into the pale heath and scrub. Straight ahead, a thin path curved between low stone walls and hawthorn. Men once called it Dunmere Cross, like the hinge of the countryside, where every road demanded a decision.

Gabriel drew the gelding to a halt and let the horse blow. He listened first. Wind rustled through the thornbush, a gull cried far off over the water, and the faint scrape of bramble on stone. No wheels. No voices. He slid from the saddle and dropped the reins for the gelding to breathe. The lantern's circle was small, and the night was honest, so he trusted the ground more than the light.

Fresh ruts cut across the older tracks, their edges still dark and damp. In one place, the near wheel had bitten deeper as if the load had shifted when the driver corrected his direction. A spray of gravel lay thrown across the verge and had not settled into the frost. He crouched. The soil was cold to his fingers and soft beneath the crust. The coach had recently passed.

He moved to the hedgerow and read it as he would read a map. Leaves were bent in the wrong direction. Two twigs snapped close together, too clean for weather, just at shoulder height where a body brushed through. He found a snag of silk on a jagged stone. Silvery green. He pressed it between his thumb and forefinger. A trace of rose clung to the thread. The scent caught in his throat, sharpening into an anger clean and clear.

She had been here.

He crossed the dip again, slower now, and set each small sign into the path in his mind. The northern lane showed bruised leaves where something wide had pushed by. The southern verge held a shallow crescent where a horse had shifted weight. No lantern wax. No crest marks. Whoever drove did not wish to be seen. If he stayed on the road, he would be on their time. If he cut across the fields, he might meet them where the inland lane pinched down.

Hoofbeats came from behind. Barrington rode in at a hard pace. His bay steamed and tossed its head. He lifted one gloved hand in a question and swung down before the horse had settled.

"Anything," he asked.

"Enough," Gabriel said. "They came through heavy and fast. North to the fork. They will not risk the storehouses if there are eyes on the bluff."

Barrington studied the ruts, the hedge, and the open dark beyond them, evaluating what might still be moving unseen. "The inland fork is quieter. Slower, though."

"They will trade speed for cover if they think we chase wheels," Gabriel said. "Hawthorn Rise cuts the field. If I cross there, I reach the inland road before they make the turn, whether they choose coast or country. I will not follow them. I will meet them."

Barrington's mouth tugged. "You sound sure."

"I am."

He reached inside his coat and took out a folded page. "Townsend brought this from Edward. I told him you were gone." He passed the paper across.

Ink and ledgers. Neat handwriting. Names down one column. Purchases down the next. Halfway down the page, two names sat together as if they had been written to chafe the eye.

Object Identified: Diamond and sapphire brooch. Sapphire etched with a raven within a geometric diamond.

Participants Listed: Bidders listed. Five in total. Among them, Erica St. Clair and Lord Ashcombe.

Outcome Reported: Sold to Lord Ashcombe.

Transfer Noted: Anne Salisbury

The pattern that had eluded them snapped into shape.

"It was never about only the brooch," Gabriel said, his voice low, the word *only* smaller than the truth.

Barrington glanced north and west. "If they stay on that track, they will hit the bend to the water inside an hour."

"And pass within a quarter mile of the old stone sheds," Gabriel said. "Too open. Too many chances to be seen. If they are clever, they turn before it."

"If they are tired, they blunder on," Barrington said. His tone was dry but not unkind. "What are you counting on?"

"Not luck," Gabriel said. "Bracken Hollow sits between the high hedges and the old oaks. The ground dips there and holds water after rain. A carriage cannot take it at speed without risking a wheel."

Recognition sharpened Barrington's gaze. "You want the hollow."

"I want to cut them off." Gabriel pointed west with two fingers. "You take the lane and hold Bracken Hollow. I ride the cut through the rise and come in from the field. We will have them trapped between us."

Barrington nodded once. "I will keep them from slipping through."

They moved without another word. Barrington whistled, and two men peeled off to ride wide and watch the rise. Another took a lantern and checked the southern verge for a false trail. Gabriel tightened the girth and set his boot. The gelding gathered under him like a held breath. One of Barrington's men brought a spare lead rope and held it up without being asked. Gabriel took it with a short thanks and slid the silk scrap into his pocket, where it warmed against his palm.

"Go," Barrington said.

Gabriel put his heels to the gelding and took the cut at a canter that lengthened into a run. Branches scraped his coat. Cold mud flicked against his boots. The hedges opened, and fields that rolled in ridges silvered with frost. He lay flat over the horse's withers and let the horse eat the ground. Wind stung his eyes and put salt on his tongue. He thought of Leticia's chin when she refused fear and shaped that refusal into speed.

The inland lane came into view ahead as a pale seam between hedges. He set a line that would bring him to the pinch where the road climbed past a low stone marker. He meant to stand there first.

THE COACH SWAYED like a ship that had forgotten calm water. Leticia kept her back against the seat and her wrists low. The straps held fast enough to bite but not to deaden her hands. She counted the road using her senses, feel, and sound rather than sight, gravel under wheels, a hollow thud, and a change in the air that tasted clean. A bridge, water flowing underneath. The coach rattled on, and gravel gave way to turf. The pace slowed over rough ground, and the frame leaned into a turn.

Erica had left them at Dunmere Cross, her work already done. Two men rode outside. Their shadows cut across the shutter with a rhythm that matched the coach. The air inside was close with damp wool, and the breath of horse sweat drifting from the roof vent.

The lane narrowed. High hedges pressed in. The straps bit as the coach dipped again. Leticia shifted to brace her feet and felt the faint tug as the hem of her gown caught on a rough seam near the lower hinge of the door. She didn't move. A breath later, she heard the faint hiss of silk giving way. She let it go.

The coach tilted into a turn. Branches scraped the sides. A

curtain of leaves reached in, and with them, the wind. Just enough to snatch the torn silk outward. If it caught somewhere, if he found it…she could only hope.

A whistle cut the wind, and a voice followed it, low and clear. "Bracken Hollow before nightfall."

The name lodged in her chest. She had never been there. She only heard the way people said it with caution. A dip in the road between a hedge and an oak. A place where wagons slowed, and riders vanished without a sound. If Gabriel guessed the route, he would choose the ground rather than the wheel tracks. If he knew the hollow, he would already be moving to get there.

She shifted and tested the rope. The guard opposite her lifted his chin in a warning and let his eyes fall again when the road smoothed. Pitch stained one of his cuffs. The other man wore a ring that flashed dull in the low light. When the wheel hit a rut, the ring turned, and the face showed plain. A small diamond with a bird inside it. A raven. She looked away before she could give anything to the expression the sight wanted from her.

The coach dropped into a deeper shade. The air cooled and smelled of moss and turned earth. The horses changed their stride. The wheels complained. Bracken Hollow was close.

Hawthorn Rise closed in like a narrow corridor. Thorns scraped at Gabriel's knees, and he kept the gelding straight and sure. Frost rang under iron hooves when the lane gave way to the open field. The ground shifted from ridge to flat, and he put his weight forward. Ahead, the lane climbed to the pinch and bent out of sight. He slowed to listen. Wind in the hedge. A dog far off. The faint grind of wheels came on the cold air. He knew it before he heard it. The night held its breath.

He turned the gelding into the hedge shadow and let his own breath steady. When the sound filled out into a rhythm, he eased the horse forward again. He was not going to follow a door that had closed behind her. He was opening the one ahead.

Back at the Cross, the wind had shifted. Barrington checked the sky and the line of hawthorn as if both could carry words. He mounted and kept two men with him. The rest would sweep the road in pairs and hold the hollow if they reached it first. He set his horse to a pace that could last and kept Dunmere Cross behind him. He had ridden with Gabriel long enough to trust the man's sense of ground.

THE COACH JOLTED. A click from outside and the horses shortened their stride. The lane dipped. Leticia pressed her shoulders into the seat and matched the sway so the rope would not bite. She fixed the name in her mind and pictured the bend that hid what lay beyond. If Gabriel came in from the field, she must keep calm long enough to be worth the risk he would take. She kept her eyes on the slit of light and her breath even.

GABRIEL REACHED THE marker stone and drew the horse into the hedge's shadow. The gelding stood calmly beneath him. He listened once more and counted. The sound grew. The carriage was approaching. The driver would not dare a reckless run through a dip with slick mud in the ruts. That meant control, and control meant time.

A shout rose ahead. A rider's voice cut the damp air, and the team's rhythm changed. The sound came to Leticia through wood and iron like a heartbeat that was not her own. The coach slowed for the dip. The light thinned. She closed her eyes for the space of a breath and saw the hollow as if she stood above it. Hedges close on either side. Oak trees leaning in. Water pooled in the low ground. No room to fly through. No room at all.

She opened her eyes. She did not pray. She counted the seconds between the wheels and the next stone. She kept the name in her head. She kept his name there, too.

Gabriel came out of the hedge shadow at a canter that snapped into a run. The gelding took the slope straight. His world narrowed to the sound of wheels and the shape of the bend. Barrington's men would hold the far side. He would take the near one. The hollow would do the rest.

He saw the coach lantern hooded. He saw the driver lean. He saw the horses' ears cut back. He did not think. He moved. The hunt had turned into a meeting, and he meant to keep it.

"Hold the hollow," Barrington called behind him.

Gabriel's answer was already in motion. "Bracken Hollow." And the night closed its fist around the name.

# Chapter Thirty-Six

T HE HOLLOW PRESSED in on all sides. Hedges rose high and close. Old oaks leaned until their branches knitted to create a low roof of shadow. The air smelled of wet earth and moss. Wheels hissed through standing water. The coach rocked and groaned as if the road itself wished to turn it back.

Inside, Leticia kept her wrists low and her breathing even. The rope bit, eased, then bit again with each sway. Leather creaked. Iron ticked against iron somewhere above the roof. Sweat from the team drifted through the roof vent and mixed with the colder scent of fern.

A man rode close on the near side. She heard the muffled scuff of his boot as he steadied himself against the panel. Another rider cut across the front. The horses shortened stride. The driver muttered and laid the whip without true force. No one wanted speed in this place. The ruts were slick. The bend hid all but a sliver of the way forward.

Words came thin through the wet air. Not whispers. And not meant for her ears.

"Easy through the dip."

"Hold for the bend."

"Bracken Hollow. Off the lane."

She fixed the name in her mind and pictured the road as Gabriel would. Hedges to the left. Water on the right. One wheel would sink deep if the driver misjudged the crown. No room for speed, but there was plenty of room for a mistake.

The coach shifted weight. The near wheel climbed the rut and dropped. A rope outside snapped tight. The horses stamped. A rider hissed at them. The sound came like a spill of gravel over stone.

Another rhythm rode beneath it. A hard, steady beat that wasn't the team. It was iron on the ground, uncut by wheels. A horse coming fast through the field, not the road. She couldn't see it. She felt it, rising through the floorboards like a second heart.

"Hold steady," the driver called.

The coach leaned again. Boots ground the hollow's grit. A shape crossed the slit of the shutter. Only a shadow. Large. Close. Gone again. A word snapped at the team. The reins creaked. Someone swore under his breath.

The world outside jumped with a new noise. Short. Close. Certain. The sound of a blow that found its mark. A second blow. A grunt cut off halfway. The horses tossed and snorted. The coach rocked as weight left the near side too quickly.

Leticia set her heels and braced against the door. The rope at her wrists rasped. Her fingers tingled. She said nothing. There was no time to say anything. The boards along the far wall trembled. Another thud shook the frame. Silence followed. Not a natural quiet. A stopped one.

The latch clicked.

Light and cold poured in as the door flew wide. A figure filled the opening, broad shoulders, dark coat with spray from the lane. Lantern light caught in the eyes that did not miss anything.

The nearer guard started to move, but Gabriel moved first. The butt of his pistol caught the man across the temple clean, silent, and final. The other froze, his eyes wide in disbelief.

"Letty," Gabriel said.

Her name in his voice unmade something tight in her chest. She pushed forward, skirts tangling, vision blurring as her eyes adjusted. He reached in and caught her at the waist. His grip was firm and sure. He lifted. The ground came up wet and uneven. He held her until both her feet found it.

He looked her over. Face. Hands. The set of her shoulders. He did not touch the rope yet. He did not look away.

"Where is Erica?" he asked.

"She left us at Dunmere Cross," Leticia said.

His jaw set. "Alone."

"I had no choice. I knew what I was doing," she said quietly. "That does not mean it was not frightening."

Across the coach, the other door flung open. Barrington's voice carried low and sharp. "Out you come."

Two men inside jerked toward the sound of Gabriel's door and lost the beat on Barrington's side. That was enough. Gabriel's hand flashed. He caught the nearer man by the coat and dragged him hard over the step. The man's boots scraped and skidded. He swung a fist that hit air. Barrington's men were already there. Two bodies closed. Arms wrenched back. A knee took the fight out of the man. He folded with a choked curse.

On the far side, Barrington hauled the second man bodily to the ground. They went down in a tangle. A third guard drove his shoulder into the captive's spine and pinned him. The rope bit home. The man spat and went still when Barrington lifted the barrel of a pistol a hand's width from his eye.

The driver raised the whip to bring it down blind and hard. Gabriel did not look. He reached and caught the leather with his left hand, twisted once, stripped it free, and tossed it into the standing water at the hollow's edge. The driver stared at his empty fist. He tried to climb down. Barrington's younger man met him at the step and pressed him against the wheel with his forearm until the driver's breath left him in a rush.

"Hands," the young man said.

The driver offered them without pride.

Leticia stood still and listened to the end of it. The hollow held sound like a bowl. It caught the last scuffle and the last hiss and the last clink of buckles. The only noises were the team's breath and the slow drip from the hedge.

Gabriel turned to her. The tightness in him had not gone

anywhere. It had only changed shape. He reached for her wrists. The small knife he kept hidden under the edge of his gauntlet flashed and was gone. The rope fell. Blood sprang in a thin line where the cord had rubbed her skin raw. He closed his hand over the mark and pressed to slow the sting.

"Can you stand?" he asked.

"Yes," she said. Her voice steadied. "I heard them say Bracken Hollow."

"We are there," he said. "And done with it."

He lifted her hands and looked again. His breath came measured. His eyes did not.

Barrington strode around the rear of the coach and stopped a few paces away. "Yours are secured," he said. "Mine are thinking about their choices." His mouth marked a wry line that did not touch his eyes. "We will make them talk in a better place."

Gabriel nodded without looking away from Leticia. "Search the coach. Look for anything they carried that is not theirs."

Barrington signaled his men. One went to the box under the driver's seat. Another checked the floorboards. A third used the butt of a knife to tap the lower paneling in a slow rhythm, listening for a hollow sound.

"I meant to draw them out."

The tightness beneath Leticia's ribs eased all at once, and she drew breath as if her lungs had been unlocked. Air rushed in like the morning tide.

Gabriel's hands lifted to her face before she could find any words. His thumbs brushed the chill along her cheekbones. He breathed in as if her nearness could fill his lungs.

His voice was rougher than he meant it to be. "You are here," he said.

"I am here," she whispered, the words catching halfway between disbelief and relief.

It was all either of them needed. His mouth took hers. No careful distance. His mouth took hers, and restraint shattered. She rose into him. Her fingers caught at his coat and pulled him closer. His arm closed across her back. Everything else fell away. The wet road. The captured men. The whisper of leaves. There was only the press and answer, the hard line of his chest, the taste of wind and fear and relief turned sweet.

He pulled back only to breathe. His forehead rested against hers. The world returned in fragments. A horse stamped. Barrington spoke quietly to a man. Water dripped from a fern into a shallow pool.

His gaze dropped to her throat. "The brooch."

Leticia's hand rose to the empty space. "She took it."

His jaw tightened once. "We leave," Gabriel said. "Now."

Barrington looked over. "If we take the road they will chase. We may not shake them."

"We do not take the road," Gabriel said. He turned to Leticia. "Can you ride?"

"Yes," she said. The word found its strength as she spoke it.

He lifted her into the saddle of the gelding. The leather creaked under her weight. He mounted behind her in one sure move. His arm caged her with the reins. His chest set firm against her back, steady and warm. For one heartbeat, he allowed himself to hold that closeness before the work returned.

"Across the lower fields," he told Barrington. "They will expect us east. We will not give it to them."

Barrington nodded. "I will take the lane and hold the next turn. We will meet at the marker beyond the rise." His gaze flicked to Leticia and softened for half a breath. "My lady."

"Thank you," she said.

Barrington was already moving. He called two men to stay and watch the captives. He sent a third to fetch the team forward and lead them out of the worst of the mud.

Gabriel set his heels. The gelding stepped out and stretched. The hedge fell away behind them. The hollow's damp chill gave over to the sharper cold of the open field. The moon broke free and painted the ridge in pale silver.

Leticia leaned back into him for balance as the pace built. It put her spine to his chest. It put his breath warm at her ear. It set the beat of his heart against her shoulder blades. The kiss still burned in her mouth. The fear still shook faintly in her hands. Both truths could live at once. She drew in air that smelled of frost and horses and the simple, clean fact of motion.

They ran until the field gave way to a narrow cut that climbed toward a marker stone worn by years of weather. Gabriel slowed to read the land. The inland lane curved ahead and dropped from sight. He lifted his head and listened. Far off and low, he caught the grind of wheels. Behind that sound lay the murmur of men. Not close. Not far. Somewhere between.

"We are ahead of them," he said.

"And Erica," Leticia asked. "She left us at the Cross."

"She is not here," Gabriel said. "But she has left her shadow on this road."

Leticia saw the ring on the guard's hand as if it still turned in the lamp light. A diamond with a bird inside it. She told him. He did not answer at once. His jaw worked. His hand tightened on the reins. He looked at the lane and at the hedge and at the dark beyond.

"You did well," he said. "You saw, and even stressed, you remembered."

She let that praise settle where the rope had bitten. It soothed more than the knife had.

Barrington's bay came up on their left at a steady canter. He drew even for a stride. "We found a false floor in the coach," he said. "Empty. They were meant to carry something or to take something away."

"Not tonight," Gabriel said.

"No," Barrington said. "Not tonight."

They rode together through a thinning hedge until the lane widened to a patch of bare ground where a milestone lay on its side. Barrington raised two fingers to his men, who had cut across by a shorter track. They spread without noise and took positions that watched both the bend and the field.

Gabriel kept the gelding in the shadow and steadied his breathing until his chest no longer burned. He could feel the tremor that ran through Leticia's shoulders begin to fade. He rested his hand for one moment at her waist, where the rope had pressed. He then took up the reins.

A thin wind came down the lane. It brought with it the sour tang of lamps that had been hooded too long and the stale smoke of men who had stood and waited for orders in a damp place. He stored the scent away. Even a small thing could matter.

The hollow behind them held its silence. The men they had left there would be moving by now under Barrington's guard. The driver would be thinking about the choices he had made. The guards would be learning how long a night could be.

Leticia looked over her shoulder. There was no fear in the movement. Only a need to see him. In the dim light, his eyes met hers. He reached again and touched her cheek with his knuckles. It was no kiss, but it carried the same heat.

"Stay close," he said.

"I do not intend to do anything else," she said.

He gave a short laugh that was more breath than sound. "Good."

The grind of distant wheels grew a shade louder. Barrington's head turned. His men lifted their chins almost in unison and took a half step toward the positions they had already chosen. No one spoke.

"Not the road," Gabriel said softly. "We keep the cut."

He nudged the gelding forward along the hedge. The horse's muscles coiled and uncoiled beneath them with the easy strength of an animal that still had miles to give. She let herself breathe with that rhythm. In. Out. In. The night opened ahead. It did not feel empty. It was as if they had chosen the path.

They reached the field's edge and slid down a narrow strip of turf that paralleled the lane. A low stone stood where water had once marked the boundary of a parish. Gabriel took them behind it and paused again. He could see the bend now and the slow gray roll of fog that caught at the hollow. The coach that would have carried her on ground not of her choosing would soon nose into that mist.

Barrington shifted his bay to the far side. "If they run," he said.

"They will not," Gabriel said. His voice held no bravado. Only knowledge. "Not through this ground. Not with the wheels they drive and the weight they carry."

He turned his head and spoke low to Leticia alone. "When they come into sight, we move only as far as we must. If it breaks, we go straight for the open. Do not look back."

"I will not," she said.

He believed her.

A shape stirred at the bend. Lantern hoods shifted. The faintest glimmer winked and died. The team shook out and set a new rhythm. The driver reached to soothe them. He did not know he soothed Leticia's horse as well. The night drew in a breath and held it.

Gabriel pressed his knees, and the gelding gathered. The world narrowed again. Not to fear. To purpose.

They waited for the bend to give up what it hid. They were ready to take it. They were ready to run with it. They were ready to cut it off.

And when the coach showed its dark nose through the mist, they moved.

And Bracken Hollow, once meant to swallow her, opened its jaws for someone else instead.

# Chapter Thirty-Seven

THICK IRON RINGS groaned as the cell gate swung open. Cold seeped from the stone floor of Sommer Castle's ancient dungeon, a chill that belonged to older centuries and harsher punishments. Somewhere down the corridor, water dripped steadily into a rusted pan.

Gabriel stepped inside. The torchlight behind him stretched his shadow across the walls in long, dark limbs. Barrington followed, boots striking with crisp authority, while Leticia remained just outside the iron bars, visible through the narrow window, her arms folded firmly, though her fingers pressed into her sleeves to keep from shaking.

The guard captured at Bracken Hollow sat on a wooden chair. His wrists were chained behind him, but his spine remained stubbornly straight until Barrington laid a gloved hand on his shoulder with a quiet pressure that made him flinch.

"Once more," Barrington said, his voice mild but edged with steel. "Why did you take her. And why Bracken Hollow?"

The man's jaw worked. His eyes slid toward Gabriel, flicked away as if meeting that gaze were a blow of its own.

"We never wanted the girl," he muttered. "We wanted what she might lead us to."

Gabriel didn't move. The pulse at his temple ticked once and stilled.

"The brooch?" Barrington pressed.

The man nodded. "The sixth piece. The last of the set. No

one knew where it had gone after Vienna. All we knew was Robbie Ashcombe handled it before his fall. And that it passed from him into her family. She might have… more than jewelry."

Leticia exhaled softly behind the wall.

"It isn't magic," the guard added quickly, as though that mattered. "But having all six together again, it was something. Proof. Power. A banner to rally behind. The Order was nothing without its symbol."

Gabriel's voice cut like a blade drawn slowly. "And once you had the brooch?"

The man licked his lips. "Tresham meant to present the full set to… influential men. Men who'll pay to resurrect what was lost. The girl would… cease to be an inconvenience."

Gabriel's stillness sharpened into danger itself. Barrington caught his sleeve, a silent warning.

Leticia stepped forward so she could be seen. Her voice was steady. "Erica was to see it done?"

The man's mouth twisted. "She said she'd earn her way back into a higher circle once the Order returned. Tresham made her promises."

Gabriel had heard enough. "Send him on to Bamburgh. Let the constable hear the rest." His gaze was colder than stone. "Alive. He is worth more talking."

Barrington nodded to his men. "Take him."

The guard was hauled to his feet and marched away.

In the next cell, Tresham clutched his coat like a professor protecting his papers, even as iron bound his wrists. He didn't look repentant, only irritated at being interrupted mid-lecture. Erica St. Clair Notley sat on the bench opposite him, her gown dirty and her lip split, still trying to look as though she held the upper hand.

Gabriel gave them no courtesy.

"You will be moved to Bamburgh by nightfall," Barrington told them. "Treason and theft from titled families carry penalties this castle is no longer authorized to dispense." His chin lifted slightly toward Tresham. "Your books and papers will be taken into custody."

Tresham snarled, lunging until his chains clanked hard. "You've no idea what you are disrupting…"

"On the contrary," Gabriel said softly, "we know exactly what we have ended."

Erica stood when Leticia stepped up to the bars. "You would see me thrown to the wolves?" she hissed.

"You chose your own path," Leticia replied. "I am simply stepping out of your way."

Erica glared…but when she saw Barrington's men arriving with chains and paperwork, her bravado wilted just a little. "May your wedding cake choke you," she hissed.

Leticia didn't even blink. "Blessings upon your next scheme," she said calmly, and turned her back.

Tresham was dragged from the cell, ranting about legacy and symbols. Erica followed two paces behind, surrounded by guards. When they were gone from sight, only the sound of their footsteps retreating along the corridor remained.

Gabriel's gaze lingered on the empty corridor. "He was the one who helped us decode Alastair's journal," he said quietly. "We trusted his insight. His discretion."

Barrington's mouth flattened. "He was brilliant," he allowed. "That's what made him so dangerous."

Silence settled in the wake of it.

Leticia's voice came, steady and clear. "He did not rebuild the Order for jewels."

Gabriel turned to her.

"He rebuilt it for access," she continued. "Position. A way into rooms that would never question him."

Barrington gave a single nod. "Influence," he said.

"And power that would not be seen until it was too late."

Gabriel studied her, something deeper than relief in his expression now. "You saw that."

Leticia held his gaze. "I understood enough."

"Enough to walk into it," he said.

She did not soften. "Not alone."

The words settled between them.

Gabriel's hand closed around hers, firm, certain. "No," he said. "Not alone."

Barrington removed his gloves and turned to Leticia. In his palm lay the brooch, gleaming in muted gold and sapphire, the sixth piece.

"It's yours by right," he said. "And I believe you've earned it back."

Leticia took it carefully. "Thank you."

"Keep it close." His smile was faint but real. "History has a habit of trying again."

Gabriel offered his arm. She laid her hand upon it with quiet pride. Together, they walked up the long stone staircase and stepped out into the castle ward. Ahead lay winter sunlight, a paved path, the promise of peace beyond the castle walls.

Gabriel did not remove his arm from around Leticia's waist until they'd crossed the drawbridge completely, as if he trusted her safety only when the portcullis had lowered behind them.

Beyond the walls lay Barrington's residence, not far, but far enough that the sharpness in his jaw had time to ease. They took the gravel path slowly. His thumb drifted over the back of her gloved hand.

"You planned to throw yourself into the heart of it, even if I hadn't found you," he said at last.

"If it meant protecting people I love... yes." Leticia's chin lifted. "I am not ashamed of that."

He stopped walking.

When she turned, he was watching her in a way he hadn't since the night before the world changed. He wasn't evaluating risks, nor planning angles, but simply seeing her.

"I was terrified," he said plainly. The honesty of it tore through the distance between them. "More than in battle. More than when any blade has come for me. Because I..." he drew a sharp breath. "…I was afraid I wouldn't reach you in time. And that…I could not have borne."

Leticia blinked. The brooch in her palm caught the sunlight, warm again at last. She slid it carefully into her reticule and stepped closer, settling her hands at the breast of his coat.

"I chose you," she whispered. "Not because you are safe. Because I would not choose a life without you."

His breath left him in a rush. "Letty."

She half-smiled. "I am not so easily broken, Gabriel."

He lowered his forehead to hers. "No. But I am breakable without you."

Her fingers curled behind his neck, soft, deep when he groaned against her mouth and gathered her closer as if only blood and bone could keep her there.

When they broke apart, both of them were breathing hard. She kept her hands fisted lightly in his lapels and did not let him move away.

"So," she said, breathless but steady. "It's been two weeks. Do you intend to marry me?"

He brushed his thumb across her jaw, reverently. "I intend to marry you before the week is out, if Barrington will lend me a priest."

A throat cleared discreetly behind them.

They turned to find Kenworth, Barrington's long-suffering valet, appearing much as though he had been waiting for the proper moment to intrude.

"My lord," Kenworth said to Gabriel, "Lady Leticia… I hesitate to interrupt, but the cake has arrived. As have the first of the wedding guests. Lord Barrington begs to know if the ceremony is, in fact, to occur as scheduled next week."

Leticia's cheeks flushed pink. Gabriel did not release her hand.

"Tell him," Leticia said, straightening her spine with the poise of a woman who had just defeated a secret society, "that it had better. I have no intention of stopping it this time."

Kenworth beamed. "Very good, my lady."

He departed with all the solemnity of a man delivering state secrets to a king.

Gabriel leaned close to Leticia's ear, his voice a promise and a vow all at once. "Before winter," he said, "you'll be mine."

She turned toward him, eyes bright, lip caught between her teeth in a smile she could no longer hide, and whispered, "Only if you are mine, too."

# Chapter Thirty-Eight

THE MORNING SUNLIGHT glinted off the carriage door as Barrington handed Mrs. Bainbridge inside. Gabriel followed, pausing to rest one gloved hand on the frame before looking back toward the portico.

Leticia stood there beside her aunt, skirts stirring in the crisp air. "It is an honor," she said, "that His Majesty himself wishes to see you both and offer his blessing."

Mrs. Bainbridge leaned out the window, laughter bright as a bell. "A royal summons and a wedding blessing in the same week, can you imagine? Do try to keep Kenworth from strangling the florists while we're gone."

"I make no promises," Leticia replied, smiling despite the knot in her chest.

Gabriel met her eyes for one heartbeat longer than was proper. "We'll not be long."

She inclined her head, but her hands folded at her waist as the carriage rolled down the long lime-lined drive, raising a storm of golden dust and fluttering leaves. She stayed where she was until the wheels vanished behind the hedge, and even the faint rhythm of hooves was gone.

Only when she stepped back inside did her breath leave her in a soft rush. The house had not rested for a moment since Tresham's capture. As if in gratitude, it had flung itself wildly into motion. Unsurprisingly, Barrington's home had become a hive of effort for his and Mrs. Bainbridge's wedding, not hers. Florists arrived with bolts of palest peach ribbon and armloads of half-closed ivory roses. Crates of china were taken to the Sommer Castle. The housekeeper muttered about guest rooms and bed linen, while the discreet tray of subtle gossip passed between underfoot-men like a torch.

Kenworth, who had already proven himself unflappable under explosions, kidnappings, and aristocratic scandal, now faced his greatest adversary, wedding chaos. He had traded his pistol for a notebook the thickness of a small brick and stalked the corridors with relentless purpose.

"I warn you, my lady," he told Leticia in the hall one afternoon, "if even one more person enters this house with a floral sample, I shall personally lock them in the potting shed."

She laughed before she could stop herself, the sound startling in its freedom.

In her absence, Mrs. Bainbridge had pressed Leticia into the role of surrogate hostess with breathtaking boldness, insisting that a future baroness ought to stand at the helm and learn to wield diplomacy as deftly as placing a cut-glass decanter. So Leticia smiled at each arrival, accepted compliments on plans that were not truly hers, and learned the necessary art of making directions sound like gentle suggestions.

By mid-week the house had swollen with counts, countesses, colonels, and at least one near-deaf dowager accustomed to speaking at cannon volume. Trunks filled with gowns thumped against carved banisters. Maids whispered, footmen hurried, and once a frantic shriek erupted when a spider was discovered in the chapel at the back of the property.

Her aunt remained calm and watchful through it all, seated on a settee as though poised for a hunt, her embroidery never once missing a stitch while her gaze took the measure of each guest. On Wednesday afternoon, when Leticia managed five blessed minutes of peace in the morning room, her aunt entered and closed the door behind them with finality.

"We must speak," her aunt said. There was no refusing that tone.

Leticia set her teacup down carefully. "Yes?"

Her aunt surprised her by sinking down on the sofa beside her, not opposite, and after a moment of silence, folded Leticia's hand into her own. The gesture was unfamiliar and unbearably tender.

"There is something I have not told you, and I cannot let you marry, or begin your life anew, while I still keep it clenched like a thief hoarding sorrow."

Leticia's pulse skipped. "What is it?"

"The brooch," her aunt said on a sigh, sounding tired beneath her determination. "Years ago, the summer after Robbie died… a man came asking questions. A man claiming he was writing a history of minor jewels. He wanted to know if Robbie had ever purchased an unusual sapphire piece, and if I knew where it might have gone." Her brows knit. "Even then, I suspected he was not what he claimed. I promised I had no idea. And I begged your mother to destroy it, or sell it, for safety's sake. She assured me it was gone." Her voice fell to a whisper. "I believed I had kept you safe."

"She gave it to me as a gift before she died," Leticia said softly. "She never said a word of danger."

"I think she believed love protected more than secrecy," her aunt replied. Tears gathered but did not fall. "I watched you walk into that soiree with it at your throat, and all my guilt came roaring back. I should have told you long before. I should never have left you ignorant of the risk."

Leticia turned their hands and squeezed her aunt's fingers gently. "There was nothing cowardly in wanting to keep me safe. You tried to remove the threat without stealing my mother's memory. I cannot condemn that."

Her aunt's relief was quiet but immense. "Do you forgive me?"

"With all my heart."

They sat so for a long moment, palms warm, before the bells rang for luncheon and the world bustled forward again without mercy.

⟫⟩⟩⟨⟨⟨

THE DAYS THAT followed blurred beneath a sweeping tide of ribbons, deliveries, and the sharp scent of rose oil. Barrington's home grew steadily more crowded and chaotic. Mrs. Bainbridge's seamstress arrived with armfuls of lace and trim while Kenworth trailed behind with the expression of a man who has stared too long into hurricane winds and begun to catalog the debris with grim determination anyway.

Kenworth paused beside her, scanning the arrangements with the air of a general surveying a battlefield he did not entirely trust.

"The ribbons are staging a rebellion, my lady," he said quietly. "They refuse symmetry."

She managed to pat his arm gingerly and advise him to breathe.

The guests arrived in elegant rolling waves, carriages bearing ladies in dove-gray and pale pistachio, gentlemen with stiff collars and sharper tongues. They offered compliments on the 'upcoming wedding,' meaning, of course, Lord Barrington and Mrs. Bainbridge, and told Leticia what a splendid future hostess she herself would be one day. She thanked each one politely, though some deeper part of her smiled to think how little they knew.

Her aunt, newly at peace, presided over everything with a kind of calm majesty. She floated from room to room, correcting place cards, soothing ruffled dowagers, and yet managing to place her fingertips lightly on Leticia's shoulder each time she passed, as if anchoring them both in this moment rather than the harrowing nights they had already survived.

Leticia worked without complaint or hesitation, taking on the quiet burdens that Mrs. Bainbridge had left behind in her haste to

London. Others remarked upon it with pleased approval. Leticia herself, between the bustle and sleepless flickers of wondering if Gabriel had arrived safely, if he was eating, if he had caught a chill, rarely had a moment alone that did not ache with longing.

On the sixth evening after Gabriel's departure, she could not sleep and wandered outside. Fog clung close to the grass, silvering everything it touched. In the distance, an owl called once. Her heart reached across the miles toward London like a lantern trying to catch fire in another man's hand.

*Come back to me,* she prayed. *And quickly.*

The house rose on the morning of the wedding to find Sommer Castle alive with preparation. The autumn sky beyond the windows was pale blue, but within the walls, the staff moved with brisk efficiency, carrying tiers of cake, arranging champagne flutes, and stringing garlands of ivy and roses along the carved beams of the great hall. The vast hearth blazed at either end, throwing warmth across the polished floor as tables were laid with linen, silver, and crystal.

Leticia, dressed in lavender silk to stand with her aunt and welcome guests, smoothed her skirts and ignored the way her pulse skipped every time a carriage rattled up the lane.

The next coach delivered a familiar laugh before its door even opened. Her cousin Felicity spilled out in a flutter of dove-gray silk, cheeks pink from travel. "Did you think I would miss Barrington's grand wedding?" she asked as she reached Leticia and kissed her cheek. Her gaze swept the garlands being carried past and the footmen struggling under crates of roses. "Heavens, if the flowers multiply any further, they'll need their own pews."

Late morning bled toward noon. Guests filled the pews in the chapel, their whispers and laughter rising like the hum of an orchestra tuning before a performance. Some speculated on delays, a misplaced reticule, a lame horse, but Leticia's nerves wound tighter with each quarter hour.

At last, the sound of hooves on gravel reached her ears.

She turned sharply. At the crest of the drive, a small traveling carriage and two mounted riders were visible. Lord Barrington rode tall and composed. The other rider was Gabriel, looking dusty, windblown, and more beautiful than any creature had a right to be. Mrs. Bainbridge waved enthusiastically from inside.

Relief shot through her so swiftly her knees went weak.

The carriage halted. Barrington dismounted first. Gabriel handed Mrs. Bainbridge down with exaggerated gallantry. They approached to stand before the assembled guests. Murmurs stilled. Fans fluttered.

Lord Barrington stepped forward, composed and clear-voiced, as the hush of the chapel deepened.

"My esteemed friends and family. Thank you for gathering so loyally on such short notice."

A few obliging chuckles met the understatement.

"Before I speak to personal matters, you know we were called to London by the king. I am proud to deliver news of official import." He paused, letting the silence settle before he continued. "His Majesty has authorized the creation of a permanent military post near Sommer-by-the-Sea."

A ripple of excitement moved through the crowd.

"The post will be led by Major Felix Townsend, whose character and service are beyond reproach. I have no doubt he will safeguard the region admirably."

Townsend inclined his head in acknowledgment as murmurs of approval spread.

"Brave hearts have broken the Order of Shadows." Barrington's gaze swept the room, pausing on each of his six men. "I am honored to have led you, worked beside you, and to call each of you my friend. Now, the Brigade has earned its rest. Still, keep a weather eye. Should trouble rise again, you may find a gold coin on your doorstep when you least expect it."

"To the Brigade," came a shout from the guest.

"To the Brigade," came the thundering answer.

When the quiet returned, a faint smile touched Barrington's lips.

"And now to matters dearer to me. While in London, we paid a visit to His Majesty. Upon learning of our intentions, he made a request, rather firmly, that the archbishop marry us at once."

A low hum of astonishment rippled through the pews.

"He delivered the order to my lady directly, before I had time to object."

Laughter bloomed.

"It is, therefore, my great pleasure to introduce my wife, the Duchess of Barrington, Honoria Bainbridge Barrington."

Honoria curtsied, radiant and composed. Her dimples were shameless.

A collective gasp flew through the chapel like birds startled from a hedge. Leticia's mouth fell open. Even her aunt emitted a thoroughly inelegant sound. The guests exchanged stunned looks, and then, all at once, burst into delighted applause.

Leticia had just enough sense to turn her wide eyes toward Gabriel.

He lifted one brow in answer, as though the true surprise was yet to begin.

# Chapter Thirty-Nine

LETICIA WAS NOT entirely convinced her heart still beat normally. It instead fluttered in place like a trapped bird, all sound and wing, as Lord Barrington calmly announced that he and Mrs. Bainbridge had married in London prior to this day. She had expected scandal, but not this scandal. Certainly not in front of a chapel full of nobility. All these people were there for their wedding. Mrs. Bainbridge had been planning this event for months. Gasps tumbled amongst the stained glass and vaulted ceiling, followed by laughter, whispered delight, and more than a few wide-eyed attempts at discretion.

Her own mouth had gone dry. Even her aunt emitted a strangled sound beside her.

The only thing that kept Leticia steady was her gaze locked on Gabriel's.

He stood just behind Barrington, not arriving late as she had feared, but standing at attention, dusty and travel-worn, his gray eyes fixed upon her with unmistakable purpose. When Barrington finished receiving astonished congratulations, and the chapel had half-settled again, Gabriel stepped forward with the quiet certainty of a man who had just chosen his course and meant to see it through.

He did not approach her. Instead, he addressed the entire congregation.

"Your Graces, ladies, gentlemen. I beg your indulgence." His voice was deep and sure. "Lord Barrington has surprised you with the announcement of his marriage. But since you are all here…and since I am fortunate enough to stand here with her…I wonder if I might ask your patience for one more surprise."

He reached into his coat and produced a folded document upon heavy cream parchment. "This is a special license from the Archbishop of Canterbury, obtained on what I freely admit was little sleep and considerable determination. It permits me to marry here and now the woman I love."

A storm of astonished chatter rolled down the pews. Several ladies fanned themselves harder.

Leticia's breath rushed in and out. He looked only at her now.

"Leticia," he said, softer so only she could hear, "Marry me today, in this chapel, so that nothing, ever again, delays our future?"

She opened her mouth, but no sound came. She swallowed, found her voice, and whispered, "Yes… yes."

He offered his hand. In a daze, she placed hers into it.

"Yes, now?" she breathed, glancing down at her plain lavender dress. "Like this?"

Gabriel's mouth curved, but before he could answer, Mrs. Bainbridge swept forward with silk in her arms. "I would be greatly offended if my gown went unused," she declared. "And after all, I am already married. It would be criminal to waste a perfectly good wedding dress."

Leticia laughed, half disbelieving, half joyous, and for a fleeting instant, she thought of another borrowed gown, worn on a night when she had not yet known where she belonged. Now, she allowed herself to be swept toward the small anteroom beside the chapel, where Mrs. Bainbridge, her aunt, and two maids descended upon her with pins and lace ties. The gown was not white, but a shade of blush silk that turned luminous in the candlelight, something warm, and utterly her. She slipped it over her head with surprisingly little fuss, and the silk settled around her waist.

Felicity darted in at the last moment, offering pins with a flourish she had clearly pilfered from one of the maids. "Stand still, cousin, or I'll be forced to improvise," she teased, though her grin betrayed delight rather than mischief.

"Almost," her aunt murmured, tugging gently at the fit.

"There," Mrs. Bainbridge declared. "Now you may be seen."

The door opened softly.

Gabriel turned. For a moment, he did not move at all. His gaze steady on Leticia.

"A borrowed gown," he said, his voice low but certain. "But this time there is no mask, and if there were, it is you I would choose. It was always you."

Leticia's breath caught. The mask, the mistaken proposal, the borrowed life, all of it undone in that single vow.

"And a name," he added, a flicker of heat and humor in his eyes. "One I offered without knowing to whom I gave it."

A quiet smile bloomed on her lips.

"I know now," he said simply. "And I'd give it again."

He opened his palm. A ring of warm gold cradled a gleaming star ruby. Its heart was touched with light. "It belonged to my grandmother," he said. "If you will permit me...it would please me to see you wear it now, and forever."

Leticia stared. "It's astonishing."

"It is uniquely ours," he said as he slipped the ring on her finger. His fingers were steady, though his breath was not. He pressed something small into her hand, a folded envelope, sealed in his script.

"Later," he murmured, too low for anyone else to hear.

She let out a shaky breath. "I am ready."

Within minutes, they stood before the altar, garlanded with roses twined through autumn ivy, candlelight gilding the carved wood as the astonished guests hushed beneath the painted rafters. The vicar's voice ran like velvet over stone as he asked Gabriel if he would take this woman, Leticia Salisbury, to be his wife.

"With all that I am," Gabriel answered, his gaze drinking in each inch of her face.

When Leticia's moment came, she spoke without tremor, "I do. With all my heart."

The rings slipped into place, his large and ancient, hers delicate and newly forged, and as the vicar's words echoed against the stone, the past fell from her shoulders as surely as the future settled into her hands. When the words were spoken and vows complete, Gabriel kissed her as though she were the only woman who had ever existed, taking her gently at first, then with growing certainty until laughter and adoring sighs filled the aisle around them.

Her arms came around his neck shamelessly. Her slippered toes tipped high. The kiss broke only when Barrington loudly cleared his throat to declare it time for cake and triumph.

Felicity swept through the knot of guests with theatrical gravity. She pressed the back of her hand to her brow and leaned toward the bride.

"Letty, quick, I'm going to swoon." She peeked slyly from beneath her fingers, lips curving. "You did warn me this day might come."

Gabriel's voice came dry, edged with wryness. "Best wait until after the cake. Kenworth has enough chaos without you toppling into it as well."

Laughter sparked around them, lighting the air, and Leticia's smile carried the memory of a jest that had at last turned into truth.

They stood before their guests arm in arm, Baron and Baroness Ashcombe, no longer divided by doubt or disguise. At last, together by choice, and by law.

# Epilogue

*The Morning After*

SUNLIGHT POURED ACROSS the bed in honeyed stripes, warming the tangled, unhurried hush of the chamber. Leticia stirred against her husband's bare chest, solid, warm, familiar in ways that still made her heart skip with disbelief. Gabriel murmured something low and sleepy, tightening his arms around her like he meant to keep her cuddled against his body forever.

"I was trying not to wake you," she whispered against his collarbone.

"You failed," he rumbled, his voice deep with sleep and satisfaction. "And now that you have, I cannot be held responsible for what happens next."

She laughed, breathless and unashamed, and pressed her lips to the pulse beating just under his jaw. It leapt for her as if his heartbeat were the answer to her kiss.

"I am your wife," she reminded him softly.

His hand curved over the slope of her hip, possessive and reverent all at once. "Best sentence in the English language."

The star-ruby caught the morning light on her finger, warm against her skin beside her wedding ring. She turned her wrist slightly, tracing the edge of the stone with her fingertip. "I still cannot believe this is real."

Gabriel tipped her chin so she had no choice but to meet his steady gaze. "Believe in this. I will love as long as I draw breath… and beyond it, if I am permitted."

Tears slipped unbidden down her cheeks, and he brushed them away with his thumb, kissing the tracks where they had fallen.

"And," he added with that wicked flicker she now recognized as her undoing, "I intend to begin showing you exactly how devoted I am the moment you finish breakfast."

"Breakfast?" she repeated, amused.

A knock sounded at the door.

Kenworth's voice floated through, dry as ever. "Begging your pardon, my lady, but victory eggs and ham have arrived on the tray. Shall I leave them at the door…or dare I risk entering?"

Leticia collapsed into Gabriel's shoulder with a muffled laugh. "Victory eggs?"

Gabriel shrugged. "We won. Kenworth is sentimental when he thinks no one is looking."

"Leave the tray," Gabriel said, without looking away from her. "And go."

"As you wish." One could almost hear Kenworth smirking behind the panel.

When his footsteps faded, Gabriel gathered her beneath the sheets once more, his lips finding hers slowly, as though time itself had finally yielded to them.

But Leticia slipped away just enough to reach for the little page she had tucked on the bedside table, folded and worn already, though she had not yet dared to open it before. The letter Gabriel had pressed into her hand with the ring.

"You thought I would forget," she teased, holding it aloft.

His arm fell across his eyes with a groan. "I hoped I could distract you."

She smiled and smoothed the paper open. "You underestimate me." Her voice softened as she read.

*I have written you truths in shadows, in fear, in longing. But tonight, I write to you in joy.*

*You have been my secret and my solace. Now I would have you be my future.*

*I am, without condition or restraint, yours. Entirely.*

Her eyes lifted from the page, shining. "Without condition or restraint," she whispered. "Yours entirely."

Gabriel caught her around the waist and rolled her against him, laughter low and unguarded. "I wrote that under duress."

"Duress?" she echoed, wicked smile curving. "You'll have to show me what kind."

His answer was another kiss, deep enough to make the letter slip from her fingers and flutter onto the rings on the side table.

Perhaps they did.

For the first time in a brutal season, danger lay behind them, love beside them, and a lifetime of bright mornings ahead.

They began it, as all good adventures ought, with a kiss…and a promise that neither intended ever to break.

## The End

# About the Author

There was never a time when *USA Today* Bestseller, RUTH A. CASIE hasn't had a story in her head. When she was little, she and her older sister would dress up and act out the ones Ruth creative. Today, Ruth writes exciting and beautifully told legendary historical romances that are both rich and engaging. Her stories feature strong women and the men who deserve them, endearing flaws and all. Her stories are full of, 'edge of your seat' suspense, mind-boggling drama, and a forever-after romance.

She lives in New Jersey with her hero, three empty bedrooms and a growing number of incomplete counted cross-stitch projects. Before she found her voice, she was a speech therapist (pun intended), client liaison for a corrugated manufacturer, and vice president at an international bank where she was a product/ marketing manager, but her favorite job is the one she's doing now—writing romance. Ruth hopes her stories become your favorite adventure.

Fun facts about Ruth:

1. She filled her passport up in one year.
2. She has three series. The Druid Knight is a time travel romance. The Stelton Legacy is a historical fantasy about the seven sons of a seventh son. Havenport Romances are contemporary romantic suspense stories. She also writes for the Pirates of Britannia connected world.
3. She did a rap with her son to "How Many Trucks Can a Tow Truck Tow If a Tow Truck Could Tow Trucks."

4. When she cooks she dances around the kitchen.
5. Her sudoku books is in the bathroom and that's all she'll say about that!

## Social Media Links:

Website:
ruthacasie.com

Instagram:
instagram.com/ruthacasie

Facebook private reader's page, Casie Café:
facebook.com/groups/963711677128537

Facebook Author Page:
facebook.com/RuthACasie

Twitter:
twitter.com/RuthACasie

BookBub:
bookbub.com/authors/ruth-a-casie

Amazon:
amazon.com/author/ruthacasie

Goodreads:
goodreads.com/author/show/4792909.Ruth_A_Casie

YouTube:
bit.ly/3hI5eQr